MICHELLE GAGNON

THE TUNNELS

D0049780

MIRA

$6.99 U.S.
$8.50 CAN.

ISBN-13:978-0-7783-2446-1
ISBN-10: 0-7783-2446-X

EAN

Praise for

MICHELLE GAGNON

"*The Tunnels* starts out scary and only gets worse—
or, if you like frightening thrillers, better. Michelle Gagnon
is a fresh and confident new voice in crime fiction,
and *The Tunnels* marks an auspicious debut."
—John Lescroart, *New York Times* bestselling author
of *The Suspect* and *The Hunt Club*

"Michelle Gagnon's stellar debut is an edge-of-your-seat
story of suspense and intrigue. FBI agent Kelly Jones
is in a race against time to stop a series of gruesome
murders on a pristine eastern college campus.
With a deftly crafted plot and a winning protagonist,
Gagnon spins a fast-moving yarn that is certain to keep
you up late. We will hear more from this
talented newcomer. Highly recommended."
—Sheldon Siegel, *New York Times* bestselling author
of *The Confession*

"Michelle Gagnon has written a tremendously fine debut
novel that's as dark, twisty and thrilling as the
tunnels she so hauntingly describes therein.
Expect to sleep with the lights on for at least a week
after you've relished the final page."
—Cornelia Read, Edgar Award nominee for
best debut novel, *A Field of Darkness*

MICHELLE GAGNON

THE TUNNELS

MIRA®

MIRA

ISBN-13: 978-0-7783-2446-1
ISBN-10:   0-7783-2446-X

THE TUNNELS

Copyright © 2007 by Michelle Gagnon.

www.MIRABooks.com

Printed in U.S.A.

For my parents

ACKNOWLEDGMENT

Although *The Tunnels* is a work of fiction, I attempted to stay true to the myths and rituals that serve as its basis— any failures to do so are sincerely regrettable.

That being said, the Ring of Ásatrú and the Warder of the Lore are entirely fictional creations. In recent years pagan religions have become increasingly popular, attracting numerous followers worldwide. This book serves as an example of how any religion can be distorted, and should in no way be construed as a slight on these practitioners or their beliefs.

I relied heavily on several sources for information on the Norse religious traditions. Snorri Sturluson's *Heimskringla: History of the Kings of Norway* and *Prose Edda* were both invaluable, as was Edred Thorsson's work *Northern Magic*. For historical background I referred to *Myths and Symbols in Pagan Europe* by H.R. Ellis Davidson and *Norse Mythology* by John Lindow.

I'd like to thank my many readers, all of whom offered invaluable feedback at various stages of the editing process, including my sisters Kate and Adrienne, Darren Fitzgerald, Tamim Ansary and everyone at the San Francisco Writer's Workshop. Thanks to Wesleyan University for an amazing college experience, and for serving as the inspiration for the setting of this book. I also owe a tremendous debt to my agent Jean V. Naggar for her continued faith in me, and to my editor Selina McLemore for seeing the potential in my manuscript.

And finally, thanks to my parents for always telling me that I could be whatever I wanted to be, and to my husband for helping me believe it.

Prologue

"Seriously? You've never been down there? And you're what, a junior?" Chad shook his head in mock surprise as his eyes lingered over her cleavage.

"No, never." Anna flushed slightly and resisted the temptation to tug at her shirt's bodice. Her roommate had talked her into borrowing it, scoffing, "Nuns show more skin than you do. Men don't dig turtlenecks." She had been right, as always. Within ten minutes Chad Peterson had backed her into a corner by the keg and offered her a refill, even though she'd barely had a sip of the beer in her hand.

"Well, I don't think we can allow you to graduate without at least one late-night visit to the chapel. It's a rite of passage, for Christ's sake." He pushed a stray lock of hair from his eyes and smiled down at her, causing her heart to thump uncomfortably hard. She nodded with more assurance than she felt and said, "Let's go."

Chad leaned toward his friend Pete and whispered something. Pete leered at her and clapped Chad on the

shoulder. "The tunnels, huh? Right on. We'll come, too."
With one arm Pete scooped up a tipsy blonde and led the
way to the rear of the frat house.

"Are you sure she's okay?" Anna asked uncertainly.
The girl's feet stumbled and twisted over each other, and
her head lolled to one side.

"Gina? She's fine, she always gets like this. The walk
will do her good," Pete said.

Chad's lips grazed Anna's hair, sending a thrill down
her spine. She swallowed hard and downed the rest of her
beer in one gulp. She'd never seen this section of the
building. The lighting was dim, their footsteps loud on the
wood floors. The alcohol was spreading a pleasurable
warmth through her bloodstream. Finally, Pete ducked
into a narrow hallway.

"Watch your heads, it's dark in here."

Anna crouched down. The passage was so narrow that
her hips almost touched the walls on either side. It was
pitch-black. Pete yelped, and the drunk girl giggled. "It's
not funny, yo. I hit my head," he murmured.

"Sorry," Gina answered in a stage whisper, then
giggled again. Anna fought a rising claustrophobia,
closing her eyes to squeeze out some of the darkness and
drawing a heavy breath of dusty air. Chad's fingers
stroked her back reassuringly, which only served to feed
her rising panic. *What was she thinking? She barely knew
these guys—and here she was heading into the bowels of
the building with them.*

"Oops…shit, this is it." There was the click of a match
being lit, and Gina was suddenly silhouetted in light.

Anna peered over her shoulders to see Pete unbolting a heavy door. A tarnished brass knocker hung in the center—was that a goat? A shiver tingled unpleasantly down her spine. Silly superstitions, she thought, trying to shake off the warnings ringing through her head. Those were old-world fears, the kind of thing her father clung to despite all of his education and business acumen. She was in Connecticut now, for God's sake. She'd left all that behind her.

The door groaned slightly as it opened. Pete issued a mock-evil laugh and rubbed his hands together.

"Knock it off, Pete," Chad said sternly. He reached around and rubbed Anna's upper arms. "Wow, you've got goose bumps."

She hadn't noticed, but it was true. "I'm cold," she lied.

Pete fumbled around inside the door, cursing under his breath, and suddenly a flashlight sliced a swath through the murk. It was a small token of comfort, she thought, proof that other people had done this before, that they were not the first venturing into uncharted terrain. Everyone had been at least once, according to Chad, and in a school of almost three thousand students that was saying quite a bit.

"Careful, it's pretty steep," Chad whispered in her ear. Gina disappeared around a bend in the stairs, and Anna hurried to catch up. The temperature dropped as they descended and she rubbed her arms, wishing she had brought a sweater. It was musty, the walls lining the stairwell not dirt as she had imagined but concrete, painted by generations of students with varying levels of skill. Names, doodles and profanity were scrawled in a spectrum of colors. Farther down they encountered crude representations of owls, bulls and other symbols she didn't recognize.

"Did you do any of these?" she asked, snipping her words off at the end, startled by how they took on a life of their own down here, amplified and distorted until she hardly recognized them.

"Not yet. They don't let you, until you graduate." Chad ran his fingers along a stark William S., 1923. "They're running out of room. We might have to start back at the bottom soon, paint over the ones that aren't so great, you know? Some are pretty cool, though. You're an art major, aren't you?"

"Art history." She was secretly stunned, hadn't counted on him knowing her name, never mind her major.

"Then you'll appreciate this."

It felt as if they descended for hours, though it was probably only ten minutes. Pete jumped the last few stairs with both feet, landing with a clank on a metal plate. "Yeeeee-haaw!" he yelled. The call thundered down the tunnel ahead of him and rushed back like a train, almost taking her breath away as it swirled around her head before diminishing.

This was it, she thought, staring past the flashlight's illuminated coil into the depths beyond. *The infamous tunnels.*

It had been a rumor at first, one confirmed by so many disparate sources that she had acknowledged their existence without any firsthand experience. Varying explanations of their origins were debated heatedly in dorm rooms and dining halls; some claimed the tunnels were built in the 1950s when many of the dorms were redone, to facilitate travel around campus during the snowy winter months. Others argued that they predated the university itself, built during the days of the Underground Railroad, later used by the university's first presidents to store illegal contraband. One rumor claimed that you could even get to the waterfront if you followed the right shaft. Anna ran her fingers along the whirls and grooves of the concrete, feeling the slickness of condensation under her fingertips. *Not the fifties, certainly,* she thought to herself as her eyes marched along a string of dates from the 1800s. Moss carpeted sections of the floor, the sponginess pushing back against her thin sandals. A line of dark steel beams vaulted the ceiling, some dangling strands of lichen that danced on drafts of air. Gina stumbled, caught herself, then bent double.

"Are you okay?" Anna asked with concern, taking her elbow.

The girl tilted her head to look at her, eyes struggling to focus. She pointed past her to something on the wall and said, "Look."

Anna followed her finger and caught her breath. An enormous painting glared down at them. It spanned the space from floor to ceiling, streaked dark brown, disquieting in its intensity. Chad squinted over her shoulder. "What the fuck? No one's supposed to paint this section, it's the oldest. Yo, Pete! You know who did this?"

Gina suddenly heaved, spraying the floor with sudsy beer. They jumped back.

"Oh, man! What the fuck! I told you not to get sick

down here! Jesus Christ—I'm gonna have to clean this up now, you know that?" The flashlight's beam jerked and bounced along the walls as Pete gesticulated, making the leering face on the wall appear to dance. "For fuck's sake. All right, let's head back."

"Dude, I promised to take her to the chapel," Chad argued, head cocked to the side.

"It's okay, really," Anna said through her fingers, covering her mouth in an attempt to filter the smell. "Some other time."

"Seriously, though, all you've got to do is get a little water…" Chad guided Pete down the tunnel away from them. Their voices became muted, the whispers curling eerily around the still air. Gina was still on her knees, hair swung in front of her face like a drape.

"Are you okay?" Anna asked tentatively.

In response, Gina nodded and sniffled.

"Here, let's get you up." Anna bent to help her.

Gina lifted a tear-streaked face and half smiled. "Thanks. I'm an idiot."

"Shh…no, it happens to everyone. Seriously. We've all been there. It's not your fault." Anna stroked her back reassuringly.

"All right, let's go." Chad reappeared at her side. He had the flashlight now, and Pete pulled Gina to her feet behind him.

"We don't have to, really."

"No," he said firmly. "I don't want this to be your last memory of the tunnels. They're too cool. Trust me, when we get to the chapel it'll be worth it. I promise."

Anna sighed. If nothing else, the incident had quelled any residual fears. They were just tunnels, no more, no less, built up in students' imaginations by generations of tall tales. And the face—well, that was just some fraternity prank. "All right. But I have to get up early to study, so let's make it quick."

Minutes later they clambered out a hatch in the chapel floor just behind the pulpit. Chad held his hand around the mouth of the flashlight, providing just enough light for them to see. "Public Safety officers," he whispered. "They make rounds every night. If I get caught again, I'm expelled."

Again? she thought, miffed, but didn't say anything.

After the dank closeness of the tunnel the chapel felt enormous, bathed blue by the patches of moonlight seeping through the windows. The ceiling hovered above them in crisscrossed arches, the pews stood silently watchful. *Chad was right,* she thought. It was wonderful, and romantic.

They started to kiss, lips grazing each other lightly as he eased her back onto the carpet. *Tomorrow morning,* she thought with barely repressed glee, *Father John will be standing right here, delivering the Mass.* Her dad believed she still attended, figuring it wasn't Greek Orthodox but it was better than nothing. It had been a simple lie, one she told him initially to gain more study time, then because she no longer believed in the fairy tale of good and evil that was dished up on a weekly basis.

She jerked upright, pulled back from her thoughts by the hand under her shirt.

"What?" Chad whispered.

"Nothing." She felt her cheeks flush. "It's just that I want to go kind of slow, okay?"

Chad shrugged. "Yeah, sure. Whatever."

They started to kiss again. This time she focused on his mouth, the slightly bitter taste of beer lingering on his tongue. He was a good kisser. *What the hell,* she thought as she let his hand make its way up her back, feeling for the clasp on her bra. *You can't stay a virgin forever.*

Footsteps, suddenly. They both froze, pulling apart to listen. It sounded like someone was in the apse behind them. *Who would be here this late?* she wondered. *Father John?* Closer now, purposeful strides echoed from behind the curtains where the priest made his entrance every Sunday.

"C'mon," Chad whispered in her ear, all the smoothness gone from his voice. He yanked her up sharply, almost making her cry out, then pushed her down the iron ladder in front of him, slamming the trapdoor shut over their heads. "We gotta run for it, before they get a look at us. Let's go, let's go!" He prodded her forward.

"The flashlight," she mumbled, but he didn't seem to hear her. *I'm going to twist an ankle in here,* she thought. *I'm going to fall and break my leg, all so this guy doesn't get some bullshit citation from Public Safety. They're not the police, they don't even have any power…*but she stayed quiet and pushed ahead.

At the bottom he squeezed past and grabbed her hand. "This way!"

She jerked along behind him, the darkness smothering

her, breath coming in gasps and gulps. *I can't breathe,* she thought. *There's not enough oxygen.* She tripped on something and heard a squeal, repressed the urge to scream herself. Rats, of course there were rats down here. It was like the subway, nothing but rats and graffiti. She tripped again and landed on one knee. Her hand slipped from Chad's grasp.

"C'mon!" he whispered.

"I—I think I'm hurt!" She eased back on her haunches, rubbing the knee, feeling it throb in response. "Chad?"

He was gone.

It took her a second to fully believe it, that he would leave her down here with no light, no map, no clue as to which of the corridors wound back to the frat house. She kicked herself for not paying attention. They had hit forks twice along the way, but he was obviously so familiar with the route she had just followed blindly along.

"Chad?" she called out plaintively. "Anyone?" She eased herself to her feet, groping for the wall with both hands. She heaved a sigh of relief when after an eternity her fingertips scraped against the gravelly surface. She should have taken the flashlight, should have demanded it. *Well, these tunnels all led somewhere,* she thought. If she just kept going, eventually she'd find a stairwell that led up into one of the buildings. And it wasn't like the university would kick her out, she mused with a grim smile. Considering who her father was, she probably couldn't get expelled if she tried.

Footsteps again, from somewhere in front of her. "Chad?" she called hopefully. He wasn't a bad guy, he was coming back for her; he had probably turned around as soon as he realized she was gone. "I'm down here, this way! Chad?"

He was closer now, moving slowly, probably trying to pinpoint which direction her voice was coming from. She listened hard, straining her ears toward the echoes. She edged along the wall, pieces of the concrete coming loose in her hands. "Hello? Who's there?"

With a jolt she remembered something: her keys! There was a mini-LCD light on her key chain, a stocking stuffer from her father last Christmas. She dug them out of her pockets, sifted through until she felt the soft plastic case, and squeezed. She caught her breath, then giggled nervously. On the wall opposite her was another face, identical to the one they had seen earlier, but even larger and darker. And freshly painted, she realized—drops were still running down it, dark streaks dripping from the beard to the floor. Once again, a feeling of foreboding trickled down her spine, and she had to suppress the inclination to run. She took a deep, shuddery breath, stepped back from the image, and turned in a slow circle. There was something there, just beyond the reach of the light. Anna squinted and took a tentative step toward it. "Are you…" she started to ask, then her eyes widened and she screamed, fingers releasing the key chain. It fell to the floor with a clatter. Darkness descended once again.

One

"What's his name?"

"Chad Peterson, a.k.a. smart-ass punk."

"Great. I can hardly wait." Kelly Jones sighed, quickening her pace as Agent Roger Morrow struggled to keep up.

"Jesus," he huffed. "It's called walking, Jones, not jogging."

"Sorry." She shrugged. "A decade of living in New York will do that to you. Relationship to the victim?"

"None, or so he claims. They hooked up at a party Saturday night, he took her into the tunnels—you know, get her a little scared and you might get lucky, that sort of thing—they heard a noise in the chapel and bolted, got separated, then Prince Charming spent the rest of the night tucked soundly in bed."

"And the girl?"

"Like I said, they got separated."

"And he didn't go back for her? What a hero. Any chance it was him?"

"Nah. Normal kid, no history of anything besides the usual prep-school bullshit. Roommate confirms he was in bed, asleep by 2:00 a.m."

"But then frat brothers will say almost anything, won't they? Give me a minute alone with him." She threw open the door of the FBI command trailer. Sunk deep into one of the swiveling chairs was a young man, face buried in his hands. He lifted his head and regarded her forlornly. It was obvious he'd been crying. Pinned to the bulletin board behind him were photos of the girl. It was a common tactic, leaving a suspect alone with the crime-scene photos. The innocent ones crumbled at the images, and the others…nine times out of ten they gave themselves away, unable to fully contain their pride. Chad Peterson appeared to belong to the former group, although Kelly wasn't letting him off the hook yet. She fixed him with a glare and planted herself in front of the chair, peering past him to examine the gruesome images of the crime scene. The trailer was sparsely furnished, desks and swivel chairs bolted to the floor, most of the wall space occupied by dry-erase and bulletin boards. A coffeepot and microwave in the corner served as the kitchen. Right now, all of the boards in the office were empty save for the one she squared off against.

This wasn't her first homicide. Since joining the Bureau a decade earlier, she had investigated dozens of deaths across the country, ranging from prostitutes dumped in shallow graves to children maimed beyond comprehension. But these shots were uniquely horrific. The girl hung from a rope coiled around one of the beams supporting the roof of the tunnel. Her naked body was splayed like a butterfly on display, head dangling forward, eyes open as if gazing down at the terror inflicted on her body. Her jaw hung abnormally slack and distended. Below the rope, her chest was carved open to expose broken ribs; the lungs were missing, an odd trophy to take, Kelly thought. Blood trailed down the girl's leg from another gash on the inside of her upper thigh. The incisions were surgical, probably done with a large hunting knife, Kelly surmised. Scrawled across the bottom of the photos in black ink was, "Anna Varelas, 20 yrs., Cauc female."

"So." She turned to the boy. "Anything you want to tell me?"

"I'm so sorry…" he began, voice strangling with emotion. "When she didn't come back, I just assumed she found another way out, you know? I never thought…" He dissolved into sobs.

Kelly twisted the top off a bottle of water and handed it to him. He took it gratefully and swallowed a few gulps, breath heaving between sips. She watched him silently. Not even De Niro could pull off a performance of this caliber. The kid was definitely clean. *Being an asshole didn't make him a killer,* she thought grimly. Which unfortunately made her job harder. "Have you seen her before?"

"Sure." He nodded his head slowly. "Around campus. But this is the first time I ever talked to her, I swear. I don't know who could've done this. I feel terrible, I never should have left her alone down there."

"No, you shouldn't have."

"I just don't get it. I've been in those tunnels a hundred times, I've never seen anything or anyone—"

"There's a first time for everything." Kelly perched on the edge of the desk facing him and crossed her arms. "So here's what we're going to do. We're going to go through your story, step by step. Anything you can remember, even if it doesn't seem important, you're going to tell me. I want to know everything you said and did, everything you heard and saw, up until the moment you got into bed. You got it?"

He cleared his throat loudly. "Sure." He finished off the water and pushed a stray hair out of his eyes, surreptitiously wiping away the last of his tears. "FBI, huh? I thought you guys only came in for the big cases."

"This is a big case."

"Well yeah, I know. But I figured one murder, the cops would handle it first, right? Aren't you guys only pulled in for federal stuff?"

She considered telling him about the other girl, then decided against it. "You don't know who she was?"

"Who, Anna? She said she went to boarding school in Switzerland."

"Right. She's Dmitri Christou's daughter." Kelly sighed inwardly at his blank stare. "The Greek shipping magnate? Makes loans that float the economies of small countries?"

"No shit?" The boy looked awed. "But I thought her last name was—"

"She was going by her mother's maiden name here, as a security precaution."

"Wow…I had no idea."

"That was the whole point. Anyway." Kelly pulled a notebook from her inside jacket pocket and flipped to a clean page. "You met around what time last night?"

"So what do you think?"

She looked up from her notes to find Morrow watching her, rocking back and forth on his heels with a half smile.

"Not our guy." She rubbed her eyes with a thumb and forefinger and suppressed a yawn.

"Told you. Long day, huh? Where'd they pull you in from?"

"Jersey."

"Oh right, the chicken guy. Nice work on that one."

"Thanks. How's Carol?"

"Counting down the days until my retirement."

"Really? I didn't think you were close." Kelly had worked a few cases with Morrow in the past, including a particularly nasty one with teenagers who took horror movies far too seriously. She wouldn't have guessed him to be a day past forty-five, bald head and paunch aside.

"Just ten years to go," he joked, rolling his eyes. "You want to talk to the other couple that was with them?"

Kelly shrugged. "You tell me. Did they see or hear anything?"

Morrow shifted his belt back below his paunch. "Naw. Those two could have seen Jack the Ripper drag someone into an alley and they wouldn't have anything to report. Their daddies must be rich, otherwise there's no way they would've gotten in here. You stop by the sites?"

Kelly shook her head. "No time yet." She nodded at the board behind her. "But a picture's worth a thousand words."

"Gruesome, huh?"

"Yeah, gruesome." Kelly sighed. Ten years of this work and it never seemed to get any easier. If anything, the killers she tracked became more creative and vicious in their cruelty. "What did the M.E. list as cause of death?"

Morrow sank into the chair opposite her. "From the looks of it he strung her up first, but the rope was knotted to choke without breaking her neck. Actual cause of death was massive blood loss. Stabbed the femoral vein and collected the blood in a bucket while she was still alive and kicking."

"Tricky stuff." Kelly chewed the end of her pen. "Could be a surgeon, someone with medical training."

"I checked, no med school here. I was thinking a butcher."

"Not a lot of those here, either," Kelly noted.

Morrow shrugged. "You never know, maybe a scholarship kid or prof with a blue-collar daddy." He walked over to the board and pointed to one of the photos, the camera zeroing in on the girl's toes dangling just above the ground. "You see these circles, here? The bigger one was left by the bucket, wax residue indicates the other two were candles. He tore her jaw in two, snapped her ribs and yanked out her lungs."

"Postmortem?"

"God, I hope so. We should know for certain this afternoon. Not the way I want to go, I'll tell you that much."

Kelly leaned in to squint at the photos. "Any sign of rape?"

Morrow shook his head. "M.E. doesn't think so, at

least definitely not with the Christou girl. Believe it or not she was still a virgin, probably the last one on campus. The other one, she's not so sure."

"Tell me more about her."

"Almost identical M.O.s. Lin Kaishen, Chinese, twenty-one-year-old senior, daughter of a U.N. diplomat. Turned up in a connecting tunnel about a half-mile away. She'd been missing for about two weeks, not that anyone knew it. Her friends assumed she went home for the break before midterm exams, parents thought she stayed to work on her thesis. We're trying to pin down exactly when she got grabbed. Not a pretty sight after the rats got to her. I've got the shots here if you want to take a look at them."

"Sure." Morrow tossed her the file. She caught it midair and flipped it open. This girl was slighter and more fine-boned, with long black hair trailing down what remained of her face. Her legs were spread, pinned to the wall with heavy black rebar. Again, the lower jaw dangled grotesquely and ribs peeked out from her torn flesh. Kelly's eyes narrowed. "Body position's different."

"And that's why they pay you the big bucks. For some reason he skipped the legs on the Christou girl. Maybe he forgot the rebar at home."

"But remembered the bucket and candles? Might mean he's refining his M.O.," Kelly mused. It generally took serial killers some time to hit their groove, so to speak. The best chance of catching them was always early on, when they hadn't yet perfected their technique and were most likely to make a mistake. With any luck, they were dealing with a newcomer here.

"So sure it's a he?" Morrow asked.

Kelly shrugged. "To mount the girls like this would take someone pretty strong, or maybe two people. What are this one's stats?"

Morrow flipped through his notebook. "According to her driver's license she was five-six, a hundred-fifteen pounds."

"Add five to that. Girls always lie about their weight." Kelly peered closely at the last photo in the batch. "What's that behind her? Was that already there?"

"That, my friend, is our best lead. And the answer to why he collects their blood. Apparently he's too cheap to invest in a set of watercolors. We found a couple of them painted down there, mostly in the tunnels leading to the chapel." He tossed her two more photos. "These were taken once the bodies were removed."

Kelly exámined one photo closely. The paint had been smudged by the girl's body, blurring the details of a crudely scrawled image. It was difficult to tell whether it was supposed to be human or animal, but it was most definitely a face of some sort. Two eyes glowered fiercely from beneath a shaggy brow, pointy ears jabbed out from the sides, and a long bedraggled beard dangled almost to the floor. Even here, under the fluorescent glow of the trailer lights, the sight of it induced a prickle at the base of her spine. She could only imagine how much worse it would look looming out from the darkness of the tunnels. "He uses the girls' blood as paint?"

Morrow nodded. "But there's a nasty twist to it. Get

this—the one behind Anna Christou? Painted in the Kaishen girl's blood."

"Lovely. So we have a frustrated artist on our hands. What about the first girl?"

"If she is the first girl. Those tunnels are a nightmare, it'll be weeks before we've covered them all. Kaishen was found by a janitor cleaning a bathroom near the tunnel entrance. You believe there's bathrooms down there?"

"Only two, in the Sommerfields."

"What the hell are Sommerfields?" Morrow raised an eyebrow.

"The dorms right at the edge of campus. Did she live there?"

Morrow flipped through his notebook while she waited. "Nope. Off-campus housing, with a couple of friends. What, did you memorize the campus map?"

She half smiled. "I lived in the Sommerfields my freshman year."

"No shit?" Morrow laughed. "You went here? Guess that's how you pulled this detail."

"Guess so. This is my first visit back, and to be honest it's not the kind of homecoming I was hoping for." Kelly's forehead crinkled as she leafed through the photos from the Kaishen crime scene. "Were her prints in either bathroom?"

"The janitor does a hell of a job, hardly any prints at all down there, the only ones we found were too degraded to match."

"So maybe our guy took her from there, maybe he grabbed her somewhere else. Same M.O., huh? The drawing was behind her?"

"Yep. Painted with the blood of an as yet unidentified female—that's the bad news. We combed the place, no sign of another body yet."

Kelly leaned back and crossed her arms over her chest. "And no other girls have been reported missing?"

"Not yet, but with classes just starting up again after midterms, it's hard to know for sure who's supposed to be here. Apparently there's no way for the school to take attendance, and lots of kids wander back late for one reason or another."

"Great. So we wait for another body to turn up."

"Looks like it," Morrow agreed.

Kelly sighed; this case was already shaping up to be a nightmare. "All right. Let's send the crime-scene pics and M.O. to ViCAP to see if they've got anything similar, maybe on another campus. Could be our guy is fixated on coeds. Send a photo of the drawing to the lab, hopefully they can tell us what the hell it is. And I want a full schematic of those tunnels—blueprints, access points, any information the university has on their origins."

A ViCAP search would tell them if other girls had been murdered in the same way anywhere in the country. Created by the FBI in the 1990s, the Violent Criminal Apprehension Program was a database that detected patterns by analyzing evidence from violent crime scenes. Before that, serial offenders like Ted Bundy could slip through the cracks just by killing in another jurisdiction. Not that Kelly expected much from the report. At this point in her career she could recite the M.O.'s of the nation's active serial killers by heart, no small feat considering there were almost a hundred running loose at any given time. A killer targeting college coeds was something she would have heard about.

Morrow bowed slightly. "Already done. Although in my professional opinion, it looks like there's some sort of freaky cult running around here. They kill a girl leaving the chapel, and any first-communion kid could tell you what that drawing looks like." He flicked his head toward the photo.

Kelly leaned in to examine it again. "You might be right, but let's see what they come up with anyway. It reminds me of something, I just can't quite put my finger on it…"

"Count Chocula?"

Kelly laughed and rolled her eyes. "I missed you Morrow, really I did. Serial crimes are no fun without you."

"And that's why *I* get the big bucks." He winked and held open the door of the trailer. "After you?"

"Where are we headed?"

"Promised the new president we'd stop by to give him an update. He's tearing his hair out, poor guy. It's only his third month on the job and two students turn up dead."

Kelly set the file down on the desk and sighed. "Welcome to the ivory tower."

Two

University president Ken Williams stood at the window, gazing through the tree branches at students playing Frisbee on the quad below. His office was located in North College, a row of brownstones comprising the oldest architecture on campus. Across the quad on his left rose the stately brick and marble library, to his right the gothic old gymnasium. In its entirety the university sprawled across a few square miles, student housing spreading tentacles in every direction. And right next door to his office was the chapel.

Ken Williams was the youngest president ever appointed by the college, though his prematurely white hair and aristocratic bearing lent him the air of someone far older than his forty years. After his cramped quarters as dean of the English Department at Northwestern, the size of his new office still overwhelmed him, a fact he took great pains to hide from his assistant. Despite the fact that it was already October, boxes of unpacked books still filled the corners, and his desk was bare save for a phone and laptop. Peter Scott, dean of the College and his right-hand man, perched on the edge of the plush leather couch opposite the window. He was maintaining a rapid-fire discourse that Ken had trouble focusing on.

"In terms of damage control, I've already spoken with both sets of parents and they agree that we should stick with the media blackout. Wu Kaishen in particular feels that too much publicity could compromise the investigation, and might focus undue attention on his position at the U.N., which at this juncture—"

"That's absurd. We have to warn them."

"What?" Dean Scott looked up from his binder with surprise.

"We should post a campus bulletin, have the Public Safety officers assume a more prominent role."

"Ken…" Dean Scott removed his glasses, pulled a soft cloth out of his blazer pocket and began cleaning them, a process he repeated whenever he needed to organize his thoughts. "We discussed this with both the authorities and the parents, and everyone agrees that publicizing the case could compromise it."

"Still, we have to do something. Rumors are already running rampant, and I'm sure our students have noticed that there's an FBI trailer parked in the lot behind the science building." President Williams turned from the window and glared at the dean over the top of his glasses. Drawn up to his full six foot three inches, he knew he cut an imposing figure. It was a trick he'd had to employ all too frequently with Dean Scott. The dean had been angling for the presidency for years, kowtowing shamelessly to the trustees. When they handed the job to an outsider, he was understandably upset. In retribution, he sought to make President Williams's daily life as unpleasant as possible. The recent murders had provided him with a fresh stock of ammunition. He'd spent most of the morning clucking to himself as he flipped through the updates from Public Safety. President Williams was finding it increasingly difficult to resist the temptation to backhand him.

Dean Scott cleared his throat and said condescendingly, "I agree that the death of Anna Christou was extremely unfortunate, particularly since her father was one of our biggest contributors last year. But it was a tragedy that could not possibly have been averted. These are still kids. If you forbid them to use the tunnels, you'll have hundreds of them down there every night."

"I give our students a little more credit than—"

The intercom on the desk crackled. "President Williams? The FBI agents have arrived."

He strolled over to the desk and pressed the intercom button. "Send them in, Annette." He glared at Dean Scott. "We'll finish this discussion later."

Kelly entered briskly with Morrow at her heels. The president was younger than she had expected. In her day the school was headed by a crusty blue-blooded patrician who only materialized at the opening and closing ceremonies each year. She strode to the desk and extended her hand. "President Williams? Special Agent Jones of the FBI. I understand you've already met Agent Morrow."

He shook her hand—a firm grip, she noted. He probably played squash or tennis regularly. "Yes, of course. Nice to meet you. I understand you're an alumna?"

"Yes."

"I'm sorry you couldn't be here under more auspicious circumstances."

"I am too."

Dean Scott cleared his throat loudly. "Agent Jones, I'm sure your colleague has already informed you of our concerns regarding media involvement in this case. Especially considering the nature of the crime and the high profile of the fathers, we hoped that—"

"And you are?" Kelly turned to him, raising an eyebrow. He was dressed expensively, sporting a tailored Italian suit that must have strained his salary. Something about him gave the impression of a toad, huge eyes behind thick glasses, sausage-like fingers protruding from his jacket sleeves.

"Peter Scott, dean of the College. As I was saying, we feel strongly that to incite a panic would be a tremendous—"

She cut him off. "I'm not here to discuss media relations with you gentlemen. I'm here to update you on the facts of the case and to glean any information you might have. Rest assured, I won't be the one calling CNN. But you've had two murders on a small campus in the space of a few weeks, not to mention another possible victim. I think you can expect national attention within a few days, if not sooner. I recommend you prepare a statement."

"Another victim?" President Williams sank heavily into his chair, the taste of bile rising in his throat. He struggled to maintain composure. "Who?"

"We don't know yet, but the killer paints this image in the blood of former victims. Does it look familiar?"

President Williams took the photo Kelly held out to him, hands shaking slightly. It wasn't one of the girls, he noted with relief, just some sort of crude painting. "No, I don't think I've ever seen anything like it."

Kelly nodded and slid the photo back into her file. "All right. Now I'm going to need a complete map of the tunnels. Have you secured the blueprints that Agent Morrow requested?"

The two men exchanged glances. Dean Scott pulled off his glasses and once again began cleaning them. "There's been a bit of a problem with that request."

"A problem?" Morrow stepped forward, brow furrowing. "Yesterday I was told they were all on file, and that your assistant was pulling them."

"Yes, I apologize for—"

"What President Williams means to say," interrupted Dean Scott, replacing his glasses carefully, "is that as it turns out, no blueprints of the tunnels currently exist. The former administration building was destroyed by a fire in the early 1900s. Our best guess is that the tunnel schematics went up in smoke." He lifted his fingers to the ceiling with a half smile.

Kelly eyed him; he seemed awfully smug for someone in his position. But what could they possibly gain by keeping the tunnel diagrams to themselves? "Surely there must be some record of the layout. If nothing else, we need to seal off as many access points as possible. I'm sure you want to prevent this from happening again."

"Yes, yes, of course." President Williams drummed his fingers on the desk. "I've already had Public Safety seal off the entrances in the fraternities, library, chapel and Sommerfields. And we've arranged for Jerome Brown to guide you through as much of the tunnels as he knows."

"Jerome Brown?" The name sounded familiar. Kelly started flipping through her notes.

Morrow leaned forward. "The same Jerome Brown who found Lin Kaishen's body?"

"That's him, yes. Jerome is apparently our resident expert on the tunnels."

"He claims to know them like the back of his hand. In fact, the other maintenance workers nicknamed him Rat," chuckled Dean Scott, shushing quickly at a stern look from the president.

"Interesting," Kelly said. "How long has Jerome worked here?"

"Over ten years. I believe he grew up here."

"Any complaints about him?"

"Not that I'm aware of." President Williams looked to Dean Scott, who shrugged and replied, "Honestly, Ken, he's a janitor. I didn't even know he was from here."

Kelly said, "I'd like a copy of his personnel file. Have you received any strange letters or calls lately?"

"Nothing comes to mind. As I'm sure you've heard, I only assumed this post a few months ago. I'm still acclimating myself to the university."

"Well, there are the AARO students. They certainly seem capable of anything," Dean Scott interjected.

President Williams threw him a withering look. "Really, Peter, I hardly think any of our students are capable of such an atrocity."

Kelly turned to Dean Scott. "What's the AARO?"

"At the induction ceremonies last month, their de facto leader marched up to the podium and slammed a bullet on it. I'm sure you remember, Ken," Dean Scott said snidely. "I recall you looking a bit pale at the time."

President Williams flushed. "The AARO is the African-American Rights Organization, a politically active student group. You have to understand, Agent Jones, these are idealistic young students. They get carried away sometimes. I'm sure things were similar during your time here."

Kelly nodded. "Still, I'd like the names of anyone who might have a grudge against the university or some of its patrons."

"Absolutely. My secretary will bring it by tomorrow."

"Tonight would be best, if you don't mind. Additionally, we'd like the names of students registered in your premed program, and background information on your scholarship students."

"What kind of background information?" Dean Scott asked.

"Family history, that sort of thing."

"I'm afraid that's where we start crossing lines, Agent Jones, in terms of privacy rights." Dean Scott tilted his head to the side.

"I'm guessing most if not all of your scholarship students also applied for Pell grants, in which case the government already has this information. You would just be expediting our retrieval of it." Kelly smiled sweetly. "The more we know early on, the faster the investigation can proceed. I'm sure you want this killer caught as quickly as possible."

"Of course." President Williams cleared his throat and stood. "Not a problem at all. I'll have them sent over tonight."

"We'll let you get back to work. If anything else occurs to you, don't hesitate to contact us," Agent Morrow said, pushing himself out of the armchair.

"Absolutely, and please keep me posted."

"What do you think?" asked Morrow as they strolled back across the quad, dodging students who lolled on the lawn soaking in the last of the Indian-summer day.

"I think that we need to have a word with Mr. Brown."

"He's next on my list, but first we've got a hot date at the morgue. Autopsies should be finished by now." Morrow glanced at his watch. "We should also check in with the girls' roommates, professors, friends…try to narrow the field."

"Fine. Let's start with the Christou girl, since that trail is warmer." Kelly stopped and squinted across the quad toward the student union. "But first, let's hit the dining hall. I'm dying for a cup of coffee."

Facing north, he carved the symbol in the air before him with the sharp blade of his knife. He saw its graceful strokes hovering for a moment before fading, the precursor to the cross, the sign of the hammer that had once reigned from Iceland to Persia, Sweden to Italy. His was the one true calling, the path every man was meant to follow since the dawn of civilization. Turning to the right, he repeated the symbol, then pivoted ninety degrees twice more to hallow each of the four cardinal points. Murmuring in the ancient tongue, eyes closed, he felt strength course through his limbs as the power of the words embraced him. The blood shone in the cup as he lifted it toward the heavens, enacting a ritual as old as time itself, one that he had recognized in his very bones the first time he saw it performed. That's when he had known this was the path to salvation—and the only way to stave off the dark forces pursuing him. He could hear them now, the whisper of their voices coming for him, the feel of their hands reaching for his robes. As he raised the vessel to his lips and drank, leaving a few drops glistening in the bottom, he forced every thought from his mind except that of the task before him. Carefully pouring the remaining draft into the blessing bowl, he dipped in a sprig of evergreen and withdrew it, sprinkling the altar with three quick twitches of his hand, then turning the wand on himself. He poured the remaining liquid onto the ground, watching the dirt eagerly lap it up, red quickly fading to brown.

Facing north again, he lifted both palms toward the heavens and said, "And so it has begun."

Three

Middlesex Hospital was located on a small hill less than a mile from campus. Kelly and Morrow found themselves wandering through a labyrinth of red buildings for a half hour before arriving at the solitary door tucked at the end of a long corridor. A tarnished plaque read MEDICAL EXAMINER CONSTANCE ANDERSON.

"Is this where they keep the dead people?" Morrow asked in a stage whisper.

"It is indeed." The crisp voice made them both jump. Kelly turned to peer down at a tiny, wizened woman. Dressed in pastel surgical scrubs, her brown eyes twinkled behind an enormous pair of glasses. She raised her hand and wagged a banana at them. "Potassium. Critical for proper regulation of the nervous system. Have you been waiting long?"

"No, we just got here."

"Well, no sense wasting time. I had the orderlies remove the girls from the freezer when you called. We better hop to it." She shooed them aside with the banana, stepped past and drew an enormous key ring from her pocket with her free hand. "Let's see here…ah." She inserted a key in the handle, twisted the knob, and threw the door open.

It was a far cry from the morgues Kelly usually visited. One side of the room clearly functioned as a de facto office; plants overflowed from the window ledge set ten feet up, and the ergonomic chair behind the battered desk was draped with an enormous filmy doily. Mingled in with anatomical diagrams was a wide assortment of cat posters: calicos dangling from trees, Siamese spilling from baskets, coon cats lolling on couches.

The other side of the room contained the standard morgue equipment, although some of it appeared ancient enough to qualify as museum pieces. A microphone dangled above two metal tables, a scale hung just to the left of a chalkboard covered with scrawled information. Hoses were tucked to the side, next to a stainless-steel tray holding surgical implements. An industrial refrigerator stood in the back corner of the room. The girls' bodies were laid out on the tables at a perpendicular angle so their heads were almost touching. There was something heartbreaking about it, Kelly thought, as if they were cloud gazing.

The medical examiner broke into a grin. "My domain," she stated dramatically, with a sweeping arm gesture. "Of course I don't generally host such illustrious company. Small town, this one. It's been months since I performed an autopsy. Those who don't succumb to natural causes usually fall victim to drunk drivers. No mystery there."

"No, ma'am," Morrow agreed.

"Oh, please." She stopped in the course of unpeeling the banana to issue a short laugh. "You may call me Constance. Do you mind if I eat before we get down to it?"

"Of course not."

She motioned to two folding chairs in front of her desk. Her eyes closed in appreciation as she bit off an enormous chunk of banana and chewed. After a moment, she opened her eyes. "Haunted, you know."

"Excuse me?" Kelly said.

"Haunted, the whole place." Constance nodded at the poster opposite her, where a striped cat in enormous pink sunglasses sat above the caption *Gimme a break!* "The hospital was built on the site of an Indian burial ground. At night they say you can hear chanting and drumbeats. Not that I believe that bunk, of course."

Kelly squirmed in her chair. "Constance, we're on a bit of a tight schedule here."

"Of course." Constance tossed the peel into the basket and pulled a baby wipe from a dispenser on her desk. After scrubbing her hands with it, she stood and smiled at them. "Terrible, what was done to those girls. Never seen anything quite like it."

They followed her to the first table. Kelly's stomach turned involuntarily. The body had turned blue and bloated slightly. A jagged row of sutures ran the length of the girl's torso. The angle of her distended lower jaw made her appear to be grinning.

"Anna Christou, twenty-year-old female. Estimated time of death is between 2:00 and 3:00 a.m. on Sunday, October 7th. Official cause of death is massive blood loss due to puncturing of the femoral vein in the left leg." She peered at them over the tops of her glasses. "Nasty, that. Bled her almost dry. Chafe marks around the neck from a slow-releasing rope, knotted to hold her in place without killing her. I'm waiting for tests on fibers, but it appears to be run-of-the-mill, you could find it in any hardware store. The jaw and rib cage were done postmortem, thank God for small blessings. I've prepared a copy of the autopsy tape if you're interested."

"Sure, that would be great." Kelly squinted at the chalkboard, but Constance's handwriting was indecipherable. "No defensive wounds?"

Constance shook her head. "Not that I found. Nails were clean, all the dried blood was her own. No trace evidence at all, in fact. Whoever your guy is, he's a careful so-and-so."

"Great," Morrow grumbled. "So basically we got nothing."

"I wouldn't say that. Ask and ye shall receive." Constance plucked two metal bowls from the side table. She held them out triumphantly, one above the other. "In bowl A, stomach contents…beer and some rather detestable-looking lasagna. Then it got interesting." She raised up the smaller bowl. "Bowl B. I initially mistook these for oversize grains of pepper."

Kelly bent over the bowl, nose wrinkling at the stench of decomposing food. Small black dots floated in the middle of a gelatinous mass. "What are they?"

"I had our lab run some tests, and you can imagine my surprise at the results. Henbane seeds."

"Henbane? What the hell is that?" Morrow peered cautiously over the rim of the bowl, two fingers holding his nostrils closed.

Constance carefully set the bowl back on the table and cleared her throat, crossed her hands in front of her, and intoned,

> *"Sleeping within my orchard*
> *My custom always of the afternoon*
> *Upon my secure hour thy uncle stole*
> *With juice of cursed hebenon in a vial*
> *And in the porches of mine ear did pour*
> *The leprous distilment."*

"Excuse me?" Morrow asked. Kelly and he regarded each other blankly.

Constance shrugged, disappointment at their ignorance apparent in her eyes. "The Ghost's speech in *Hamlet*, of course. The cursed hebenon, henbane. A poison in large doses, mildly hallucinogenic in smaller amounts."

"So you think the girl was doing drugs?"

"I believe it's more likely they were fed to her. A few were still caught in her throat. The seeds possess strong sedative properties, a medieval version of Rohypnol," Constance explained.

"Did that match the tox-screen results?"

"Based on tests of her urine and ocular fluid, I'd say the seeds were introduced within hours of death, no signs of anything else in her system aside from the beer. And here's the interesting thing—they were in the other girl's stomach, too." Constance arched an eyebrow.

"So we've got some sort of medieval date rapist on our hands. Fantastic." Morrow scribbled on his pad. "Can we trace the seeds?"

Constance shook her head. "No sign of rape on either girl, as I wrote in my report. As far as the seeds go, a quick search of the Internet uncovered numerous possible sources. Amazing the things you can buy online. Just last week I ordered a dishwasher."

"Well, congratulations," Morrow said uncertainly. "If there's anything else, could you call us?" He handed over one of his business cards.

Constance wagged a finger at him. "Not so fast, young man. I was saving the best for last." She crossed the room and threw open the refrigerator door. "Let's see…oh, here it is." She withdrew two other silver bowls and nudged the door closed with her hip.

Kelly took one from her. Inside was a congealed mound of granola. "What is it?"

"Contents of Lin Kaishen's stomach. At first I simply thought it was oatmeal, but the lab found an odd composition to it. There are over thirty different kinds of seeds here, mostly of nonnative origin. Barley, linseed, gold of pleasure, knotgrass, and of course, the henbane seeds. He must have given her a last supper of sorts. Very strange."

"What's that?" asked Morrow, squinting at a narrow black line in the second bowl. It resembled a furry twig.

"Ah, the pièce de résistance…." Constance gingerly

pinched it between tweezers and brandished it in front of her face, grinning. "Found this mixed in with the gruel—tail feather of the *Corvus corax*."

"The what?"

Constance twirled it by the stem. "Common raven. Now isn't that just the oddest thing?"

Four

"Mr. Brown? FBI Agents Morrow and Jones. We just need a minute of your time." Jerome Brown peered at their badges with distrust, bent almost double to restrain a wiry pitbull growling fiercely through the small crack in the door.

"He don't like strangers," Jerome said flatly. "Wait here."

Kelly looked at Morrow, who shrugged and muttered, "I told you he was a character."

A minute later they heard the chain slide back, and the door opened to reveal an older black man dressed in a spotless green jumpsuit. He was over six feet tall, with closely trimmed white hair, deep-set eyes and a thin scar lining one side of his face. Kelly noted that his left arm ended at the elbow, which explained why the local PD didn't consider him a suspect.

"Vietnam," Jerome said, following her eyes. "Don't slow me down none, though. The president said you'd be stopping by. Well, come on in." He waved them by with his good arm and relocked the door. For a man who lived in a relatively safe small town, Kelly noted, his house was fortified with two dead bolts and a high-end chain lock. "This is about the girl, right?" He shook his head sorrowfully. "Hoped to never see anything like that again."

"You've seen something like it before?" Kelly perched on the edge of the chair he pointed to. The house was small and sparsely furnished but immaculate. Other than the worn green chair she occupied, there was a small sofa, coffee table, ottoman and television set. The only decorations on the wall were a yellowing framed newspaper clipping and a glass case with three mounted medals. Through the open kitchen door she saw a small table and folding chair. A copy of *National Geographic* rested atop the neat stack of magazines on the coffee table. She heard the sounds of snuffling and scratching from behind the other door.

"Not exactly like that, but there were some terrible things in 'Nam. Thought for a minute I was seeing things, her being Asian and all." Jerome scratched his upper lip thoughtfully. "Can I get you folks some coffee or something?"

"No thanks, we just had some." Morrow smiled wanly. "Tell me something, when was the last time you were in that tunnel?"

"Oh, I'd say a few weeks earlier. That bathroom doesn't get cleaned too regular, not many kids use it."

"That's strange. It was spotless when forensics went tnrough it."

Jerome shrugged. "Cleaned it afterward. Police didn't say not to."

Morrow chimed in. "He's right, locals didn't consider it part of the crime scene."

"Okay. Then it would be helpful if you could help us draw a map, Jerome," Kelly said. "Everyone says you're the resident expert on the tunnels, and we need to find out what's down there."

"I can't draw much…" Jerome hedged.

"You won't have to. We have a computer program that does that part for you." Kelly watched him carefully—*definitely jumpy,* she thought. When he shifted, muscles strained against the polyester confines of his jumpsuit. With his disability he couldn't have mounted the girls on the wall, but he could have been an accomplice. Serial-killing teams were rare but not unheard of: the Hillside Strangler murders in L.A. were committed by two men. "We'll set you up with someone from our team. It should only take a few hours."

"Tomorrow I got to work." He shook his head.

"President Williams told us it was fine, the other workers will cover your areas for as long as we need you. Consider this a mini-vacation." Morrow clapped his hands together. "So tomorrow morning then, at our trailer? Let's say 8:00 a.m.?"

Jerome nodded slowly but didn't appear pleased.

Kelly paused at the door and turned back. "Mr. Brown, why do you spend so much time down in the tunnels?" She thought she saw something flash behind his heavily lidded eyes, then quickly subside.

He shifted his weight from one foot to the other. "It's quiet down there."

"Not lately it isn't," Morrow noted.

Jerome cast his eyes downward. "I ain't seen nothing down there."

"Aside from the girl," Kelly said.

"Right. Just the girl."

"What do you make of him?" Morrow asked sotto voce as they stepped off the porch.

Kelly listened to the bolts and chains sliding back into place. "I'd like to find out more about his record in Vietnam."

"What are you thinking? Accomplice?"

"Possibly. He might've been a medic, or a surgeon's assistant. We should keep an eye on him."

"I'll assign a detail. Should we call it a day?" Morrow yawned dramatically. "If I'm tired, you must be ready to keel over."

"Not yet. How far to the Christou girl's house?"

"Few blocks that way. Oak Street." Morrow pointed.

Kelly looked at her watch. "It's seven o'clock. I say we talk to the housemates tonight. We'll have a better chance of catching them at home."

"Aye, aye, Cap'n." Morrow mock-saluted and marched ahead of her.

Kelly suppressed a grin and tried to block out thoughts of the hot shower waiting for her back at the motel. She was known for driving a case relentlessly, a trait that didn't endear her to colleagues but resulted in a higher success rate than anyone else in her department. Over the years her contemporaries shifted out of fieldwork to settle down and have families, while she continued clocking thousands of frequent-flier miles. She lost contact with most of her friends outside the Bureau, and pulled out of romances as soon as they got serious. It was only at times like this, at the beginning of a case when all she could see ahead was the twisted snarl of events and people awaiting her, that the accumulated stress of those years took their toll and she just wanted to crawl into bed and sleep for a week. As they approached the door to 69 Oak Street, she shook off the thoughts with the memory of what brought her here, to this career, all those years ago. As Morrow rang the bell, she felt her resolve return.

The door slowly creaked open to reveal a hulking man in his early twenties, heavily bearded, round lips hanging open. He held on to the door with one hand, swaying slightly and staring at them blankly.

"Agents Morrow and Jones, FBI," Morrow said authoritatively.

In the background a girl called out, "Josh, is someone here? Josh? Oh, for Christ's sake…" A girl with short brown dreadlocks bustled into the room. Dressed in stained gray sweatpants and a T-shirt with the university logo emblazoned across the front, she pulled Josh aside by his shirtsleeve. "You'll have to excuse him, he's having one of his bad days. Hello, Agent Morrow. And you are?" She raised her eyebrows at Kelly.

"Agent Jones," said Kelly as she flipped open her badge.

On closer inspection the girl looked as though she hadn't slept for days, dark pouches framing red eyes. "I'm Kim Mitchell, Anna's housemate. Please, come in. Can I get you something?" Issued in a flat tone of voice, her courtesy sounded mechanical.

Kelly stepped into the living room and watched Josh shuffle away. A minute later, a door closed upstairs. Kim followed Kelly's gaze. "Clozapine. You should have known him before—the bounciest, funnest guy you ever met, seriously. Then he just cracked. Schizophrenia. Personally, I think he should have taken at least a semester off to deal, you know? But his parents just kind of dumped him here. He's taking Anna's death pretty hard, drinking, which he really shouldn't do on meds. I keep calling his folks but they won't return my calls. Anyway…did you want anything? I was just putting the water on for some tea."

Despite her prattle, Kelly could tell that she'd been crying. "Tea sounds lovely, thanks."

Kim scurried off to the kitchen. The sounds of running water and the clattering of pots and pans indicated that some cleanup was necessary before tea could be served. While they waited, Kelly studied the room. In stark contrast to Jerome's apartment, this living room was strictly campus-chic. A motley assortment of furniture, some of which appeared to have served generations of former students, filled almost every inch of space. The walls were painted a deep orange, and stood in stark contrast to the moldy-looking green carpet on the floor. Papers and books covered almost every spare inch of space, spilling over tables and peeking out from under chairs. Dirty bowls and glasses completed the portrait of every parent's nightmare.

"You'd think Christou's kid could afford something better, huh?" Morrow said, hands on his hips. "I shudder to think that in a few years I'm abandoning my daughter to this fate."

"I recommend calling before you visit." Kelly smiled. She hadn't seen Morrow's daughter in years, but dimly recalled a ten-year-old blonde with her father's round face.

Kim bustled into the room bearing a tray loaded with three steaming mugs. "I hope chamomile is okay, it's all we've got left. I haven't really had the heart to do any shopping…" Her voice trailed off, and a tear snaked its way down her cheek. "Oh God, there I go again. I'm sorry. It's just, Anna and I were roommates since freshman year. I still can't believe…" She sniffled. Morrow handed her his handkerchief. "Oh, thanks. Just give me a minute." She waved a hand in front of her eyes. "Okay, I'm ready. So, what do you need to know?"

"First of all, I'm wondering how many people knew Anna was Dmitri Christou's daughter?"

"Ohmigod, you don't think that's why she was killed, do you?" Kim clapped a hand to her mouth.

"We're just trying to gather as much information as possible," Kelly said.

"Wow. Josh and I knew, of course, but the three of us have been, like, inseparable since frosh year. Other than that, I don't really know. Anna was pretty secretive, she always said people got really weird when they found out, so she wouldn't tell them if she could avoid it. I think pretty much everyone in the administration knew, of course, because they always tripped over themselves whenever they saw her. Was another girl killed? I heard a rumor they found someone else."

Kelly and Morrow exchanged looks. He wrapped his

hands around a tea mug and said, "Tell me about Josh. What was their relationship like?"

Kim shook her head fiercely. "Uh-uh, not what you're thinking. Josh might have had a thing for Anna way back when, but he was totally over it. Being schizophrenic doesn't make him dangerous, I wouldn't live with him if I thought he was."

"Of course you wouldn't," Kelly said reassuringly. "We're just trying to get a better sense of what Anna's day-to-day life was like. Did all three of you go to the party together?"

"Just Anna and I, Josh stayed home." Kim examined the floor. "He wasn't feeling well, so he decided not to go at the last minute. He doesn't really like frat parties, anyway. I think that's why he's so upset. He thinks if he was there, it wouldn't have happened, even though I keep telling him that's totally untrue."

"Why would he think that?" Kelly asked.

"He thinks he could've protected her. He keeps saying he wouldn't have let her just go off with some guy."

Kelly nodded and patted Kim's hand. No matter what the girl said, a schizophrenic harboring an unrequited crush was definitely worth looking into. And if the killer had been someone close to Anna, it made sense that he would be harboring a guilty conscience. She made a mental note to put a police detail on Josh, and to see if he could be linked to the Kaishen girl. "Do you remember anything else from that night, Kim? Anyone at the party strike you as strange or out of place?"

"Like I told the other guy, I was pretty drunk. I didn't

even really notice when she left," she said, voice cracking at the end.

"What other guy?" Morrow asked sharply.

"You know, the other FBI guy. He was here earlier today, asking the same questions." Kim looked from one of them to the other. "He was FBI, right? I gave him cookies…"

"Did he show you a badge?" Kelly asked.

Kim nodded emphatically. "Uh-huh, but I didn't exactly examine it, you know? I mean, I think it was the same as yours."

"Any chance you remember his name?" Morrow asked. "Or what he looked like?"

"Ohmigod…it wasn't him, was it? Are we in danger?" Kim appeared on the verge of panic.

"I'm sure it's nothing to worry about, probably just a mix-up at the office." Morrow put a steadying hand on her arm. "Just in case, we'll assign someone to watch your house, okay? They'll keep an eye out for anything suspicious."

Smooth, Kelly thought. Morrow just provided them with a good explanation for why a police car would be stationed outside.

"Okay." Kim sounded uncertain.

"And if you think of anything, even if it doesn't seem important, don't hesitate to call." Morrow smiled reassuringly as he handed her his card. "My cell phone number is on the back. Anytime, day or night."

"Thanks." Kim wiped her cheek with the back of one hand. "Anna's dad arrives tomorrow. I'm trying to organize some sort of memorial, you know? But I don't want to do it in the chapel, obviously."

"Well, let us know. We'd love to attend." Morrow patted the girl's knee and stood.

"Thanks for your time." Kelly carefully set her tea mug back on the tray and headed for the door.

"Sure."

As they stood on the porch, Kelly heard two dead bolts turn in succession; Kim wasn't taking any chances. The temperature had dropped with the sun. She buttoned up her jacket, shivering slightly. "Anytime, day or night?" She raised an eyebrow at Morrow.

"I live to serve." Morrow grinned, bowing slightly from the waist. "Besides, she reminds me of my little girl."

As they started down the path to the street, Kelly felt eyes on her back. She stopped and turned to face the house. Framed by light in an upstairs window, Josh stood watching them. He raised a beer bottle to his lips, then slowly lowered the blinds.

Morrow followed her eyes. "Prime suspect, huh?"

Kelly nodded slowly. "I'd like that car here by tonight. Let's also look into his background, see if he has any medical training or experience with butchering."

Morrow nodded. "On it. So far the locals have proven surprisingly helpful, if not completely competent."

"It's a shame about the bathroom, we might've gotten something there," Kelly agreed. "We're the only agents assigned here, right?"

Morrow shrugged. "Far as I know."

"So it sounds like we've got company. I need you to sniff around, find out who's playing at being FBI. We need to scare him off before he interferes any further. And

I think that's it for today." Kelly checked her watch again. It was almost eight o'clock. A gnawing feeling in her stomach served as a nagging reminder that she hadn't eaten anything but a bagel since breakfast.

"You want to grab something to eat?" Morrow asked. "I hear there's a great barbecue place on campus."

Kelly repressed a smile; Morrow's appetite was legendary around the New York office. "I think I'll just get something at the motel. Long day tomorrow." More than anything, Kelly wanted a shower and a good night's sleep. Hopefully the motel had room service. A burger would be perfect right now, she thought. A nice juicy burger and a shower, and she could face whatever tomorrow had in store for her.

As it turned out, the only available food at the motel was dispensed by a vending machine at the end of the hall. Kelly sighed as she deliberated between a Snickers bar and a Twix. Not what she had in mind, but she was too tired to drive anywhere. As she soaped up in the shower ten minutes later, she let her thoughts wander over the case. Two possible suspects so far, and that was only considering the people on campus; there were a few thousand residents in the surrounding town, and countless more in a five-mile radius. And then there was the painting done in the blood of a third, unknown victim. On a campus this size, another missing girl should have been reported by now, which left the possibility that the victim came from somewhere else. But an exhaustive search of the tunnels hadn't uncovered another body. So where had the killer disposed of her?

She was also bothered by the timeline: two murders in two weeks was atypical for a serial killer; usually there was a cooling-off period of months or even years before they killed again. Either the perpetrator had hid past crimes well, or he had recently graduated from lesser crimes to murder. Most serial killers also had a type, and they tended to stick to their own race; killing an Asian, then a Caucasian, was rare. The victims were the daughters of a Chinese diplomat and of a Greek shipping magnate: on the face of it, all they had in common was powerful fathers. Was it possible that was a coincidence? Or was someone targeting these girls to fulfill a grudge, and if so, what was the connection?

Generally serial killers were classified into two types: organized versus disorganized. The disorganized ones were always the easiest to catch: exhibiting low- to mid-range IQs, they left behind a chaotic crime scene and an abundance of forensic evidence, acting mainly when the opportunity arose. On the other side were the organized killers; intelligent, well-educated, and typically male, they spent weeks or months tracking their victim. Organized killers maintained an impenetrable facade, living seemingly normal lives by day while they indulged their dark secret by night. Almost invariably when one was caught, neighbors expressed shock because "he seemed like such a nice man." Despite the fact that the United States possessed only six percent of the world's population, it was home to three-quarters of all serial killers, with at least thirty-five actively hunting at any given time. Some criminologists claimed that a third of the annual murder rate could be attributed to serial killers.

As Kelly brushed her teeth, she wrinkled her nose at the mirror. This killer was perplexing. Clearly organized, since there was hardly any forensic evidence left behind, and the murders were highly ritualized. But he also acted impulsively, because no one could have predicted that Anna Christou would enter the tunnels that night. Had he lured Lin Kaishen into the tunnels, or captured her somewhere else before staging the murder? Kelly tried to force the questions from her mind as she felt the encroaching beginnings of a migraine. The report from the profiler was due the next day. She wasn't hopeful, but with any luck it would narrow down what she was looking for. As she sank into bed and flipped off the light, she tried to block the images of the mangled girls from her mind. Eventually she sank into a deep, dreamless sleep.

"Ken? Come to bed, Ken."

His wife stood in the open doorway, holding her robe closed with both hands as she regarded him with concern. He had barely slept the past few nights. When he took the job and moved them cross-country, he thought his biggest obstacles would be stabilizing the university's diminishing endowment and fighting the standard tenure battles with professors. Instead, two of his students were dead, and his presidency was about to be thrust into the national spotlight. Worse yet, every night as he started to drift off to sleep, he imagined he could hear the screams of those poor girls from deep in the caverns below his house. Until a few days ago he'd barely been aware that the tunnels existed. Now he swore he could feel them, hear them, lurking underground. That morning he had installed a dead bolt on the outside of the cellar door as his wife eyed him, eyebrows raised over her coffee mug.

"Really, Ken, the most important thing is to get some sleep. You can't do anything else tonight." Elizabeth came over and took his hand, gently guiding him back into the bedroom. He curled up in her arms, listening as her breathing evened out and deepened. Outside the window, a fall wind whispered through the leaves. Despite his flannel pajamas and their thick down comforter, he started to shiver uncontrollably.

He swirled the brush around the top of the bucket, breaking the slight film that had developed over it. It wasn't cold enough. He needed someplace cooler to keep it, he pondered, somewhere it wouldn't be found. After a few moments of methodical stirring, it started to ease up under his hands. He saw the heartbeat in it, bringing it back to life. The girl had looked like an angel, he thought, so young, so pretty.

He settled back into his seat at the table and carefully straightened out the block of wood before him. He ran his fingers over the coarse grain: yew wood, the tree of eternal life, Yggdrasil. As he lifted the knife, his eyes half-closed and he began to whisper a chant, voice rising and falling. The cat stopped its grooming and lifted its head to watch him. Wood shavings curled out of the grooves formed as he went over them again and again, digging in deeper with each stroke of the knife. Finally, his eyes opened and he blinked. In a daze he dipped the brush into the bucket—

one, two, three times—then carefully wiped stray globs off on the edge before running the brush across the wood in long, even sweeps. He felt his hand being guided, his insides settling into a meditative calm with each stroke. Finished, he set the brush to one side, careful to lay the bristles on a paper towel. Lifting the wood above his head, he raised his eyes to the ceiling. The cat jumped from its perch in alarm at the sudden booming of a loud, clear voice that seemed to emanate from deep within. After a moment the silence returned. Lowering the wood back to the table, he raised his knife and slowly drew a ring around it, then repeated the gesture twice more.

As he cleaned up, carefully pressing the edges of the lid onto the bucket, a few drops of blood seeped over the rim and ran down the side. He stopped their escape with one finger, retracing their route to the top. He couldn't resist sucking the last bit off his finger.

Five

Kelly awoke shortly after dawn the next day. Shards of sunlight pierced the Venetian blinds. Rubbing her eyes, she crossed the room and pulled on the cord, revealing the highway in the foreground, grassy fields extending into the distance. Not the best view, but all things considered not bad.

Within five minutes she had dressed in Lycra leggings and a pullover and strapped on her running shoes. If she remembered correctly, a hundred yards from the motel she could pick up the woodsy trail she ran on when she was a student. After stretching briefly, she checked her watch for the time and set off. It was a gorgeous day, the leaves still damp with dew, low-hanging fog clinging to bushes. She took long deep breaths—three counts in, three out—enjoying the loamy scent of soil and late-season wildflowers perfuming the air. She had forgotten how beautiful it could be out here. Years of city living had acclimated her to a constant barrage of smog and sound, but what struck her now was the stillness. She had loved it here, she remembered. Her student years had easily been some of the best of her life, a brief window when it seemed she might finally put her past behind her. She shook the memories off and focused on the path. Winding through a thick patch of woods bordering campus, it intermittently ran alongside and skipped over a small stream. She felt the ground spring back against her shoes as she pushed off, her pace steady and even. She ran four miles a day, a regimen she stuck to regardless of where in the country her job landed her or what the day held in store. It was the only concession she allowed herself, her own form of meditation. Sometimes she thought her daily run was the only thing that kept her sane in the face of so much pain and misery.

It was a little past seven when she pulled open the door of the trailer, long auburn hair still wet from her shower, coffee cup clasped in one hand. Kelly intended to spend an hour or two reviewing the crime-scene photos and initial interviews. She sensed that she was missing something, but couldn't put her finger on what it was.

"Good morning."

Surprised, she almost dropped her coffee. Tilted back in a chair with his feet propped up on her desk was a man in his forties, handsome, with salt-and-pepper hair and pale blue eyes. Her files were scattered across the desktop, and he held a sheaf of papers in one hand. "Kelly Jones, I presume?" In one fluid motion he slid his feet to the floor and crossed the trailer, right hand extended. "Jake Riley, formerly of the FBI, currently of Mr. Christou's personal security team. Nice to meet a colleague."

She ignored his hand. "What the hell are you doing in here, Mr. Riley?"

Jake let his hand drop, though his grin widened. "Excellent question. Mr. Christou sent me to look into the circumstances surrounding his daughter's death. His good friends at the Bureau offered him all the help and support they thought he might need. And that's how I came into possession—" he held up a key to the trailer door "—of this."

Kelly fought to control her rage. "I would have appreciated a heads-up before you helped yourself to my files."

"Sorry about that. I wasn't sure where you were staying." He tapped the papers on the table to straighten them, then handed them to her. "So what's on the docket for today?"

"Let me make something clear, Mr. Riley—"

"Jake."

Kelly found his air of bemusement irritating beyond belief. "This is an FBI investigation. Until I hear directly from my superiors, your job is to stay out of our way. I'm assuming it was you that scared the hell out of Kim Mitchell?"

"Not my intention. What did you make of the other roommate, Josh? I've managed to secure a copy of his medical records, if you want to take a look…" Jake rummaged through a worn blue backpack and withdrew a red folder. "Peace offering?" he asked, holding it out to her.

Kelly kept her arms crossed in front of her chest. "I thought that was privileged information."

Jake shrugged. "One of the benefits of leaving the Bureau—the rules are a little more fluid for me now. Hey, don't look at me like that." He held up his hands. "Nothing shady going on here. His parents offered me those records, and since his diagnosis they've been reinstated as his legal guardians. No harm, no foul."

Kelly reluctantly accepted the folder, tempted to look but not wanting to be indebted to this jerk. "They just gave them to you? Why, to help convict their son of murder?"

"Well, I might have told one or two little white lies, but—"

"Knock, knock!" Morrow clambered into the trailer, balancing a tray of steaming coffee cups in one hand, a box of donuts tucked under his arm. "Best thing about this job so far—there's a Dunkin' Donuts on the way to campus. Hey, Riley. I see you two have met."

"So far Ms. Jones seems less than thrilled by my presence. It is Ms., isn't it?" Jake cocked an eyebrow.

Kelly ignored him and turned to Morrow. "When did you find out about this?"

Morrow shrugged. "Got the e-mail this morning, probably one waiting in your in-box, too. Hey, this is a good thing." He turned to Riley. "We were worried there might be an overzealous P.I. screwing things up for us."

"Not that this is much better," Kelly said under her breath, as she took a seat and flipped open her laptop. She eavesdropped as Morrow and Riley chatted over donuts. Apparently they'd worked togehter on a few cases in the past together and enjoyed an easy camaraderie. She tried to shrug off how much their rapport was bothering her. There were three messages in her e-mail in-box, one from ViCAP. Plugging in the M.O. for this case had only elicited partial matches, nothing that looked particularly promising: a string of young girls choked, then stabbed in Minneapolis, but they were all prostitutes; and another set of murders in Texas involving teenage boys hung from trees. Neither sounded like her guy. There was an e-mail from her superior, Assistant Special Agent in Charge Bowen. Morrow always joked that ASAC really stood for Assholes Stuck At Corporate. Bowen's message informed her of Jake Riley's involvement with the case, and included a thinly veiled threat of what would happen if she didn't cooperate fully. Too little, too late, she thought angrily. He should have told her this over the phone when he assigned her the case. Bowen had only been her boss for a few months now, but he was turning out to be the worst sort of ASAC, one with virtually no field experience who advanced thanks to his ass-kissing skills. Finally, Constance had sent an updated report on the third blood type found under the Kaishen girl. A side note mentioned that whoever the unidentified girl was, she had been pregnant at the time of the killing. *Great,* Kelly thought with a sigh. The media was going to lap this up when word leaked out.

"Any word from the locals on missing persons?" Kelly asked, interrupting Riley mid-sentence. He was regaling Morrow with the story of his latest adventure, pursuing a team of international arms dealers who'd tried to infiltrate Christou's shipping network.

"All business, isn't she?" Riley said with a wink at Morrow.

"You don't know the half of it," chuckled Morrow. After seeing the expression on Kelly's face he cleared his throat. "Local PD doesn't have any missing person reports matching our profile. In fact, they only have one report total, and that's a deadbeat dad. This place is a modern-day Mayberry. The captain might join our little tour today if he can tear himself away from his desk. I assume you're coming as well?" he asked Riley, who nodded.

On a whiteboard were three columns, one entitled "Christou," the next "Kaishen," the last headed "Jane Doe." Each column listed all the evidence pertaining to the victims. Under the Jane Doe column, Kelly erased the word *Local?* The news was discouraging; it meant their third victim probably came from somewhere else entirely, which could bog down the investigation in jurisdictional battles if and when they did find her body. Something else troubled Kelly: if a high-profile girl had gone missing in the last month, it would be common knowledge by now. Chances were the unidentified girl belonged to what was unofficially termed the "less-dead," victims whose disappearances were rarely reported, such as runaways, prostitutes and illegal immigrants. That meant their killer was now targeting a different type of prey, possibly in a bid for fame. Kelly turned her attention to a map of Connecticut tacked up beside the board. "Let's widen the search—statewide first, then bordering states if that doesn't turn up anything."

"Have the profilers weighed in yet?" asked Jake.

"This afternoon at the earliest," Morrow said through a mouthful of jelly donut.

"Let me guess—we're looking for a white male, age twenty to forty, lives alone, though he might be married. He holds down a steady job, planned out the killing in meticulous detail, which is why we have no forensics, and probably took some sort of trophy, unless the blood and lungs were enough. Organized, doesn't discriminate by race, probably wet the bed as a kid and had some trouble with his mommy. Can you believe it takes them more than ten minutes to come up with that? Ever notice how all the serial killer profiles are almost identical?" Jake sipped his coffee with a self-satisfied smile.

What an asshole, Kelly thought. She pursed her lips and clicked her laptop shut. "Can you pass me the photos from both scenes?"

Morrow and Riley exchanged glances. *Great,* she thought. The boys' club had already formed against her. "Listen, Jones, I really don't mean to be stepping on your toes here…" Jake said.

"Have a donut, Kelly. C'mon, let's all be friends." Morrow passed her the open box. She reluctantly dug out a cruller and nibbled at it. "In this case, I say the more manpower, the better," Morrow concluded.

"Jerome will be here soon. I want to go over this stuff one more time before we have to cover these boards." The men nodded, and Riley silently passed her the files. She buried herself in them, flipping slowly through photo after photo, seeing the girls' anguish in every shot.

Six

Jerome materialized at the trailer door exactly one minute before eight o'clock He was dressed in his work jumpsuit. *Probably hoping this won't take all day,* thought Kelly. She wondered why he was so eager to clean toilets. In his good hand he held a battered silver lunch box, which he carefully set on a desk. He nodded at them each in succession. "Morning. You folks ready to go, or should we do the drawing?"

"Let's walk the tunnels first, I'm itching to get out of this trailer. I don't think the good captain is going to show anyway. Kelly? You agree?" asked Morrow, jumping to his feet.

She nodded her assent and they set off behind Jerome. Kelly followed on his heels with Morrow and Riley bringing up the rear, still trading stories from the past few years. The low cloud cover had already burned off and the day was heating up. They passed sleepy-looking students on their way to class, bags slung from one shoulder, who turned and stared after them. Word must be out, Kelly thought, if the campus grapevine was anything like it used to be. Their trailer was hardly inconspicuous, but Kelly had talked Dean Scott out of moving it off campus, convincing him that in terms of convenience they needed to be as close to the center of things as possible.

Jerome led them across the street and into the Sommerfields quad. The grassy slopes were encircled by three-story dorms and classrooms constructed from the dark brown blocks that were popular in the late sixties. Despite the inherent ugliness of the architecture, the stone paths and manicured gardens gave the area a glen-like feel. Kelly half smiled as she took in the patch of grass bathed in sunlight next to Sommerfield One; she used to while away afternoons there, she remembered with a pang of nostalgia. She and her roommate would flip through their books and chat while surreptitiously watching a circle of boys nearby play Hacky Sack.

Jerome held open the door at the entrance to the College of Letters building for her. Despite the fact that it was Tuesday and classes were in session, the halls were oddly hushed. She followed Jerome down a staircase, sliding her hands along the metal banister as a flood of memories returned. She'd been to a party here herself, her freshman year. A keg was packed in an ice-filled trash can and set in a shower stall in the boys' bathroom. She had worn her new Levi's, and spent the evening flirting with the captain of the hockey team. Kelly turned to Morrow. "Check with Lin's roommates, find out if there was a party in this dorm around when she disappeared."

"Gotcha," Morrow said, noting it down.

At the bottom of the stairwell stood two beige metal doors. A chain looped through their handles was clasped with an industrial padlock. "This is it," Jerome said solemnly, digging an enormous key ring out of his pocket and awkwardly sorting through it for the right key. Kelly resisted the urge to help him. Having located it, he undid the padlock and slid the chains out. They fell to the floor with a metallic clatter that made her flinch. He pulled the door open and nodded for her to enter.

It was pitch-black inside. For a moment she couldn't find the button on her flashlight and felt the darkness closing in around her, causing her heart to race. *This is what they felt,* she thought. *How heavy the darkness can be.* Her flashlight clicked on and she played it across the walls. It was just as she remembered it, the same faded paint chronicling the lives and passions of legions of students. A rainbow arced through the words, *"Matt + Patti,"* quotes from John Lennon and Karl Marx proclaimed peace and communism, a panther leaped from the boundaries of the circle her light cast.

"Wow." From behind her Morrow issued a long whistle. "There wasn't anything like this at City College, I'll tell you that much."

She heard Riley's low laugh, and for the first time felt comforted by the fact that he had come along; down here, she preferred strength in numbers.

"This way." Jerome's face loomed out of the darkness. She felt him ease past her, and followed closely behind. Less than ten yards in she heard him say, "Watch out for my equipment." Right in front of her was a bucket with a mop and bottle of cleaning solution tucked inside. As she skirted it, Jerome said, "No closets down here. It's easier than taking it up and down the stairs."

After about five minutes his footsteps stopped, and his light froze on a section of the wall. "I found her here," he said quietly.

They stood in silence gazing at it, shoulder to shoulder. The image looked much larger than it had in the photos, Kelly thought. The center of it was smeared, but the edges were distinct. She had hoped that seeing it in person would give her some sense of what or who it was supposed to be. It was a face, and there was something satanic about it as Morrow had noted, but there was another element too, a feral quality in the nose and eyes. "Pretty intricate, the way the lines interconnect," she said quietly. "He clearly took his time on it."

"So he paints it, then comes back later and kills the girl? It doesn't make a lot of sense," Jake said thoughtfully. "He probably drugged the Kaishen girl, then brought her down here. But he couldn't have known Anna would be in the tunnels."

"No, but maybe he followed her. Seized the opportunity when it presented itself," Kelly said as she carefully walked in a half circle around the painting. The outline of the gallon-size bucket was clear, as were the smaller waxy circles where the candles had been set. The rest of the floor was sticky with blood. Some of it had sprayed on the walls surrounding the painting, almost giving the impression of a halo around the leering face. "Pretty far in," she noted, turning thoughtfully to Jerome. "You clean back here?"

He had stepped out of the light; only the whites of his eyes were visible. "Thought I heard something," he responded sullenly.

"Yeah? Like what?" Morrow asked.

"Probably just rats," Jerome said after a minute. "Figured I'd set some traps, then I seen the girl."

Kelly waited for him to continue but he lapsed into silence. She considered pressing him, but by this afternoon she'd have his military record in her hands. Then she'd know if he was worth questioning further.

"Does this tunnel link up with the chapel?" asked Riley, his voice unnaturally loud in the small space.

"They all link up somewhere," said Jerome in a monotone.

Morrow fell into step beside her as they continued. "Creepy, huh?" he said in a stage whisper. "Give me a shallow grave next to a highway any day of the week." At the look on her face he realized his mistake. "Oh shit, Kelly, I'm sorry. I wasn't thinking—"

"It's fine. Forget it," she said gruffly, quickening her pace to pull ahead of him again. The donut she ate earlier had settled into a lump in her stomach. Periodically it threatened to rise up the back of her throat.

They walked for ten more minutes through what felt like miles of tunnels before hitting a fork. "This way." Jerome ducked into the tunnel on the right. *What were they under now?* she wondered. *The science building?*

The president's office? The darkness was so cloying she had lost her bearings.

She almost walked straight into Jerome. He had stopped again and stood facing the wall. The drawings in this section of the tunnel were older, she noticed. Quotes from Baudelaire and Blake surrounded silhouettes of young men in caps, probably self-portraits, she thought. They marched down the hallway, fading into the same grim painting, dark brown blood clinging to what remained of their faces.

"This was where they found Anna." Riley stated flatly. He was different here, Kelly noticed, watching him out of the corner of her eye. She wondered how long he had worked for Christou, and how well he had known the girl. She made a mental note to do a background check on him when she got back to the trailer. The image was exactly the same, though somewhat larger by her estimation. There was the same bucket mark on the floor, the same halo. On either side the waxy remnants of two candles marked outposts in a sea of dried blood.

"Yup." Jerome nodded slowly. "She must've got turned around down here. The tunnel to the chapel is that way…" He gestured with his flashlight, waving it down the length of the tunnel. "But to get back to the fraternity, she should've taken a right."

"She got lost," murmured Morrow. "Poor kid."

"Yessir." Jerome heaved a heavy breath. "Well, if you folks don't mind, we should get to drawing that map. I'd like to get some work done today…"

"The chapel. I want to see the chapel," Kelly said firmly. Jerome shrugged and brushed past her.

* * *

He eased open the trapdoor, flooding the mouth of the tunnel with sunlight. Kelly gulped deep breaths of fresh air as she climbed out, clicking off her flashlight as she shielded her eyes and waited for them to adjust. Dust motes danced in the rays pouring through the clear leaded-glass windows set high along the walls of the chapel. Lush red curtains swept from ceiling to floor, facing austere wooden pews that led to an enormous wrought-iron door. She hadn't set foot in here once during her four years at the school, Kelly realized as she looked around. It was beautiful. Someone cleared their throat behind her, and she turned to see a slight man in his forties wearing a turtleneck, blazer and corduroy pants. He stood behind the altar, fingers drumming against the top of it, eyeing them quizzically through round metal glasses.

"You must be Father John?" Morrow asked as he dusted off his hands.

"Yes, well." Father John looked from one of them to the other. "I'm guessing you're those FBI agents everyone has been talking about. Hello, Jerome."

"Morning, Father John," Jerome said, bowing his head slightly.

"So you're following the path of our poor dear Anna. Such a wonderful girl. I can't imagine for the life of me how such a thing happened."

"Were you aware, Father, that students were coming in here after hours?" asked Riley, stepping forward.

Father John nervously examined the floor. "Obviously we don't encourage that sort of thing. We keep the main doors locked at night. But I like to think that the chapel is always available to students in need…of course now the entry is padlocked on the inside."

"Right." Morrow ran a hand through his remaining hair. "We understand that Anna Christou used to attend services?"

"Yes, she was very devoted her first year here." The priest lowered his eyes. "But unfortunately, like so many others she eventually stopped attending regularly."

"How many students do you generally see at Sunday Mass?" asked Kelly.

"Oh, on average I'd say about fifteen or twenty. It's very different now than it used to be. Back in the day, there were never fewer than a hundred. But then these are different times, aren't they?" Father John smiled weakly.

"I suppose so. Did she come to services with anyone in particular?"

Father John tilted his head to the side, contemplating. "Not that I remember, no," he said after a moment.

"When was the last time you saw her?" Kelly pressed.

He hesitated, then said, "Now that you mention it, it was the Sunday prior to her disappearance. I remember, because she made a point of speaking to me after Mass."

"About what?" Kelly asked.

"She was concerned about a friend of hers. Apparently he was acting increasingly strangely. I recommended that she refer him to the school's mental health counselors."

"I thought counseling fell under your purview," Morrow noted.

The priest smiled thinly. "She had made it clear that he was not a Christian, so I felt that a layperson would be more appropriate."

"Thanks for your time, Father." Kelly smiled reassuringly at him. He looked badly shaken, and she felt for him; it couldn't have been easy, knowing that a killer had infiltrated his sanctuary.

They left through the doors at the rear of the chapel and made their way across campus to the trailer.

"What time is it—Jesus, eleven o'clock already?" Morrow said as he checked his watch. "Is it too soon for a lunch break?"

Kelly absentmindedly kicked up a few mid-fall leaves as she walked, staring at the ground. "I was hoping we might speak to a few of the girls' professors first, but I suppose it can wait."

"Does that mean I can get back to work?" asked Jerome hopefully.

"Sorry, Jerome, we still need you to help with those drawings. Join us for lunch? Morrow's buying," Kelly said consolingly.

"The hell I am…" Morrow guffawed.

"All right then, it's on me."

"I brought my lunch, in the trailer…" Jerome shuffled his feet uncomfortably. She laid a hand on his good arm. "Please. It's the least we can do, to thank you for your help." Jerome recoiled visibly at her touch.

"Office hours are usually in the afternoon," Riley said, falling in step beside her. "I think your best bets are Professor Birnbaum for the Kaishen girl—that was her thesis adviser, rumor has it they were close. Anna had just started her major, but her adviser last year was Vivian Westlake in art history. I've got a copy of both of their schedules from this semester and last back in the trailer."

"Thanks," Kelly said begrudgingly. She had requested copies of those documents herself but was told they would take a few days. Clearly Dmitri Christou's money greased the wheels of bureaucracy.

"So? Lunch?" Morrow rubbed his belly and grinned at them.

In spite of herself, Kelly smiled. "Sure. I need to stop by the trailer first to grab my wallet, then let's hit that barbecue place you mentioned last night. I'm starving."

"I don't have much of an appetite," Riley said. "I might as well follow up some other leads, meet you back at the trailer later."

Kelly noticed he was subdued after their visit to the tunnels. "Don't go off cowboying," she warned.

"Who, me?" Riley responded with a forced grin. "Never."

Seven

Perched on the curb next to their trailer sat a petite blond girl in her early twenties dressed in a white oxford shirt, jeans and loafers. She was furiously scribbling notes in a small binder. As they approached, she jumped to her feet and removed a pair of owlish black reading glasses.

"Excuse me, are you the FBI agents working this case?" she stammered. "Claire Denisof, editor in chief of the *Cardinal*. That's, uh, our school newspaper. I was wondering if you could answer a few questions."

She looked unsure of herself, and Kelly repressed a smile. "Nice to meet you, Claire. Unfortunately, we can't comment on the investigation at this time."

"Oh, okay." The girl looked crestfallen. "But is there any way you could just confirm a couple of things for me? I'm hearing there's another girl, besides Anna. Is there any way you could give me her name?"

Kelly and Morrow glanced at each other. The parents had been informed, and the girls weren't minors. Despite the news blackout, there wasn't much harm in confirming what many of the students already knew. Rumors were often worse than the truth, especially on such a small campus.

Kelly pictured the pinched set of Dean Scott's jaw when he opened the *Cardinal* the next day. *What the hell, why not give the scoop to a student,* she thought. The kid could use the help, considering that within a day the university would mark the front lines for every major media outlet in the country. "Lin Kaishen was found during our search of the tunnels. She was a senior."

"Oh, that's fantastic!" Claire's face reddened with embarrassment. "I mean, how interesting." Claire squinted as she recorded the name in her book. "Is that L-y-n-n—"

"L-i-n, actually."

"Thanks." She glanced up again. "There are rumors going around that they were cut up pretty badly."

"I'm afraid I've told you all I can." Kelly paused with one hand on the door. "But you should write this—we've sealed off all known entrances to the tunnels. If anyone comes across other access points, they should inform us immediately. If they have any information regarding either girl, they can contact me directly through the switchboard. And most importantly stay out of the tunnels at all costs, report any suspicious behavior, and be careful. Don't walk around alone at night."

"Okay, got it. And you are?" Claire poised her pen above the pad.

"Special Agent Kelly Jones."

"Great. Thanks so much, Agent Jones, I really appreciate it. And if anything else comes up could you call me?"

"We'll be updating the media regularly as the investigation continues." Kelly smiled to herself as she closed the trailer door.

"The media, huh?" Morrow chuckled.

"Honestly, she'll probably turn out to be the most professional of the bunch," Kelly said.

"True," Morrow agreed. "Although I do love that foxy little thing from CNN. Do you suppose she'll be showing up?"

"As our official media intermediary you'll find out soon enough."

"Crap, I knew you were going to saddle me with that," Morrow grumbled. "So are we going to lunch, or what?"

Her black hair swished back and forth as she walked, books propped against one hip, a bright red purse slung from her shoulder. She waved and smiled at people as she sashayed slowly down the long, diagonal path connecting campus with some of the outlying buildings. *On her way to French class,* he thought. *She'll be five minutes late, as always.*

He followed at a discreet distance, not that she would have noticed him anyway. At this time of day the grassy slopes on either side of the path were filled with students chattering and laughing over lunch, while others raced to their midday classes. He adjusted his hat and glanced down at his notebook. After that, Philosophy 101, then a break until her four o'clock aerobics class, after which she would probably spend the evening in the library. *Fourth floor, carrel three,* he thought. *It would be so easy.*

He was distracted by the sight of the FBI agents strolling past, painfully obvious in their dark suits amid the thicket of students. His eyes narrowed as he watched the woman leading them. Her hair was the color of blood, and she walked with long, certain strides. Sensible shoes for a woman, he noticed. *Good,* he thought. *She'll need them.*

Eight

"This one leads to the old gym. And there's a fork in it, right about…here." Jerome pointed at the screen. "That part goes all the way to the waterfront."

"The waterfront? Are you shitting me?" Morrow shook his head as he inputted the new information. Lunch had provided a welcome break from the grim morning; now they were back at work, constructing a map. A labyrinth of lines crossed the screen, with X's detailing access points. "Have we locked that one off yet?"

"Not yet." Kelly leaned over his shoulder. It had only been a half hour, and already their diagram spilled past the overlay of the campus on-screen. She hadn't realized the tunnels were so extensive. She'd never ventured beyond the Sommerfields during her time on campus. "Let's call the captain and see if he can get someone down there right away."

"Yeah, good luck with that," Morrow scoffed. "Now he's acting as if this entire thing is one huge imposition. I get the sense that before this his biggest call was a kitten stuck in a tree. He keeps claiming he doesn't have the manpower."

"If he balks, make it clear that we'll go over his head to the mayor." Kelly shrugged. Dealing with local police departments was frequently the most frustrating part of her job. Either she ended up with a cowboy determined to break the case himself, or with a yokel who resented the fact that his shiny cars were actually being put to work. She understood where those sentiments came from but hated the delay caused when she had to smooth ruffled feathers. With any luck they'd crack this thing in a few weeks.

"And that one there ends up at the Gingerbread House." Jerome nodded sagely. Kelly was impressed that he was able to do this from memory; he had clearly spent a substantial amount of time wandering around beneath campus. What she still couldn't figure out was why.

"Gingerbread House? Seriously?" Morrow laughed. "Man, what made you decide to come here, Kelly? Do the brochures sell it as Candyland for college kids?"

"Something like that." Kelly put the finishing touches on a formal but scathing e-mail to ASAC Bowen, filling in the subject heading "Re: Jake Riley." She'd work with him, but she wasn't happy about it, and she wanted that made clear. She'd taken enough crappy assignments in the past, and turned around enough impossible cases. It was insulting to be saddled with some maverick civilian, even if he was a former agent. She hit *Send,* then stretched her arms over her head. "I'm going to talk to the good professors. Want to come along?"

"And leave all this?" Morrow gestured at the monitor

with a sweeping arm. "Never. Jerome and me have some male bonding to do."

Jerome appeared wildly uncomfortable at the suggestion.

"Why don't we divide and conquer. You take Birnbaum, and I'll grill the art history lady," Jake said without glancing up from his laptop. Kelly leaned back in her chair and peeked over his shoulder. He appeared to be playing some sort of video game.

She rolled her eyes. "That's all right, I think I can handle it."

He stopped and looked at her. "Now that's just silly. I know this is your operation, but you can't expect me to sit here twiddling my thumbs."

She heaved a heavy sigh. "Fine, suit yourself. Let's meet back here in an hour or so." She pulled on her jacket and left, resisting the urge to slam the door.

The air was cool outside the trailer, tree shadows already lengthening even though it was only two o'clock. Kelly fastened the top button of her blazer and set off for the Religion Department on the lower end of campus. Set back from the street, fragments of redbrick squinted out from a thick cloak of ivy that had been trimmed around the windows and doors. *Maybe not Ivy League,* she thought, *but they certainly aspire to be.* The building was two stories, probably the former home of wealthy local landowners. She eased open the unlocked front door and found herself in a long hallway lined with thick Persian carpeting. An enormous crystal chandelier illuminated dark oil paintings, all depicting glowering religious figures.

"Hello? Anyone here?" Four French doors led off the

main hallway, and a staircase on her right climbed to the second floor. In front of that she spotted an incongruous office bulletin board, with pegged white letters indicating professors' names and office numbers. She scanned through until she found Professor Birnbaum, Suite 201.

Upstairs was a similar hallway, minus the chandelier. Solid oak doors emblazoned with the names of professors were interspersed between classrooms. She peered in one door to find an animated young woman marching in front of a blackboard, pounding on the surface with a piece of chalk to punctuate her points.

"And *that* is why Christianity has been, since its inception, *negligent* in its *acknowledgment* of women's contributions."

Kelly smiled to herself; in some respects, the campus hadn't changed a bit.

"Excuse me? May I help you?" She turned to find a tall, thin man with nervous eyes and a beaked nose peering at her. He clutched a small black satchel in one hand and clasped a stack of books in the other.

"I hope so. I'm looking for Professor Birnbaum?"

He blinked at her. She got the impression that he was considering ditching the books and making a run for it. "Yes?"

"Are you Professor Birnbaum?" The British accent perfectly matched his appearance, she thought. In his tweed jacket and scuffed loafers, he could easily pass for John Cleese's younger brother.

"Yes, I am. Now, how may I help you? Oh, my goodness." He shook his head. "This must be about Lin. I'm so sorry. The first few months on campus are always a bit distracting for me, the shift from research to teaching, all those new students to remember. I thought you looked a bit old for a student. Not that you look old," he continued hurriedly. "Just too old to be a senior. Although I suppose you could be a graduate student, couldn't you…?" His voice trailed off.

Kelly flashed her badge. "Special Agent Jones, Professor Birnbaum. And yes, this is about Lin."

The professor tried to extend his hand, realized he was burdened by both books and a briefcase, and executed an apologetic shrug instead. "Please, if you'll follow me this way, to my office.…"

He stopped at the last door on the left, pressing the case against the wall with one knee as he awkwardly fished in his pocket for a key.

"Can I help you?" Kelly offered.

"Thank you but no, I'm fine. So many new books this year, there's been a surge in religious interest lately due to rising tensions in the Middle East. Fervor inspiring more fervor, which is not always a good thing," he concluded pensively. He finally located the key, slid it in the lock and turned it.

The door swung open to reveal a small, ten-by-ten-foot space. Bookshelves ran floor to ceiling across two walls, while directly opposite the door a single window flooded the room with light. Stacks of books covered almost every available space, rising up to knee height in some places. A tiny, frail-looking desk tucked in a corner of the room appeared on the verge of succumbing to the onslaught of books. A sturdy wooden chair, campus-issue, faced the desk. The only other decoration was a small desk lamp and an ancient typewriter, both coated in a fine layer of dust.

"You don't have a computer?" Kelly asked as she tentatively tapped one of the keys. It smacked against the roller with a satisfying click.

"Beastly things," he said with a shudder. "I handwrite my notes to students, and do the mandatory correspondence in the computer laboratory." He deposited the stack of books under his arm onto one of the smaller piles and put a finger to his lips, apparently making a mental note of where to find them later.

"So I understand you were Lin Kaishen's thesis adviser?"

"Yes, indeed. Please." He indicated the chair opposite his desk. "Have a seat." He waited until she had settled into the chair before sitting himself. "Poor Lin. She was such a bright girl."

Kelly noticed that he had a nervous habit of rubbing his thumb and forefinger together. "What was she working on?"

His eyes lit up. "Oh, it was a fascinating topic. She was studying the origins of Falun Gong, and the oppresion its practioners suffered in China. Not my field, really, but I was able to point her toward a wealth of information. Needless to say, her father was less than supportive of this line of research." He seemed to relax as he spoke, his voice quickening and becoming more animated.

"Why is that?" Kelly asked.

"She mentioned once that he worried someone outside the school might find out, that some of her research could reflect unfavorably upon him. I thought it was very brave of her to press forward despite his objections. Not many girls in her position would have done the same." A look of sadness crossed his face.

"I have to ask, Professor Birnbaum," Kelly said gently. "Was your relationship with Lin strictly teacher/student?"

He sat bolt upright in his chair. "I know what you're insinuating, Agent Jones, and I understand you're just doing your job. But you must believe that I take the code of conduct very seriously. I have never once, in more than a decade of teaching here, had anything but the most proper relations with my students."

The denial was a little too vehement, she thought. That didn't necessarily mean he was guilty, probably just aware of the rumors surrounding their relationship. "But you did spend a good deal of time together, from what I understand. More than a faculty adviser generally spends with a student."

He sighed and leaned forward across his desk. "You must understand, Ms. Jones, when Lin first arrived at the school her English skills were fairly weak. As one of the few Mandarin-speaking professors on campus, I took her under my wing, so to speak. But there was never anything inappropriate in our exchanges."

"Where did you learn to speak Mandarin?"

"When I was a boy I spent some time in Taiwan. My father was stationed at the British embassy there for a few years. That was another commonality we shared, both children of diplomats. It can make for an extraordinarily difficult upbringing."

The professor's explanation sounded plausible enough. But Lin had been a pretty girl, judging by the photo her roommate had provided. Surely the temptation must have been there. "Are you married, Professor?"

"No, never. Agent Jones, I will do everything in my power to help your investigation, but I must insist that you cross me off your list as a suspect. If you don't, I fear you will waste countless hours, while the real killer remains at large. Please." He looked at her beseechingly. "It's critical that you not waste time."

"Just a few more questions and then we're done." Kelly returned his gaze steadily until he lowered his eyes to the desk. "When did you last see Lin?"

"My, that must have been…almost three weeks ago. Was it a Tuesday? I believe it was—let me check." He rooted a small pocket calendar out of his satchel and flipped it open. "Ah yes. I went to New York on Wednesday for a symposium, so it must have been Tuesday."

"Evening or afternoon?" she pressed.

"It was around three in the afternoon."

"And she seemed fine?"

"Yes, in fact she seemed very positive about how the semester was progressing. She remained on campus this summer, I think largely to avoid her family, but it can be a bit lonely here in the off months. Is that all? I really must be getting to class…"

"One last thing, Professor." He stiffened as she slid a photo out of its sheath and handed it across the desk. "Do you recognize this?"

His eyes narrowed as he squinted at it. A long moment

passed before he answered, "No, I can't say I do, although it is reminiscent of something…" He looked past her at the stack of books, leaped to his feet and walked to the largest pile in the corner near the door. His finger danced down the bindings as he murmured the titles to himself. After a moment he stood, puzzled. "That's odd. I must have lent it out." He returned to the desk. "You see here, at the edges. That's classic Celtic symbolism, the twistings of eternity, although the face itself…" He peered at the picture again, holding it so close that his nose almost brushed the page. "It is extraordinary. I don't suppose I could have a copy?" He looked up at her hopefully.

Kelly weighed the request in her mind. There wasn't any harm in it that she could see, as long as he didn't hand it over to CNN. If he was the killer, he'd seen it already anyway. Chances were someone with his background would be able to identify it before the notoriously slow FBI lab. "I suppose, on the condition that you keep it to yourself. We're not going to release it to the press. But if you think you can trace it…"

"It's a puzzle, isn't it? It harkens back to so many ancient cultures." He shook his head. "I understand completely the need for secrecy. You have my word, Agent Jones." He shook her hand after carefully setting the photo down in the center of his desk.

She left the office just as a flood of students entered the corridor from one of the classrooms. Kelly waited for them to pass. The outfits were slightly different, but otherwise it was like reliving a stage of her youth. Birkenstocks and jeans were still the rage, she noted, as were the same Guatemalan purses and beaded knapsacks she had once owned. Most of the girls wore their hair long and loose, the boys mop-topped and ragged. At the end of the file shuffled a tall boy who looked like he was trying to cave into his own skin. She recognized him immediately.

"Josh?" He turned and peered at her uncertainly, lids hanging low over his eyes. "It's Special Agent Jones. We met briefly last night." He continued watching her without saying a word. "Do you have a minute to talk?"

He shrugged his shoulders and turned his back to the wall. He propped one foot against it and tilted his head back, slowly closing his eyes as if drifting off to sleep.

"So I understand you and Anna were close."

He nodded his head almost imperceptibly.

"Is that a yes?" she asked, crossing her arms in front of her.

He let his head drop forward so that he was looking her full in the face. His eyes were clearer today, she thought; he was probably sober. "Yes." His voice rasped slightly, as though it hadn't been used for some time.

"But you weren't with her the night she died?" Kelly pressed.

"Kim told you that already. I heard her." He spoke carefully, enunciating every word.

"Josh, I'm sure you understand that any information you give us could help catch Anna's killer."

"I don't have any information." He looked past her now, down the hall toward the stairs.

"Oh, Joshua! I was hoping to see you today…" Professor Birnbaum stood in his office doorway, clutching the satchel once again. "So you've met Agent Jones."

Josh spoke to the floor. "She wants to know about Anna."

"Yes, yes I know."

"I wasn't aware that Josh was a religion major," Kelly said to the professor, her gaze holding steady on Josh.

"Oh yes, he's one of our new converts—aren't you, Joshua?" Professor Birnbaum chuckled slightly.

"So I suppose that means you knew Lin Kaishen, too?"

"She was in my Buddhism class last year," Josh droned.

"That's right, I'd almost forgotten that!" Professor Birnbaum said. Kelly noted a forced brightness in his tone. "It was a large introductory class, of course—over fifty students, unusually large for our department. But then there's been tremendous interest in Buddhism recently. That's the thing about religion, you know— always a different one on top. I think the aspect of reincarnation particularly appeals to people today, perhaps more than ever…" His voice trailed off.

The three of them stood for a moment in silence, the only sound the rhythmic clucking of the grandfather clock downstairs.

"What do you want me to tell you?" Josh finally asked.

"What do you want to tell me?" Their eyes were locked now. The boy knew something, Kelly was sure of it.

"Joshua?"

Josh broke his gaze to turn toward the professor. "I've got to go," he mumbled. "You know where to find me."

They watched his retreat down the corridor. Professor

Birnbaum looked perplexed. "Poor lad, he's had a tough time of it. First the diagnosis, now this—"

"You seem to take a lot of students under your wing, Professor," Kelly commented. She tried to gauge his reaction. Was he anxious by nature, or could he be involved somehow?

He crossed the yards between them with a few quick steps and stopped just short of her. "I'm a teacher, Agent Jones. I realize that in the American system professors and students coexist at a safe distance from each other, but where I was schooled it was a very different story. I've devoted my life to this place, to these people." He waved the satchel in an arc. "I wish that I knew more about what happened to those poor girls, but I don't, and despite his mental state I'm sure Joshua doesn't either. Now, if you'll excuse me, I must be getting to class." He straightened his lapels with one hand and stormed past her.

She listened to his steps skittering down the staircase. *Quite an exit,* she thought to herself.

Nine

Morrow and Riley looked up as she entered the trailer. "Shit, it's getting cold outside. Close that behind you," Morrow said, shuddering against the blast of cold air that followed her in. "Anything?"

"Yes, actually." She made a show of sitting at her desk, opening her laptop and turning it on.

"Well?" Morrow asked impatiently.

"Josh Schwartz is a religion major. He had a class with Lin Kaishen last fall."

"Ooh, that *is* interesting." Morrow rubbed his hands together.

"I thought so. Anything from the art history teacher?" she tossed over her shoulder.

Riley shrugged. "Nothing. Except that she strongly suspects the girls' deaths have something to do with a right-wing, antifeminist conspiracy. But then again, that was my theory all along."

Kelly grinned in spite of herself.

"Aha!" Jake leaned forward in his chair, pointing at her emphatically. "Finally, she cracks a smile. I knew it would happen one of these days—"

"Don't get too excited. There's only a remote chance it might happen again." Kelly pursed her lips in an attempt to stop the smile. It was hard, though. Only her second day on a serial case, and she had narrowed the field to a few prime suspects. At this pace they might set a Bureau record.

"By the way, Jerome's military records came in." Morrow held up a file.

"Anything there?"

Morrow shook his head. "No medical or surgical training. Apparently our boy Jerome was a serious badass though—Special Forces before he lost the arm. Those medals on his wall are for real."

"Any criminal history?"

"Not so much as a parking ticket. Other than a yearly tax return and a driver's license, we don't have anything on him. You want me to keep digging?"

"No, let's focus on the kid for now." She flipped open Josh's medical file for a closer examination. Apparently the boy had spent most of the summer in a psych ward upstate. His parents checked him out on August thirtieth, and classes began the next day. So much for quality time, she mused. You had to wonder about a kid whose parents were so eager to be rid of him. "We need to find out if he went home for midterm break," she said aloud as she made a notation.

"Consider it done. And I've got more good news for

you—we got that list of premed students from the higher-ups, and guess who just changed majors this year?" Morrow said.

"Josh Schwartz?"

"The one and only. Fulfilled more than half the prerequisites, then quit. And last semester he managed to pull a B minus in biology."

"Doesn't biology include dissection?" Jake asked.

"It did when I took it. Morrow, why don't you have a chat with the biology professor, find out what kind of training Josh might have had," Kelly said.

"Got it."

The hairs on the back of her neck stirred. She glanced back to find Jake reading over her shoulder. He shook his head. "It's funny, I met Josh a few times. He's an odd duck, but murder seems out of his league."

"He is mentally ill."

"Yeah, but I never got the sense that he was dangerous."

"His schizophrenia was only diagnosed recently. Maybe the disease is manifesting itself differently now," Kelly responded. Her skin tingled slightly. Jake smelled good, she'd give him that, a combination of aftershave and mint. "There's something strange about Lin's adviser, too. He's mentoring Josh, and he's got a bad case of nerves. Might be something there."

"Huh, interesting." Jake leaned over farther. "If you'd like I could shake the trees, see what falls out."

Kelly debated. She preferred going by the book, but so far the information Jake had provided was moving the case forward more rapidly than if they strictly followed procedure. And she was under orders to integrate him into their investigation, she reflected smugly. The thought made her grin as she said, "That would be helpful."

Morrow raised his hands to the ceiling, palms up. "Should I leave you two alone?"

Kelly flushed and closed the file as Jake stepped back.

Morrow continued his mock tirade. "For Chrissakes, I spent practically the whole goddamn day knocking out this map of the tunnels. And Jerome, God love him, isn't exactly the best company. Don't get me wrong, I appreciate the strong silent type, but something about that guy gives me the heebie-jeebies. And to top it off, I'm feeling like a third wheel."

"Stow it, Morrow," Jake grumbled.

Kelly resisted the urge to squirm in her seat. *I mean, really,* she thought. Jake wasn't even her type. She avoided his eyes and kept her voice firm. "Let's stay on topic. I want to keep the details on both houses for now, and if the locals can spare another, assign it to Birnbaum's place."

"I'll see what I can do, but in all honesty I'm not sure they have more than two cars," Morrow grunted.

"Try them. If they say no, we'll wait and see if it's worth shuffling the cars around. For now, Birnbaum's house isn't the highest priority."

"So are we pulling the kid in?" Morrow asked.

Kelly tapped a pen on the table. "His parents might not care, but I have a feeling the administration isn't going to take kindly to us questioning Josh with what we've got. I say we spend tomorrow doing some more digging, see what comes up."

"Agreed." Jake nodded.

"So are we done for today?" Morrow asked hopefully. "I'd love to catch the big game."

"'Fraid not." Jake stood and tucked his shirt into his pants. Kelly watched him in spite of herself. *Good build,* she thought. *The body of a swimmer.* "Mr. Christou arrived at his hotel a half hour ago. I'm going to give him an update, and thought you might want to come along."

Kelly closed her eyes. This was her least favorite part of the job, dealing with the survivors. But if she didn't go she was guaranteed another venomous e-mail from ASAC Bowen.

"I'm guessing he's not at the lovely Motel 6," Morrow grumbled while trying to shake some of the wrinkles from his jacket.

"Nope. We're at the Radisson, over in Cromwell."

"Oh we are, are we? I bet they have room service there," Morrow said.

"Sure. But the swimming pool is a little small for my taste." Jake grinned. "Anyway, we should get going. He's expecting us."

The drive to Cromwell took fifteen minutes. As soon as they left the city limits, the postindustrial decay of the town quickly faded into a countryside of rolling pastures and small farms. Some of the trees had already turned, their leaves glowing ephemeral red and orange in the fading light. *Magic hour,* Kelly thought to herself, when the light seemed to imbue the scenery with an otherworldly hue. She had dated a nature photographer for a few months who would only shoot in that final hour before sunset, when he claimed the spirits of the landscape shone closest to their surface. What was his name again? She searched her mind…she hadn't dated much recently, her work didn't allow time for that. And it was difficult. They always wanted to hear about her cases, but responded either with rising horror or a disconcerting fascination when she went into detail. In the end it was just easier being alone. Now that both her parents had died, her immersion in the job was so complete that sometimes she returned home after weeks on the road to find an empty answering machine. Not that she minded. For her this was more than a job, it was a calling, an opportunity to give other families the answers she had been denied.

The Radisson was far more opulent than their lodgings, though still a far cry from what the Greek shipping magnate was probably accustomed to. They were escorted to the penthouse by two beefy security guards, who nodded to their compatriots guarding the door. Dmitri Christou stood at the far end of the room, his back to them, staring out the windows that enveloped the suite. He was smaller than Kelly had expected, a full head shorter than her and built like a bulldog. He turned to face them, features haggard and drawn under a thick black beard. Jake walked forward to meet him, and the two men shook hands. Christou bowed his head while Jake whispered something in his ear. He gave a sharp nod, clapped Jake on the shoulder, and crossed the room.

"So you are the agents assigned to my daughter's

case." He spoke English with the short clip of someone educated at Oxford.

"Yes, sir," Kelly said. He shook both of their hands firmly; a man used to making deals, Kelly thought. A handshake clearly meant something to him. His eyes were deep pools of sadness. She had only seen him before in photos snapped at honorary dinners where he'd made one of his enormous donations. In each he looked hale and larger than life, a wide grin splitting his face almost in two. Standing before her now was a pale shadow of that man. "I'm so sorry for your loss," she said.

He met her eyes. "Thank you. I trust Jake has been helpful? He has proven invaluable to me over the years."

"It's been a pleasure working with him," Morrow interjected with a sidelong glance at her.

"I realize it is early in the investigation, but is there anything you can tell me about your progress?" Dmitri asked. His voice sounded strained, as though he was struggling to contain powerful emotions.

Kelly pictured his daughter's gaping jaw and split chest, and hoped that Constance would be able to clean Anna up before her father saw her. "We do have some solid leads, but nothing substantial enough to share," Kelly answered. She cut her eyes at Jake. On the ride over she'd stressed the importance of keeping a lid on what they knew for now. She could only hope he'd listened. Jake studiously avoided her gaze.

Dmitri nodded heavily, as if the movement alone required a great deal of effort. He quickly turned his head away from them, blinking. "I'm so sorry, I've forgotten myself. Can I offer you something to eat or drink?" He gestured toward the bar that discreetly occupied a corner of the room.

They murmured, "No, thank you," in unison.

Dmitri rubbed his beard. "It's difficult to believe that any of this is real. Jake recommended Anna have more protection here. But she resisted, not wanting to call attention to herself, and I relented. I should never have given in…"

"It's not your fault, Dmitri." Jake clasped the other man's shoulder with one hand.

Kelly shifted uncomfortably, resisting the temptation to glance at her watch. Open displays of emotion always made her uncomfortable. She'd so much rather be back at the trailer, doing more research for the case.

"I was wondering…" Dmitri paused and glanced at Jake, his voice wavering slightly as he continued. "Could I speak with Agent Jones alone for a moment?"

Kelly hoped the surprise didn't register on her face. Morrow and Jake excused themselves and disappeared into the adjoining room. Kelly sank onto the couch that Dmitri directed her to. He waited until she was settled, then sat opposite her in a plush leather armchair. He clasped his hands together and leaned forward, eyeing her eagerly. *What could this possibly be about?* she wondered.

"Agent Jones," he began. "This is a bit awkward for me. If what I ask is inappropriate, please, say so immediately and we will speak no more of it. But from what Jake has told me, about your…family history, I think you might have some experience with these things."

Kelly caught her breath. With a rush of realization she

suddenly understood why he had wanted to speak to her alone. How did Jake find out? Despite his uncanny ability to uncover information there was no way he could have accessed her FBI file, and the newspaper archives didn't go back that far. She felt a flash of rage; she'd been working this case, allowing him full access as ordered, and he'd been wasting time checking up on her. Dmitri Christou was staring at her hopefully, waiting for a response. All those old feelings bubbled to the surface again, and she felt the hot sting of tears lurking just behind her eyes.

"Mr. Christou…I'm sorry, I mean no offense, but that is something I don't really feel comfortable discussing."

His face collapsed in on itself in disappointment, and he rubbed his right hand down one cheek, probably to prevent more tears, she thought.

"I can say this," she continued. "I will do everything in my power to find the person responsible. I promise you that."

"I appreciate that, very much." He stood and paced back and forth in front of the dark fireplace. "Anna was a very dear girl, my only child. I wish now—" He stopped and shook his head. "She was so very young. And we had so little time together."

Kelly sat silently. Suddenly she wanted desperately to leave, to run from the room and keep going. It had been years since she had experienced that rush of claustrophobia, the walls pressing in from all sides, the desperation to flee what she knew was impossible to outrun. She had thought that part of her life was behind her. And now, seated in front of this man who controlled more wealth and power than most presidents, she was once again reduced to that eight-year-old girl eavesdropping on the stairs, listening to the police tell her parents that her brother wasn't coming home.

"If you'll excuse me." Dmitri turned abruptly and strode from the room, to a door that she guessed led to the bathroom. She examined her fingernails as she tried to regulate her breathing, slowing her heart rate back to normal. *It's been almost thirty years,* she thought. *It's been a lifetime since then.* In spite of herself she did the math in her head. Alex would have been forty-one this year. She could picture him as the head of a company; unlike her, he'd had a way with people. He'd be married, with a beautiful wife and two kids. He'd play basketball on the weekends, and would invite her to visit for Christmas.

"Hey, is everything okay? What was that all about?" She looked up to find Morrow regarding her with concern, his hand on her shoulder. She shrugged it off.

"Everything's fine. He just had a question for me."

Jake stood in the doorway, arms crossed over his chest. She scowled at him and pushed herself off the couch, straightening her pant legs and snapping her blazer back into place. "Let's go."

They left Jake at the hotel. Morrow drove while she sat and stared out the side window. The last rays of sunset drove shards of pink through the scattering of clouds in the sky. The horizon was dark, lightening in gradations as she looked past it to the crescent moon. "You want to stop for food?" Morrow said as they turned onto the main road through town. "I hear Burger King has some exciting new dinner options."

"I don't think so. You can drop me back at the trailer, I have a little more work to do."

"You sure?" Morrow looked concerned. "You want some company?"

"No, go on ahead. It's been a long day. I'll just grab something on campus."

"Suit yourself." He popped a piece of gum in his mouth and clicked on the radio.

Ten

Kelly stood under a streetlight for a moment after he drove off, gulping deep breaths of night air. She struggled to hold a flood of memories at bay. She and Alex building sandcastles at the beach, brushing their teeth side by side in the bathroom mirror; the sight of his bike lying abandoned in their front yard for weeks after he disappeared. He had left for his paper route at seven in the morning, as always, but never made it to school. The alarm wasn't raised until noon, when the school's secretary finally got around to calling their mother at home. Back then, the police refused to get involved until twenty-four hours had passed. She had sat in the kitchen watching her mother phone all his friends, each call raising the level of hysteria in her voice. Her father, home from work at three in the afternoon for the first time she could remember, retracing the paper route house by house, asking if anyone had seen anything that morning. No one had.

That night she lay in bed feeling the heavy silence

from the bedroom next door. She counted the headlights that bounced across her ceiling, watched them skim along her ballet posters as each car rounded the corner. Any moment now, she thought, the doorbell would ring and Alex would be standing there, grinning apologetically, with some crazy explanation for it all. They lived in a small town in New England, the kind of place where this sort of thing never happened. She didn't remember falling asleep, but opened her eyes to sunlight streaming through the window. She had missed the bus; her parents had forgotten to wake her. Downstairs, her parents sat in silence at the table. They stared down into their coffee, faces drawn, a look of ultimate defeat. It had frightened her. As quietly as possible she poured herself a bowl of cereal and ate it, letting the pieces soften in her mouth before chewing so as not to disturb them.

They kept her out of school all week. Neighbors stopped by with food and expressions of sympathy, her grandmother flew in from Cleveland and established a post in the guest room. She threw out all the uneaten food, drew baths for Kelly, manned the phones so that her mother could nap. The following Monday, the pall that had descended on their house felt impenetrable, as though it had always been there, and Kelly could no longer remember what her life had been like before. Her father drove her to school, his eyes following her anxiously until she reached the entrance. She turned and waved timidly at him. He lifted his hand slightly in return and tried to muster a weak smile. And so it went on for weeks, months, classmates' whispers hushing as soon as she was within earshot, former friends avoiding her as though she had some sort of disease.

And then one afternoon she arrived home from the bus stop, leaves crunching under her feet as she turned up the block and saw the police car sitting in their driveway. She ran the rest of the way to the house, throwing open the door with excitement, expecting to see Alex there, hair tousled, hugging their parents. Two police officers stood uncomfortably in the middle of their living room, facing her parents. Her mother rocked back and forth on the couch, hands to her face, while her father glared at the floor. When he saw her, he turned and said ferociously, "Go upstairs!" And she understood that Alex was never coming home.

Orion was rising over the campus, the only constellation that she and Alex had ever been able to pick out with any accuracy. Kelly raised her head to watch the stars poking holes in the sky. A hunting dog had uncovered her brother's body. He had been buried in a shallow grave off a deserted county road. Terrible things had been done to him. The police surmised that he had been kept prisoner for weeks, and was raped and tortured repeatedly before the final blow killed him. They had never caught him, the man who took Alex.

Her parents had grown distant, both from her and from each other. Alex's room became a shrine, remaining unchanged until her mother's death five years ago. Every year on his birthday they drove in silence to his grave, a small ebony stone set under a tree in the grassy local cemetery, with just his name and dates carved into the surface. She had thrown herself into school, hoping that the strings of A's she brought home might elicit some sort of response from her parents, but they never seemed to fully see her again. There was always a faraway look in their eyes, and she understood that when he died Alex took a piece of them with him, and for that, she sometimes found herself hating him.

Kelly inhaled a deep, shuddering breath and opened the trailer door. Inside, she sifted through files until she found the photos of the drawings on the tunnel walls. She picked up the phone and dialed.

The girl descended the steps slowly, cradling a cell phone to her ear with one hand, balancing a load of books in the other. Her hair hung loose tonight, long black curls swinging from side to side as she walked. Her voice rose and fell animatedly as she spoke, punctuating remarks with an occasional giggle. That would be the boyfriend, he thought, a mindless jock with carved features and an empty head. He waited until she had passed him, then slipped out from behind a tree and followed her, staying a few yards back. It was a dark night, with just a sliver of a moon. With a final goodbye she flipped the phone closed and tucked it in her pocket. Pulling her jacket tightly around her, books tucked against her chest, she walked quickly. She must be cold in that skirt, he thought. The curse of vanity; she never wore clothing appropriate to the weather.

She crossed High Street and walked downhill, disappearing periodically into the shadows between streetlights. He quickened his pace, closing the distance between them. She was almost at the tall hedge lining the bottom of the street when she darted her head back. He stepped behind a tree and watched as she stopped and scanned behind her, eyes crossing over him in the night. In his dark clothing he was invisible. After a moment she continued walking, her strides long and fast, just short of a jog. He could taste her fear in the air.

She lived on the outskirts of campus. At this hour the houses she passed were dark, their inhabitants already in bed. There would be no one to hear should she scream. She turned right on the next corner, the final block before her house. He was just a few yards behind her now, skimming the treeline. He dug in his pocket for the cloth, already soaked in camphor.

A police car was parked down the street from her house, he noticed with consternation. A single officer sat behind the wheel sipping from a thermos. Her pace slowed and she lifted a hand in a small wave to the officer, who nodded back. She turned up the path to her house. He continued walking, casual now, feeling the policeman's eyes on his back as he put his hands in his pockets. Tomorrow night, then. Nothing would stop him then.

Eleven

President Williams rubbed his throbbing temples as he stared down at the headline blaring from the front page of the *Cardinal:* Campus Murders: Serial Killer Suspected.

"It's the same in the *Hartford Courant* and the *Advocate,*" Dean Scott said, jabbing an angry finger at the headline. "And thanks to the goddamn AP, it's running on page three in most of the national papers."

"I know. Parents have been calling all morning." President Williams sighed heavily. "We knew it was going to get out sooner or later."

"We need to take a strong stance, let the parents know they have nothing to worry about." Dean Scott crossed his hands behind his back and rocked on his feet.

"But they do have something to worry about," President Williams said heavily. He had hardly slept the past three nights; the voices from underneath his house were getting louder. They called to him just as he was on the verge of falling asleep.

"Nonsense. These are isolated incidents. We need to release a statement saying that the campus is perfectly safe, that we're doing everything in our power to protect the students."

"Would you send your daughter here?" President Williams asked, raising his eyebrows. His own daughter, Shannon, was safely ensconced in boarding school at Exeter. He'd gotten in the habit of calling her every night around bedtime. She sounded increasingly annoyed at his pleas to not leave her room after dark.

Dean Scott shrugged. "I don't have any children."

President Williams drummed his fingers on the laminated-wood finish. "I'm considering suspending classes, recommending that students return home until we can guarantee their safety."

Dean Scott gasped. "That's ludicrous! In almost two hundred years classes have never been suspended before. You're overreacting…"

President Williams glared back at him. "Am I? And what do I say to the next parent whose daughter ends up dead?"

"Ken, be reasonable." Dean Scott plopped down in his chair, fighting to keep his voice level. "We have students here from dozens of countries and from all fifty states. Many of them won't be able to return home in a timely manner. In addition to which, what do we do with the academic calendar? We can't extend the school year—the dates for graduation have already been set. If we curtail classes, parents will start demanding reimbursement for time missed, and according to the FBI this investigation could take weeks or months.

We're already facing a budget crisis. If you do this, we could lose millions. You would in essence be bankrupting the university."

"That might be preferable to the alternative."

Dean Scott scoffed. "Hardly. Listen to me very carefully. The activities of this school did not come to a halt during either of two world wars, and that was when we were an all-male university. What kind of message does it send if we close down now?" Seeing the president's resolve waver, he pushed onward. "Why don't we do this. I've spoken with the head of Public Safety, and he's agreed to provide escorts for students concerned about their safety. We can recommend that no one walk around campus alone at night. One of the student groups has also offered to walk students to and from the library and the dorms. The access points to the tunnels have all been sealed. FBI agents are investigating, and practically the entire local police force is patrolling campus. For the moment, I think it's safe to say the danger has been averted."

The president stared out the window. The sycamore tree outside his office was whipping in the wind, leaves clinging frantically to their branches. The sky hung heavy with a gray curtain of clouds. A storm was brewing. By nightfall, the rain would be falling in sheets. He sighed heavily. "Fine. We'll issue the statement. But if another student goes missing…"

"Whoever did this was probably just a transient. They'd have to be mad to try again," Dean Scott said curtly.

"Why don't I find that comforting?" President Williams muttered.

* * *

"What time did they find her?" Kelly asked, slightly breathless as she trotted down the pier. A police boat waited at the end, tossing in the waves kicked up by the wind. It was a bitter day. Overnight the temperature had dropped almost twenty degrees, and she shivered slightly in her FBI windbreaker. The phone call from ASAC Bowen had awoken her from a bad night's sleep. The mutilated body of an adult female had just surfaced off the coast of Bridgeport, forty-five miles south of the university. He thought it sounded like her killer, and wanted her there A.S.A.P. to grab jurisdiction if it was a match.

The homicide detective responded, "A fishing boat came across her as they headed out this morning around 5:00 a.m. From the looks of her she's been in for a long time, a few weeks at least."

Morrow huffed slightly as he struggled to keep up. His own windbreaker was slightly worn at the cuffs and appeared to date back to a time when he was considerably more svelte.

A group of local law enforcement officers waited for them at the end of the pier with an air of hushed expectation. From the expressions on their faces, it was clear that none of them had seen anything like this before. One cop stood by himself, hands on his knees, bent double. His back rose and fell as he heaved. The rest stood in a half circle around a blue body bag branded, PROPERTY OF BRIDGEPORT MEDICAL EXAMINER. The group shifted back slightly as Kelly dropped to one knee and unzipped the bag.

Inside were the remains of a girl. Her body, bluish and bloated beyond any human likeness after weeks in saltwater, appeared to be bursting at the seams. Kelly pulled on a pair of gloves and checked the leg: there was a deep gouge directly above the femoral vein. There was a single puncture wound in the chest, which was otherwise intact. If this was the same killer, he had since refined his M.O. to include removing the rib cage. She tried to avoid looking at the face, most of which had been gnawed away by small fish and whatever else had gotten to her down there. Kelly pulled a stray piece of seaweed gingerly from the girl's hair and sighed before nodding to the M.E. to close the bag. The homicide detective walked them back to the end of the pier, a small excitable man who introduced himself as Ed Taylor.

"We don't get much of this sort of thing down here," he explained as he walked alongside her, taking two steps to her one. "Every once in a while a jumper. That's what I thought at first, but then I saw the abrasions on her neck. You figure she might be one of yours?" He hopped off the pier into the parking lot and stopped in front of Kelly.

"Maybe. Let me know if you get a hit off missing persons, or if you manage any sort of ID."

Detective Taylor shook his head. "Not likely. Dental records maybe, but there's not much left to her fingers."

"I'm going to need you to send anything you recover to the FBI lab at Quantico. Especially the DNA samples and blood typing. The sooner the better on those."

"I don't know how the chief will feel about that," he

hedged. "He's awful gung ho on this case. Serial murder like this, everyone wants to pose for the cameras, if you know what I mean."

"In this particular case we have jurisdiction. Don't worry, I'll explain it to him." Kelly rubbed her eyes. She hadn't left the office until well past midnight, then spent the remaining hours wrestling with nightmares of fumbling through dark spaces on her hands and knees, occasionally catching a glimpse of a ghoulish face leering at her from the shadows.

"Yeah, okay," Taylor answered with a hint of resentment. "I'll get them to do an autopsy by tomorrow at the latest."

"Today would be best," Kelly said smoothly. He opened his mouth to balk but she continued without pause, "If it's too much trouble, we could always have our own people perform the autopsy."

"No," he said after a beat. "I'll have our guy get on it."

"Thanks, I appreciate it," Kelly said. It wasn't her job to make friends, she thought. Serial murder might be exciting for the locals, but she'd witnessed so many instances of brutality now that the glamour of working such a case had faded long ago. She just needed to make sure they stayed out of her way so she could do her job.

"So what do you think?" Morrow asked as he started the car. "Victim numero uno?"

"Looks like it. At least, number one that we know about." She tilted her seat back and closed her eyes. "Mind if I nap on the drive back?"

"Well, I was looking forward to an animated discussion of the Middle East peace process, but if you must…"

Morrow looked at her out of the corner of his eye. "Didn't sleep well last night?"

"Not really, no."

"Me neither." He shook his head. "This one's really getting under my skin."

Twelve

Kelly awoke to find rain pelting the car windows as Morrow eased into the parking lot. "Storm started early," he commented.

He guided the car in and out of a host of news vans, all pointing their satellite towers toward the cascading heavens. A herd of newscasters clutched their hats and jackets against the gusts, swaying slightly as they spoke into a gaggle of cameras and pointed out the command trailer and the science building behind it.

"Shit," Kelly muttered. "We're going to have to cordon off this area."

"Ah, the Fourth Estate," Morrow said gravely. "They just embody dignity, don't they?"

Kelly smiled wanly at him. "Ready to be our media rep?"

"Are you kidding? I live for this kind of attention."

As she climbed out of the passenger seat the cluster of reporters shoved microphones in her face. She pushed them aside impatiently. Their voices rose above each other and merged with the sound of the wind, creating a jumble of unintelligible phrases. "Is it safe girl water dead?" "Serial tunnels president think more?" "Slashed Christou choked fathers home?"

With great ceremony Morrow stepped from the car, snapped open an enormous black umbrella, and planted himself in front of the FBI emblem emblazoned across the side of the trailer. "If you please!" he said, voice booming. All heads turned to him. "I am Special Agent Roger Morrow with the Federal Bureau of Investigation. I will answer your questions to the best of my ability, one at a time. However—" he paused "—due to the inclement weather conditions, and the fact that I have yet to ingest my second cup of coffee, I'd like to recommend that we move this inside, to a room in the science center that has been reserved for this express purpose."

Scattered laughter followed his remarks. Kelly heard the voices diminish, headed into the building off the parking lot. As she pulled the trailer door open the wind grabbed it from her hands and whacked it against the metal side, issuing a dull clang. She wrestled with it for a moment, then yanked it shut behind her. She turned to find Jake Riley and Claire Denisof watching her.

"What's going on?" she asked warily as she tried to collect herself. The shock of going straight from a nap to a gauntlet of reporters had left her feeling slightly off-kilter.

"Well, young Claire here—" Jake pointed at her "—was standing out in the rain waiting for you to get back, and I felt it wasn't very gentlemanly to leave her vulnerable to walking pneumonia."

Kelly struggled not to make a scene in front of the girl. Jake had pinned tarps over the boards that held the crime-scene photos and other case information. But allowing press into the trailer went completely against Bureau policy, even if that press consisted of a college newspaper with a circulation under three thousand. Claire sat cross-legged in a chair, notebook open on her lap, looking wide-eyed and a little afraid. "This isn't a good time, Claire. You'll have to come back later."

Claire opened her mouth to protest, then closed it when she saw the expression on Kelly's face. She nodded, zipped up her backpack and stood. "So maybe I'll just wait outside…"

"Agent Morrow is giving a full briefing in the science center. There's no point waiting here."

"Um, all right. I guess I'll go over there, then."

As soon as the door shut behind her, Kelly whirled and hissed at Jake, "What the hell do you think you're doing?"

"Easy now, give me a second to explain." He held up his hands defensively as she angrily swept wet tendrils of hair away from her face. "The kid was getting overrun by the pros, and I thought it would be a kick for her to see the inside of the trailer. Besides, it turns out she has some information for us."

Kelly was livid. This kind of blatant disregard for Bureau policy was no doubt what got him kicked out in the first place. "Bullshit. Let me remind you that you're here as a courtesy. I'm not going to stand by while you flagrantly abuse the rules. If she saw anything, and it turns up on the front page of the *Cardinal* tomorrow—"

"She didn't. I took care of that before I let her in."

"What, by covering the board?"

"Give me a little credit. I closed the files, too." He grinned.

She fought an overpowering urge to slap the smile off his face. "You don't have to take this case seriously, but know that I'm not going to let you get in my way just because your boss pulled some strings."

His features suddenly hardened. "You have no idea how I feel about this case. Jesus. I heard you were a hard-ass, but this endless need you have for pissing all over your territory is getting tiresome. What I care about is finding Anna's killer, period." He stormed out of the trailer.

A minute after he left, there was a tentative knock at the door. Kelly heaved a sigh, collected herself, and opened it. Claire was standing there, shoulders huddled, blinking the rain out of her eyes.

"What is it, Claire?" Kelly asked impatiently. "I've got a lot of work to do."

Claire shifted from one foot to the other. "Well, I was talking to some people, and you know Josh Schwartz, Anna's housemate? His schizophrenia didn't surface until last spring, right before classes let out."

"We already know that, thanks," Kelly said, cutting her off and starting to close the door.

Claire blocked it with her elbow and cleared her throat. "There's more. Rumor has it that he almost didn't get to come back this year. His parents had to pull some serious strings with the former president. Josh was dating a senior, Jenny Halwell? And a few people I spoke with said he attacked her."

"Attacked her how?" Kelly asked.

"That's the thing. He attacked her with a knife, while she was sleeping. She woke up and he had slit her wrists—he had slit his own, too. I guess he said that they should die together because the world was such a terrible place." She pulled the hood of her raincoat farther forward to protect her face. "I tracked down Dean Scott today, but all he would say is that the administration can't confirm or deny anything due to privacy issues. And I guess Jenny didn't report it. Her old roommate said that Josh's parents wrote her a big check. She's in New York now, but I couldn't find out exactly where." She scanned Kelly's face for some reaction.

Kelly took care to keep her face blank. "Thank you, Claire. That's very helpful."

"Oh, yeah, sure, of course." Claire continued hurriedly, "Mr. Riley mentioned that you drove down to Bridgeport this morning. Could you tell me why?"

"Nope, not yet." Kelly eyed her; she had provided them with some valuable information. "Tell you what, leave me your number and you'll be the first call I make when the information is released."

"Yeah? Great." Claire scrambled in her bag for a pen and scribbled a number on her pad.

Kelly took the damp piece of paper and nodded. "Now I really have to get back to work."

"Sure. I'm getting pretty wet out here, anyway." Claire smiled weakly and lifted her hand in a wave before trotting off toward the science center. Kelly pulled the door closed and plopped down in a chair, debating. Generally she liked to have a case rock solid before questioning a suspect. The more information she had during the initial interrogation, the more likely she could startle something out of them before lawyers got involved. But here, the danger of something happening to another student was strong enough that she felt obligated to take action earlier than usual. And Josh met all the criteria so far: he was a former medical student who knew how to use a knife. He was roommates with one victim and classmates with another. And he suffered from a mental illness that could potentially make him a danger to himself and others; in fact, he had already attacked another girl.

Morrow opened the door and shook himself like a dog, sending droplets of rain flying. "Brrr," he said, stomping off to the small bathroom at the rear of the trailer.

A minute later he reemerged, drying his face with a small hand towel. "Why don't I ever get assigned to cases in Arizona, or Hawaii? Maybe I should put in for a transfer." He saw the expression on Kelly's face. "You got something?"

She nodded. "Let's bring Josh Schwartz in."

Thirteen

President Williams walked the file over personally. He had a hard time controlling his elation despite the circumstances. It was horrible to think that a student was involved, but if this entire mess could be put to rest quickly, with justice for the families…he rapped twice on the door of the trailer.

Inside were the two FBI agents he had spoken with before, in addition to a man he didn't recognize. "Hello," he said, stepping forward and extending his hand. "Ken Williams, president of the University."

"Jake Riley." The two men shook hands. "I work for Dmitri Christou."

"Of course." President Williams nodded sharply. He held up the folder. "The record of Joshua Schwartz's disciplinary proceedings. I assure you, I had no idea that any of this had taken place. How the girl was persuaded not to press charges is frankly beyond me. I have no idea what the previous administration was thinking."

"They were probably thinking 'new gym,'" Morrow said as he took the file with both hands. "We understand that the Schwartzes made a sizable donation to the school shortly after Josh's incident last year."

"Yes, well. That sort of thing won't be happening on my watch. Particularly not after all this." He gestured toward the inside of the trailer. A bulletin board spanned one side, with photos and notes pinned on it. He averted his eyes to avoid seeing anything that might permeate his already terrible nightmares. "Have you spoken with the parents?"

They exchanged glances. "Seeing as how he's not a minor, we thought it best to speak to him directly first," Morrow said carefully.

"Certainly. I understand completely." President Williams felt a pang of guilt as he said it; in the spirit of in loco parentis, he should insist on having someone accompany the boy. But on the other hand, his main responsibility was to protect the other students. And legally, Josh was an adult. He brushed the sentiment aside. "Well, then…if you need anything else, don't hesitate to call."

"Thanks." The agents looked distracted, barely glancing up at him as they pored over the student record. He strolled back to his office, skirting the puddles that had formed along the path. For the first time in recent memory, he hummed a song softly to himself.

Josh Schwartz glowered at them from the depths of his chair.

"So, Josh. Been taking your meds lately?" Kelly asked politely.

"I don't have to say anything to you," Josh grumbled as he bent his head to examine his fingernails.

"Here's the thing, Josh. If you've got nothing to hide, why not talk to us? You might be able to help us figure out who killed Anna. You and Anna were close, right?"

Josh shrugged.

"I'm sorry, I didn't hear you," Kelly prodded.

He glared up at her. "Yeah. We were close."

"All right then." Kelly perched on the edge of the table. They were in a small conference room in the science center that the president had set aside for their use. It was here that Morrow had held his press conference earlier, framed by the orange plastic chairs tucked under a long Formica table. Hardly ideal for an interrogation, Kelly thought, but the Middletown Police Department was so small that most suspects were questioned at individual detective's desks. And Kelly hoped that by staying in his comfort zone on campus, Josh might be lulled into complacency.

Morrow and Jake sat at the opposite end of the table. So far Josh had been completely intractable. He had expressed no surprise when they appeared at the door of his house, shrugging on his coat and opening the door before they had even rung the bell. Now he faced them defiantly.

"Why didn't you go to the party with Anna and Kim that night, Josh?" Kelly asked.

He shrugged. "Didn't feel like it."

"No? You sure you didn't change your mind, maybe show up later?"

"Nope." He glowered at her.

Morrow leaned forward conspiratorially. "Hey, if it

were me, I show up at the party and the girl that I like has gone off with some other guy, I'd be pretty upset. And you know what, Josh? If you didn't mean to hurt her, maybe just wanted to talk to her, and something went wrong... well, we'd take that into consideration, wouldn't we, Agent Jones?"

Kelly nodded her head gravely. "Absolutely."

Josh picked at a chipped piece of Formica that protruded from the tabletop, his face impassive. But Kelly saw something flicker in his eyes.

She and Morrow exchanged glances. It was time to start laying their cards on the table, make the kid realize he was backed into a corner. Maybe then he'd talk.

"What about Jenny, Josh? Any particular reason you tried to kill her?" Kelly leaned in toward him. Josh appeared rooted to his seat, not shifting back even though her face now hovered inches from his.

"I was sick then. The medicine helps," Josh spit out, his tone vastly different from the other times they had spoken with him. There was intelligence in his eyes, Kelly thought. Intelligence and anger.

"I've interviewed a lot of people, Josh. And the one thing I've found is that they usually have a reason for doing the things they do." One at a time, Kelly carefully laid the crime-scene photos on the table in front of him.

Josh picked up the shot of Lin and perused it with interest. His eyes darted over to the photo of Anna. Kelly saw a flash of recognition cross his face before the mask descended again. He flipped the shot over and realigned it with the others, facedown.

"What was your reason, Josh?" she asked.

Suddenly the door was thrown open. On the threshold stood a man nattily attired in an expensive navy suit, hair slicked back from his forehead, wire glasses framing flinty eyes. *Shit,* Kelly thought. *A lawyer.* He strode confidently into the room and set his hand on Josh's shoulder. "Alan Winters, counsel for Mr. Schwartz."

"Who called you?" Riley asked, his tone flat.

"Josh's parents were contacted by his housemate and I assure you, they were alarmed to learn of the Gestapo tactics employed in removing my client from his house. Needless to say, I hope procedure was followed to the letter. Might I ask what Mr. Schwartz is charged with?"

"He's not charged with anything yet," Kelly said calmly. "We're just asking him a few questions."

The lawyer looked her up and down appraisingly. "I see. If you'll excuse us, I'd like to speak with my client privately."

They all pushed back their chairs and rose from the table. Kelly noted that with one finger Josh was tracing a box around the photos. She stopped in front of him on her way out of the room and held out her hand. He raised his eyebrows, stacked the photos into a neat pile and handed them to her. He didn't release them when she grabbed hold, pulling Kelly slightly toward him. Josh rubbed a thumb across the top photo, the one depicting the cryptic drawing smeared on the tunnel walls. He murmured urgently, "I know him." His eyes flared at her.

"Sounds like a confession to me, Counselor," Morrow bleated cheerfully.

"Josh, shut your mouth. You will not say another word," the attorney hissed.

"It doesn't matter anyway." Josh shrugged, voice monotone again. The fire in his eyes faded abruptly, and he released the pictures. "None of it matters." He sank lower in his chair, eyelids falling like hoods over his irises.

Kelly felt as if the wind had been knocked from her by the intensity of his stare. She was spooked, not because she was sure he was the killer, but because suddenly she wasn't. Unless he was the coldest sociopath she had ever come in contact with, and there had been more than a few, his tone indicated something far more troubling. She hesitated at the threshold and turned to ask one more question, but Mr. Winters cleared his throat encouragingly and she closed the door behind her. The windowed top half of the door was covered by a makeshift blind composed of taped-together copies of the school's performing arts schedule. Through it she could make out the silhouette of the lawyer and his client, heads huddled together like lovers.

"What do you think he meant by that?" Riley asked.

"I'm not sure," Kelly replied uncertainly. With his lawyer present, there wasn't much more they could do with him that night. "Did the report on the first victim come in yet from Bridgeport?"

Morrow nodded. "They faxed the results over, but it doesn't look like they found much. The blood type matches the drawing under Lin Kaishen, but it's too soon to say for DNA."

"I'm going to head back to the trailer to check out the report." Kelly cast a regretful look back at the door, annoyed that the interview had been cut short. She started to walk briskly down the hall. Morrow and Jake fell in step behind her. "Morrow, why don't you see if you can track down Jennifer Halwell, the ex in New York. I want more information on the incident between her and Josh last year."

"Got it. Oh, by the way." He snapped his fingers together as though just remembering something. "That crazy M.E. called."

"Constance?"

"Yeah. She was going on and on about the missing rib cages. Said it related to some medieval thing, a bloody eagle or something like that."

"A what?" Kelly furrowed her brow.

Morrow shrugged. "Hey, don't blame the messenger. I wrote down what she said, put it with the report. But if you ask me she's a crazy cat lady with too much time on her hands."

"She's thorough, though, and she seems competent enough," Kelly mused. "Maybe she found something helpful."

"What should I do?" Jake asked, sounding nonplussed.

Kelly paused and glanced at him. "You seem to enjoy spending time with the student body. Why don't you talk to some of Josh's fellow premed and religion majors, see what they can tell us about him."

Jake glared at her. She smiled sweetly in return and strolled out of the building.

Fourteen

"For a floater, she was in pretty good shape." Detective Taylor's enthusiasm was palpable even over the phone. "But we're out of luck on the prints. Did you get the autopsy report I faxed over? I sent a copy to the FBI lab too, just like you asked."

"Yes, thanks for doing that. Anything else?"

"No fibers or hairs, natch. Caucasian female, blood type A positive, deep incisions at the leg and chest, marks consistent with strangulation. Based on the rate of decomp she was in the water for a month, maybe more. Our guy couldn't say exactly…if you want your team to take a shot at it they might have more luck."

Kelly closed her eyes and pictured the corpse that had been pulled from the ocean. It sounded like their guy: the M.O.'s were almost identical. Bridgeport was less than an hour away. There were three other universities along the road between the two towns, and another few dozen scattered across the state. Were there more girls drifting along on the tides, waiting to be discovered? "Hopefully we'll get an ID soon," she said.

"Maybe. So far we haven't had any hits in our local database, and no missing girls within fifty miles match her description. I'm double-checking with hospitals, she was pregnant, so there might be a hit on prenatal-care clinics. Her dental work was definitely foreign. Our M.E. figures she's an illegal from the former Eastern Bloc. If anything else turns up, I'll call you."

"Thanks, Detective Taylor." *That was odd,* Kelly thought. *Another foreign student, possibly? Or an immigrant who ended up in the wrong place at the wrong time?*

"Call me Ed. Listen, if you'd like to grab dinner while you're in town, I could drive up. It's not far."

Kelly rolled her eyes. She could never understand why some men considered their mutual field of death as a great opportunity to ask her out. "Thanks, but I'm busy with the investigation. With any luck we'll wrap this up in the next few days."

"Well, a rain check then. If you want my number—"

"I have it on caller ID. Thanks again for your help."

Clearly disappointed, he mumbled a goodbye. Kelly turned back to the map of the tunnels that had been spread across the opposite wall inside the trailer, composed of twelve tacked-together sheets of 8x11 paper. The locations where the girls had been found were marked in red on the walls. Access points in green included the chapel, the library, under the president's house, three frat houses and several other dorms: as far as they knew, every vulnerable entrance had been sealed with military-issue padlocks. The third victim had yet to be ID'd, and she still had no answers on what the drawing represented. Now that Josh had lawyered up, there wasn't much else she could do. Morrow had practically begged to be allowed a good night's sleep, and Jake had left for the Radisson, probably to update Dmitri Christou.

The report from the FBI profiling team had finally come in, and she quickly flipped through it. The profilers had produced a portrait not unlike the one Jake had mocked, much to Kelly's private consternation. They were looking for a Caucasian male, age twenty-five to forty. That was a no-brainer: over ninety percent of serial killers were white males in that age range. He most likely had moved to town recently, and something specific had sparked his outburst of violence, anything from losing his job to undergoing a divorce or breakup. Beyond that, the speculation grew ever more hazy, ranging from what kind of car he might drive to what kind of clothing he might favor.

She closed the file and saw a Post-It stuck on top. Scrawled in Morrow's handwriting, it read: *Constance called. Blood eagle ritual: during ancient sacrifices, rib cages cut from spine and snapped to resemble wings. Call for more info.* Ancient sacrifices, she thought, pursing her lips as something niggled at the corner of her brain. She saw Josh's face again, that odd half smile, the flashing eyes. She sifted through the papers on top of her desk for his file. Joshua Schwartz, junior, religion major. Professor Birnbaum was listed as his faculty adviser. On an impulse she called the switchboard and had them connect her to his home extension.

"Yes?"

"Professor Birnbaum? Special Agent Jones here."

"Agent Jones, I'm so happy you called. I just heard that you interrogated Joshua, and I must say you've made an egregious error."

Word travels fast, Kelly thought. She wondered if Josh had called the professor, or if someone else had told him. "You know about the attack on his girlfriend last year?"

There was silence on the other end of the line. Professor Birnbaum cleared his throat and said, "Well, yes, I was at his disciplinary hearing. But when properly medicated, I assure you he's completely harmless."

Kelly fought to keep the impatience from her voice. "Professor Birnbaum, I'm not calling for an opinion on Josh's state of mind. Have you ever heard of a blood eagle?"

There was a long pause. "Why do you ask?" he finally said.

"The term came up in the course of our investigation."

"It did? How interesting." Kelly heard a tapping sound in the background, and pictured him emptying a pipe bowl. "The blood eagle was a particularly vicious method of execution. The victim's ribs were severed at the spine, then broken so that they resembled blood-stained wings. Lastly his lungs were removed, and salt was sprinkled on the wound. Terrible way to die. Dear God," he said, realization dawning in his voice. "Is that how Lin—?"

"Was that method of execution associated with a particular religion?" Kelly asked, dodging the question.

"Not with a religion per se. It appears most frequently in the Norse sagas, and in some of the skaldic poetry. I believe

King Ella of Northumbria was a victim. It was traditionally used by sons to avenge the deaths of their fathers."

"And what is Josh studying?"

"He's a religion major…" the professor hedged.

"Right, I know. But has he narrowed that down to a specific religion, in preparation for his thesis?"

She felt him deliberating on the other end of the wire. "As a junior it's a bit soon for that."

"Really? Because I distinctly remember going over options with my thesis adviser at the beginning of junior year."

There was a pause as he digested what she had said. "I had forgotten you attended school here," he finally said begrudgingly, "Joshua has demonstrated an interest in the old Norse religions. But I assure you that is purely coincidental. He read *Njal's Saga* for one of my seminars last year and was quite taken with it."

"That is incredibly coincidental," Kelly noted wryly.

"Agent Jones, there are several other students specializing in the ancient pagan religions, offhand I can think of ten. And as I said before, the blood eagle was strictly used by sons avenging the deaths of their fathers. I spoke with Joshua's father prior to midterms, and he's alive and well," the professor retorted.

"Could the drawing I showed you earlier relate to these mythologies?" Kelly asked, changing the subject.

"Perhaps." Some of the tension drained from his voice as he continued, "Although few visual representations from that time period have survived. Even the texts we study were all written centuries after the events they record, when the religion had already been superseded by Christianity. Wonderful mythologies, nevertheless. Joshua was doing an independent-study course this year, under my supervision. He was focusing on the Aesirs."

"The Aesirs?"

"Yes, sort of the Norse version of the Greek gods. Thor is the one most people have heard of, but there are dozens of them, ranging from Loki the God of mischief to Bragi, the God of poetry." The professor's voice warmed to the topic. "I know that he was having difficulty with the research. Regrettably, our library has a dearth of information on the subject. When we last spoke he mentioned the possibility of traveling to Iceland next summer in an attempt to view more primary sources. I do hope that this won't prevent that…"

And why would a triple homicide interfere with his travel plans? Kelly thought. "Thank you, Professor."

"Agent Jones? Please consider what I've said. I know you're just doing your job, but Joshua is an extremely sensitive young man. Anna's death has hit him hard, especially after the year he's had."

The professor sounded genuinely concerned, and Kelly wondered again at the exceedingly close relationship he fostered with his students. "I'll keep it in mind. And I'd appreciate it if you'd drop off a list of the other students studying Norse religions by tomorrow morning."

She hung up the phone, cutting off his objection, and swiveled in her chair so that she was facing the crime-scene photos. The single shot of the painted face stared back at her, leering. "Who are you?" she said aloud.

Fifteen

Tiffany Agostanelli tossed the textbook across the room in frustration. Psych 101 was a bunch of bullshit, anyone could see that. She wished she'd never let her father talk her into taking it.

She considered making herself a snack in the kitchen, but decided against it after pulling up her shirt while facing the full-length mirror propped against the bedroom wall. Her long black hair fell in banana curls halfway down her back, framing what her father always referred to as Botticelli-esque beauty. She possessed flawless pale skin and blue eyes that were set off even more by carefully applied eyeliner. Tiffany sighed at her reflection: love handles, she could smell 'em coming even if they weren't totally visible yet. It was her mother's fault, all that pasta she raised them on left Tiffany with too many fat cells. It had taken her all summer to lose the freshman fifteen (in her case, the freshman twenty) and she had no intention of going back on Jenny Craig ever again. She pulled her sweatshirt back down, shivering slightly. It was already so goddamn cold, too cold for Octber. Her roommates refused to turn on the heat yet, claiming it was too expensive and rolling their eyes when she offered to have her father pay the bill. They had been a mistake, too. Nice enough in the dorm last year, but way too prissy when it came to sharing a small house. She should have lived with boys, even though her father would have freaked. She should have gone to the University of Miami, when it came right down to it. Students there were probably still on the beach in bikinis, studying while they worked on their tans. She sighed. If she really worked her magic over Thanksgiving, maybe Daddy would let her transfer there next semester, before the real cold came.

She froze at a sound outside the window. A sharp ping, like a stone hitting the aluminum siding. She waited for it to repeat, then relaxed after a moment when it didn't. Probably just a squirrel or something. Ever since those girls were killed, everyone had been on edge. It was all anyone talked about anymore, before classes, in the dining hall, even at the campus movie theater last night, which had gone ahead with showing *Silence of the Lambs*. Not cool, she thought, but no one else seemed to mind, girls squealing and boys cringing at the gruesome shit on-screen. She wasn't freaked, not really, but the other night she could have sworn she heard someone behind her on the way home from the library.

Again, a hard rap from outside, louder this time. Her room was on the first floor in the back of the house, three doors down from where that girl Anna lived. She didn't know her but had seen her, nodded sometimes when they crossed paths. Freaky. For the first time she wished her roommates were around. One had some sort of tutoring thing, and the other was volunteering to walk students home from the library. Her dad was all freaked out and wanted her to come home, but she had no intention of leaving before homecoming, and that was just a few weeks away. She had made the cheerleading squad this year, and despite the low attendance at games she felt like she was finally having a somewhat normal college experience.

She heard the front door open and secretly heaved a sigh of relief—at least someone was home. Those other girls had both been alone, that's what everyone was saying, safety in numbers and all that. "Jen? Sandy?" she called out, trying to sound pleasant and upbeat even though then they'd know something was up. "Hey, you mind if I turn up the heat?"

No response. That was strange, she thought. She knew they didn't like her, but they usually answered when she spoke to them. "Hey, Jen? I ate your last yogurt—I hope that's okay. I'll replace it tomorrow."

Still no answer. "For fuck's sake," she muttered out loud. University of Miami, definitely; she couldn't stand to live in this house for a whole year. It would serve them right to get some loser exchange student after she left, too. Hardly anyone wanted to switch housing midyear, so they'd be stuck with the dregs. She jammed her feet into L.L. Bean moccasins and shuffled out into the hall. The rest of the house was dark, she'd gone into her room early and forgotten to turn on the lights. A flicker of fear stirred at the base of her spine. This was silly. It had been years since she was afraid of the dark; even though she wasn't crazy about sleeping in a pitch-black room, she could do it if she had to. The switch was down the hall on the left, right next to the living room door. She brushed her fingers along the wallpaper, feeling her way. The glow of a street-light illuminated a section of the wall facing the living room, which was comforting. Just a few more feet now.

Suddenly, a shadow was cast down the center of the incoming light. It was huge, black—and didn't look anything like Jen. Tiffany backed away quickly, retracing her steps down the hall. She had a bolt on her door, a flimsy one but it should work. She tried to move silently. Maybe he thought she was still in her room. Maybe it was nothing, just a normal burglar or something. Two more steps, just one more…she crossed the threshold into her room and struggled with the latch. There were footsteps in the hall now, the floorboards creaked ominously. The latch slid into place and she whirled around. Where was the phone? Shit! It wasn't on the base, she had used it earlier to call home. She tore through a pile of clothes on the floor—not there. Biting her lip, she debated what to do—should she just start screaming? Someone might hear, maybe the neighbors, or that cop who was parked down the street the other night….

A thud at the door, something large knocking against it. An involuntary squeak passed her lips. She was frozen, incapable of moving, the way she was sometimes in nightmares. A second thump brought her to her senses. She hit the page button on the base, and heard the phone beeping reassuringly from inside the closet. She raced across the room and found it on the second shelf amid her stacks of shoes. Frantically she dialed 911, realizing on the second attempt that there was no dial tone. Her cell phone! It was in her purse, which was…out in the living room, on a chair where she'd thrown it when she came in that afternoon. She felt a terrible sinking in the pit of her stomach. As she raced to the window her voice burbled up unnaturally, more of a squeak than a scream, "Help! Someone please help me please God someone…"

At the next thump, the wood around the bolt started to splinter. She tore off the shade in her haste and threw the window up, her screams now at full volume. "You mother-fucker leave me alone! Go away you sick fuck! Someone pleeease!!!"

She was halfway out when she heard a rending sound behind her. One leg over the ledge, just a short drop down, she might sprain an ankle but who the fuck cared, it would be fine by homecoming anyway…and then there was a hand on her leg, holding it much too tightly, cutting off her circulation. Another hand, grabbing a clump of her hair, almost tearing it out by the roots as she struggled with him. He heaved her back into the room where she landed hard on the floor. She looked up at him, panting. He was shrouded in black, a strange mask covering his features, black gloves on his hands. He was pulling something out from under the robe, some sort of rag. She kicked backward away from him, trying to scrabble across the floor as she said in the most menacing tone she could muster, "If this is some sort of fraternity initiation bullshit, I swear to God I'll—" He slapped the rag down over her nose. He faded out of focus as her eyes rolled back, taking in him framed by her Monet prints, black in the middle of flowers, darkness and colors, until both vanished into a tiny point of light.

Sixteen

The phone was ringing. Jake rolled over in bed and squinted at the clock: 3:00 a.m. *Crap,* he thought as he extended a hand toward the cradle. Good news never came calling in the middle of the night.

It was Jones, sounding typically pissy. "There's a girl missing. Meet me at 75 Oak Street as soon as you can." The receiver clicked. Another girl. He fell back against the pillow and rubbed his eyes with one hand as his brain sluggishly processed the information. Exhaling deeply, he flicked on the bedside lamp and threw his feet over the side, allowing himself a quick stretch before shuffling to the bathroom. As he brushed his teeth, Anna's face darted around his peripheral vision. He'd been forcing the memories away, compartmentalizing them to deal with later, but at night they were strongest and came flying at him from all sides. He'd only known her for three years, but it felt like longer; in a lot of ways she'd been a surrogate little sister.

His mind kept drifting back to how they met. At the time his life had been in shambles. He'd been booted from the FBI, the only life he'd ever wanted irretrievably gone. They'd even denied his pension, leaving him scrounging for odd jobs and sinking into a bottle every night. Then out of the blue Dmitri Christou had called, begging Jake for help. His voice choked and faltered as he described the situation. Anna had disappeared from the grounds of her Swiss boarding school, there had been a ransom demand, somehow Dmitri's security team had screwed up the money drop and now he feared for her life. Within a few hours Jake was on a first-class flight to Switzerland. A limo transported him to a five-star hotel, where he was settled into an enormous suite. Jake stood before the picture windows overlooking the Alps, scarcely able to remember what his life had been like just twelve hours earlier.

It had taken only two days to track her down, thanks to help from a buddy in the CIA. They were holding her in a remote cabin tucked in a valley a few towns away. He'd led a small force on the strike, deploying the two men that Dmitri still trusted; the fight was over quickly. He found Anna tied to a cot in the back, cold and teary but unharmed. Dmitri Christou had rewarded him with a position as head of security, and Anna graced him with a teenage crush that he found endearing. He had taught her to flyfish the summer before, when the whole family vacationed in Patagonia. She spent most of the time padding around after him, cheeks flushed whenever he met her gaze. She was just starting to come into her own, belatedly losing her teenage gawkiness. She would have been lovely someday. He had saved her once, only to have her suffer a fate far worse. And now he had every intention of making the bastard responsible pay dearly.

Within five minutes Jake had pulled on jeans and a sweatshirt and was out the door. As he drove he flipped through the news stations, waiting to hear if one of the resident vultures had picked up the story yet. The top item was still the earthquake in Iran, so he figured they had another few hours before the scene was swarming with camera crews. Jones had only said the girl was missing, not that she'd been killed, so they might still be able to save her.

Jones's attitude irked him to no end, even though he understood its origins. He'd seen it before, with the relatives of other victims. They cut off all human contact to avoid getting hurt again. Whole families became like a group of snowmen, each still standing but isolated from the others, frozen in their own little world. He wondered what she might have been like if she hadn't lost her brother. It was a shame, really; he'd always been a sucker for big brown eyes, and he'd had to physically restrain himself on more than one occasion from running a hand through that incredible hair. Too bad she was such a hard-ass.

He pulled up at the address Jones had given him. Anna's house was just a few doors down the street. As he got out of the car he nodded toward the cop parked by the curb. The guy raised a coffee cup in a salute. Heading up the walk, he tried to steel himself for whatever might be inside; this part of the job he definitely did not miss.

The house was small and set back from the street, surrounded by towering pines on both sides. Good cover for an intruder, he thought. And with two hits on the same block, chances were the killer lived or worked nearby. The front door was intact and didn't appear to be tampered with, no crime tape barred it yet. There was a glass window that could have been shattered to slide back the dead bolt, but the perp hadn't needed to do that, he either picked the lock, had a key or was let in. Jake heard muted voices coming from the back of the house and followed the sound to a girl's bedroom. Two police deputies, a forensics agent, Morrow and Jones were crowded into the room. He pulled a pair of latex gloves and paper booties from the box by the door and slipped them on. They all looked up when he entered. Morrow waved a halfhearted hello, Jones merely nodded. He watched her eyes run over the walls, resting briefly on the window shade on the floor. A fine white powder covered most surfaces.

"Who is she?" he asked, leaning forward to peer at a photo of a pretty, dark-haired girl in a blue high-school-graduation robe.

"Tiffany Agostanelli, daughter of Boston mob boss Vinny Agostanelli. Her roommates got home around midnight and found the place like this." Morrow gestured around the room with one gloved hand, his voice atypically devoid of humor. "He picked the lock to get in. No blood, but it looks like there was a hell of a struggle."

"She almost made it out," Jake said, spotting the broken window shade.

In the closet Kelly picked up and examined a pair of Jimmy Choo sandals that screamed chic. She estimated the clothing on hangers alone at several thousand dollars, not to mention a collection of shoes worthy of Paris Hilton. Kelly recognized this girl. She had grown up with a whole host of Tiffany Agostanellis, girls whose whole world consisted of clothes and boys. Despite that, as her eyes trailed over the stuffed animals tucked on a shelf next to textbooks, her heart cringed.

"His M.O. is changing. He's getting bolder," Kelly murmured.

Morrow said, "I still like the Schwartz kid for it. He knew the previous two victims, and lives right down the street from this one."

"Maybe." Kelly shook her head in frustration. "But it's still too circumstantial. We don't have enough to arrest him, and there's no way his lawyer will give us the time of day. All we can do is keep a close watch on him, try to find this girl before he completes his cycle."

"Do we know where he is now?" Jake asked.

Morrow said, "Hasn't left the house, at least not that the local has seen. And we didn't find anything."

"You got in there?"

"Yep, right away." Morrow nodded. "Thanks to 'exigent circumstances.'"

"What exigent circumstances?" Jake asked.

"Thought I heard a scream from the basement." Morrow winked at Jake.

Jake glanced at Kelly. "Wow, I'm impressed Agent Jones. So much for standard operating procedure."

Kelly flushed. "I'm sure his lawyer will have a field day with it, and it got us nowhere."

"The kid was just sitting there smirking at us while he sucked on a jug of wine," Morrow said with disgust.

"Sorry I missed it." Jake scanned the room. "So how'd he do it, then?"

"He could have slipped out back, ducked through a few backyards, grabbed the girl, and stowed her somewhere," Kelly said.

"How did the cop not see that?" Jake asked, perplexed.

Morrow grunted. "Can't see a damn thing from where he's sitting, the door's blocked by trees." He wiped his nose and continued wryly, "He didn't hear anything either, but then again his radio was so loud he didn't hear us until we rapped on his window."

They stood in silence for a moment. Kelly sighed. "We're done here." She started down the hall. Jake and Morrow followed her.

"So we've got the daughters of Dmitri Christou, Wu Kaishen and Vinny Agostanelli, in addition to our Jane Doe. All wealthy, powerful men from very different backgrounds. What I don't get is, why the daughters?" Morrow asked as they strolled back across campus to the command trailer. Their breath froze in the air.

"What do you mean?" Kelly asked.

"Well, why not the sons? If you want to get back at a guy, it would make sense to go after the kid that'll carry on the family name, don't you think? Especially since the motivation doesn't seem to be sexual."

"You're right," Kelly said pensively. "And why these

three in particular? On the face of it, they have nothing in common. The timeline's getting shorter, too—almost two weeks between the first two victims, now another in less than a week."

"Not good," Morrow agreed. "It's starting to look more like a spree killer than a serial murderer."

In silence they filed back into the trailer.

"So what next?" Morrow asked.

Kelly leaned against a desk and crossed her arms over her chest. "Chances are he took her into the tunnels for the ritual, or dumped her in the water like the first one. Morrow, I want you to get a team of divers out to the river, start dragging it. And I want all entrances and exits to the tunnels double-checked, make sure they're still padlocked. We'll also do a full search just in case he found a way in."

"That's a lot of territory to cover," Morrow pointed out. "Took the locals a few days last time, and even then they weren't sure they explored them all."

"That's why we're going to be better organized, with more manpower. Let's find out what the local PD can spare, and I'll call President Williams to see how many Public Safety officers we can rely on. And the New York field office is sending reinforcements."

"Wonderful. How I love a cavalry." Morrow stretched his arms above his head, then released them and rubbed his neck with one hand. "See if they can send the ice queen, that tall blond rookie—"

"You mean there's more than one ice queen working in the New York office?" Jake said.

Kelly fixed him with a flat stare. Jake cleared his

throat. The humor felt, and sounded, stilted. Time was against them now. He cleared his throat. "Has someone told her father?"

Morrow said, "Based on his somewhat spotty history with our organization, we decided to leave that to ASAC Bowen." Under his breath, he continued, "I have too much to live for."

They exchanged glances. Vinny Agostanelli had risen to prominence after a particularly bloody period of mafia infighting that left him the last man standing. His stranglehold on New England was complete: any prostitution, drug running or gaming north of Manhattan was cleared through him or necks were broken. His operation rivaled those in New York and Miami. Rumor had it that he dealt with traitors by personally slicing off their heads with a meat cleaver, then leaving the headless corpses in the trunk of their cars at whatever airport was handy. He was a man that would not take the disappearance of his only daughter well.

"What can I do?" Jake asked.

"Talk to the roommates, find out if there's any connection between her and the other girls, or if she knows Josh. It might be a good idea to call her father, too, see if he has any enemies that he's willing to name."

"Not likely," Jake said.

"Well, it's worth a try." Kelly smothered a yawn before continuing, "Also make a point of telling him that we won't appreciate any outside assistance on the investigation. A guy like him will probably try to get involved, and we don't want that. Tell him we have a solid lead we're following up, but obviously don't say who. I'm going to try to find an extremely friendly judge to give us a warrant for Josh's house and car so we can search more thoroughly. If he is the one doing this, there has to be some sign of it."

Morrow snorted. "Good luck. If there's one thing I know about judges, it's that they don't like to be awoken before dawn."

"Not the one I have in mind. And I don't know about you guys, but I'm dying for a cup of coffee."

"I'll go," Morrow grunted. "Otherwise we might end up with some of that healthy crap, when everyone knows an investigation like this requires donuts."

"Fine." Kelly settled into her chair. "Let's get to work."

Tiffany's head felt terribly heavy and swollen, as though it was stuffed with cotton. She tried to reach up her hands to rub her eyes, only to discover that they were bound tightly behind her back. Her feet, too, once she tried them. It all came back in a rush: the man in the mask, a rag covering her mouth, suffocating her. She was in pain, so at least she wasn't dead yet. She felt a flutter of panic in her stomach and started to hyperventilate. Not now, she thought to herself—now she had to figure out how to get the hell out of here, because there was no way she was going to let herself be split open like a fucking kebab. Not Tiffany Agostanelli—not in this fucking lifetime. She allowed herself a moment of grim pleasure at the thought of what would happen to this sicko once her father got hold of him, then focused on the problem at hand.

She was in a box of some sort; it felt like wood when she kicked it. She wriggled around a bit and found she couldn't shift much, she was jammed in pretty tightly. Some sort of leather strap was wrapped around her wrists, a belt maybe. She felt for some kind of clasp, but her fingers were too short to reach. It was so dark, she couldn't tell how much space she had above her. Tiffany lifted her head up, squeezing her stomach muscles together, silently thankful that she forced herself through two hundred crunches a day; about two feet up, her head knocked against the top. Plenty of room, this should be a piece of cake. One of her father's favorite pastimes involved explaining how to get out of situations roughly similar to this, though his tales usually involved car trunks. She lay back down and drew her knees in to her chest, then strained her arms down and around them. It felt as though her shoulders were going to tear off and her eyes welled with tears. Just at the point when the pain became unbearable her arms eased around her feet and her hands were in front of her. She reached them out toward the ceiling—it was wood, she tried not to think of coffins but that's what this felt like, a coffin. She pushed tentatively against the lid, not wanting to alert that asshole if he was still out there, then more forcefully when there was no response. It didn't budge. She needed more room, there was something jammed in here next to her, some sort of cloth. She groped along it. It felt like burlap, rough against her fingers, some sort of stuffing he was using to hold her in place. She shifted on her side to face it, bracing her back against the wall as she shoved with her hands and feet to make more room. It shifted slightly, but when she released it the cloth flopped back against the bottom with a deadening thud. She froze—cloth alone usually didn't make that kind of noise. She carefully reached her hands out again, feeling a hard lump at the top. It was round, she ran her fingers over it and heard the crinkle of plastic, then felt a raised ridge, an ear, it was an ear, he had put her in a fucking coffin with a fucking dead person, oh God oh God oh God…and she was screaming, pounding desperately at the top, her manicured fingernails breaking and streaming blood down her hands as she clawed at the wood.

Upstairs in the kitchen, he turned his head toward the sound. She was awake, wonderful, he had worried that she might not recover so quickly. Amazing these young ones, so strong. He dipped his spoon back into the bowl and ladled out more soup, blowing on it with three short, quick breaths before inserting the spoon in his mouth. After dinner he would start her on the seeds—they did a remarkable job of calming the girls down. It was then that they sensed their larger role in all this, and realized that their lives were to have a higher purpose after all. His head bobbed slightly in time to her screams. *Not tonight, little one,* he thought to himself. *I'm afraid you'll have to wait until tomorrow.*

Seventeen

Kelly was alone in the trailer. Morrow had dropped off the donuts, then gone down to the river to supervise the diving team that had just arrived. Jake was interviewing Tiffany's roommates in the science center. She stretched her arms above her head and arched her back; God, what she would do for a solid night's sleep. But until they found Tiffany, there wouldn't be a respite. And with every hour that passed, the chances of finding her alive diminished. They really needed to get the search teams organized and in the tunnels, but assembling everyone was taking longer than anticipated. She had assigned a plainclothes officer to stake out the rear of Josh's house, and to follow him discreetly throughout the day. If he was noticed, Josh's lawyer would scream harassment; she silently prayed that Josh would be as out of it as he usually appeared.

Kelly tapped a finger on the desk while staring at her cell phone, willing it to ring. She was waiting for a call back from a judge who owed her a favor. His wife had said he was still out on his morning row; hopefully he'd return soon, and she'd have her warrant. She had a feeling that everything she needed to wrap up this case was concealed somewhere in Josh's house.

She shuffled through the files for what seemed the umpteenth time. Her fingers paused at the photograph of the strange drawing; she still had no answer for what it represented. The other night she had faxed it to an old friend at the University of Chicago who specialized in religious iconography. She hadn't heard back from him yet; she picked up her cell phone, debating the merits of getting an answer from Brian versus keeping the line clear for the judge. Brian would understand if she had to hang up quickly.

It was an hour earlier in Chicago, and Brian was less than thrilled to be awoken at 6:00 a.m. "Jesus, Kelly, do you have any idea what time it is?"

"Sorry, Brian, but you know I wouldn't be calling unless it was an emergency."

"Shit. You spooks and your emergencies. I suppose national security is at risk? Will anyone be losing their civil rights if I help you?"

"I'm not exactly a spook, and you know it."

"Whatever."

In the background, Kelly heard a muffled female voice grumbling—apparently Brian had spent the night hard at work with another thesis student. There were shuffling footsteps, then the sound of a door shutting. Kelly smiled. She could almost picture him running a hand through rumpled hair after pulling on his glasses. They'd hooked up briefly years earlier when she was on loan to the Chicago office, chasing down a violent pedophile. Unlike most of her other affairs, the relationship had ended amicably. "All right, I'm officially awake. I suppose this is about that image you faxed over?"

"Good guess."

"Well it's not like you ever call just to see how I'm doing. So far I've gotten nowhere with it. It's pretty rough, so unfortunately it's open to interpretation. It could be Celtic, or Greek. There's a lot of crossover with the early religions. Not really my thing, you know. I mainly deal with the Eastern sects."

"I think it might date from the Middle Ages."

"Yeah, you mentioned that. I sent it to a friend that specializes in that time period. We're having midterms here, though, so it might be a few days."

Kelly tried to keep the aggravation from her voice. "I don't really have a few days, Brian. Another girl has gone missing."

There was silence on the other end of the line for a moment. His voice was serious as he continued, "I'm sorry to hear that, Kelly. I'll see what I can find out."

"Thanks, I appreciate it."

The phone beeped, and she glanced at the caller ID; it was Judge Rice calling her back. "Gotta go, Brian. Talk to you later."

She smiled to herself as the judge's voice boomed through the line. He sounded like he was in a good mood. If she played her cards right she might be able to go through Josh's house before the search of the tunnels got underway.

* * *

"God, I'm getting sick of this street," Jake said darkly as they pulled up to the curb.

Kelly didn't answer. The early-morning light reflected gold off the front windows, blocking the view inside. Two orderlies sat on an empty gurney parked on the lawn next to the walkway. She nodded to them as she strolled past. A single deputy asked their names, noted them in his log, then stepped aside to let them in the front door. All of the lights were on, illuminating a thin layer of dust she hadn't noticed the other night. The house was weighed down by an eerie hush that she immediately recognized, the calm that descended after violence. Through the kitchen door she saw Kim, her face buried in the chest of a uniformed officer, sobbing. Kelly set her jaw and headed upstairs.

A photographer was still chronicling the scene in the bedroom at the top of the stairs. The local police captain stood by the window, staring pensively down at the splayed body of Josh Schwartz.

He glanced up as they entered. "Morning."

Kelly extended a hand. "Captain Morley, Special Agent Jones. Sorry we haven't met sooner."

He shrugged. "It's been busy."

She nodded in agreement. "It has. Thanks for making your men so available."

"Not a problem. Don't suppose that girl's turned up yet?"

Kelly had already slipped to one knee beside Josh as she eased on a pair of latex gloves. "No, I'm afraid not. What time was he found?" She examined Josh analytically: blank eyes staring at the ceiling, lips slightly ajar. His lower arms were a horror of slashes, blood congealed around long, deep gouges. *He knew what he was doing this time,* she thought. *No mistakes.*

"Roommate came in around eight to wake him up for class. She's pretty shook up." The captain tugged absent-mindedly at the corner of his moustache.

There was the sound of a toilet flushing down the hall, then Constance Anderson strode into the room. She was wearing a pair of jeans with a stretchy waistband and an inexpertly knit wool sweater. "Agent Jones, good to see you again. Too bad it couldn't be under better circumstances."

Kelly smiled thinly. "Do we have a time of death yet?"

Constance nodded. "Rigor is just setting in. Based on that and body temp, I'd say between 5:00 and 6:00 a.m. this morning."

"Definitely a suicide," Kelly said, more of a statement then a question.

"Without a doubt. Slit his wrists open with that." Constance pointed a chubby finger at the long, thin knife still clenched in Josh's right hand. She paused before continuing, "Left it there for you to see yourself. Based on my initial examination I'd say it's strikingly similar to the weapon used on the girls."

"What's that?" Jake asked, pointing to Josh's other hand. Kelly looked closer: some wires poked out from his left fist.

"Ah, an observant male, what a rare find." Constance grunted as she lowered herself to the other side of the body with some effort. She gingerly unclasped the fingers, careful not to disturb anything. Two wires were bound together, one straight, one twisted at an angle.

They all leaned in. "What the hell is it?" Captain Morley asked after a moment.

"It looks like a Roman numeral." Jake squinted at it. "What's the D stand for?"

"Five hundred." Kelly and Constance responded in unison.

"So…five hundred what? Five hundred girls?" Jake asked.

"Might have something to do with the address where he's keeping Tiffany," Kelly said as she straightened. "Captain Morley, if possible I'd like a complete listing of local buildings with the number five hundred in their address."

"Sure," he said uncertainly. "There's probably a lot of them, though…."

"That's not a problem, we have a support team coming in this afternoon."

"You think he left a message saying where to find her?" Jake said doubtfully. "Seems a little strange. Why not just write a note?"

Kelly glanced at him. "You have another theory?"

"Nope, you're the boss."

She examined him closely. "You still don't think Josh did it."

"I didn't say that." Jake shook his head. "Honestly, I don't know what to believe anymore."

Kelly turned back to the captain. "Has forensics already been through here?"

He nodded. "Finished a while ago."

"And the parents have been notified?"

Captain Morley nodded. "Just spoke to them. They're driving down, said they'd be here late morning."

Kelly nodded briskly and scanned the room with her eyes. "All right, then. Constance, why don't you call in your people and get him out of here."

Constance nodded briskly and left the room.

Kelly started sifting through one of the piles of papers stacked by the bed.

"What are you doing?" Jake asked.

"I have a search warrant, not that we need it anymore since this is a potential crime scene. So start looking for anything indicating where he might have taken her. Keep your eyes peeled for that symbol, or the number five hundred. Diaries, photographs, class notes." She glanced up at him. "And let's try to get it done before his parents show up."

Jake waited a beat, gazing at Josh's body, then shrugged. "I'll start in the closet."

"Great. When we finish up here we'll look downstairs, then head out to his car." As she worked, Kelly thought about what Josh had said in the interview the day before, and her own moment of doubt. Suicide was certainly the act of a guilty conscience, and the knife looked like a match. Had he already killed Tiffany in a final act of violence, then turned the knife on himself? Or was she stashed somewhere, drugged and helpless? Kelly set her jaw. Either way they had to find her, and soon.

Eighteen

Over the course of the day, a fleet of blue Hoover cars rolled into the parking lot outside the trailer, spilling agents onto the pavement. Most were members of an elite Hostage Rescue Squad, though a few were from Kelly's unit in the New York office. As the late-afternoon shadows lengthened, three groups converged outside the trailer: FBI agents in blue windbreakers, Middletown police officers in somber gray uniforms, and university Public Safety officers in drab brown pants and jackets. As he rocked back and forth on his heels taking in the scene, Morrow issued a sharp laugh and shook his head. "Christ," he said to no one in particular. "It looks like a goddamn Hertz agency out here."

Morrow had opted to match each local with an FBI agent, which would, he thought with a smile, make for some interesting bedfellows. While chatting nervously with each other, each unit surreptitiously eyed the other players. Around 5:00 p.m., Morrow stepped forward and waved a sheaf of papers in the air. "Your assignments, ladies and gentlemen. Your section of the tunnels is marked in blue, shortest route there is in red. We're operating on the assumption that Tiffany Agostanelli is still alive. Radio service is spotty down there, so if you find anything and can't reach central command on channel 20, one member of the team will head back here to report to me while the other stays on-site to secure the scene."

As he wandered through the crowd handing out sheets of paper to outstretched hands, a chorus of voices began throwing names into the air. "Officer Smith?" "Agent Bradley?" "Yeah, over here…" The introductions were brusque and formal. Kelly sighed as she looked them over; it should be enough, she hoped. Twenty-five teams would spread throughout the far-flung tentacles of the tunnels. With any luck the search for a body would only take a day or so. Not a body, she reminded herself: Tiffany.

Vinny Agostanelli suddenly appeared and elbowed his way through the crowd, trailing hushed whispers behind him. "Where's my assignment?" A dozen men stood behind him, all square-shouldered with slicked-back hair. They stood with their hands crossed in front of their crotches, eyes staring straight ahead.

Kelly blocked his advance. "Mr. Agostanelli, I'm afraid we can't allow civilians to participate. This is a law enforcement operation."

"Who're you?" He stared down his nose at her.

"Special Agent Jones, FBI. I'm sorry, Mr. Agostanelli, I'm going to have to ask you to —"

"Free country, right? Tell you what, you don't want to

give us 'assignments'—" he flashed his fingers to indicate quotes "—we'll just cover the spots you can't get to."

"Mr. Agostanelli, there's reason to believe that the man who abducted your daughter is extremely dangerous."

At that, the men behind him burst into guffaws. Vinny held up a hand to silence them. "Don't worry, sweetheart, I handle dangerous men in my line of work every day. And if we get to him first, Jesus himself won't be able to save him."

Kelly swallowed hard. The entire crowd, composed almost entirely of men, was watching to see how she'd handle this overt challenge to her authority. "Mr. Agostanelli, I understand that you're concerned about your daughter, but don't force me to take you and your— friends—into custody. I really can't have you interfering."

"Hey, forget I said anything." He reached a hand into his coat pocket. "We'll just go exercise our rights as citizens. You find Tiffany before we do, you call that number right there." He handed her a business card. Raised print on white linen read simply: VINCENT AGOSTINELLI JR. (617) 555-0302.

Kelly stifled a sigh of resignation. "We'll keep you posted. But in the meanwhile, the more you let us do our jobs, the better our chances of finding her." His eyes met hers for a moment, and underneath the bravado she recognized someone in a great deal of emotional pain. She lowered her voice. "I promise I'm going to do everything in my power to find your daughter and bring her back alive."

He looked down at the hand she had unconsciously placed on his arm and set his own on top of it, squeezing firmly. Then without another word, he turned and walked away, his men falling in step behind him.

"Looks like you made a new friend," Jake commented, looking over her shoulder. "Part of me almost hopes they do find him first."

Deep down part of her did, too. She caught herself thinking that it was more than her father had ever done for Alex, a thought followed immediately by a wave of guilt and shame. Kelly squared her shoulders and took a deep breath. "Let's get this show on the road."

Kelly played her flashlight across the rubble: another dead end. She sighed. They'd spent the past three hours trying to cover a stretch of tunnel leading to the freshmen dorms, only to discover that Jerome's map possessed some serious inaccuracies. This was the third section that had ended abruptly in a messy pile of concrete and dirt, and she was becoming increasingly frustrated with back-tracking. Now she understood why it took so much time for the locals to search the tunnels before, and why they still weren't certain they had explored every corner. It was a mess down here. She squinted at the map again, trying to find an alternate route.

"All right, let's turn back, see if we can get there by this side tunnel…" she said after a moment of scrutiny.

She was partnered with one of the Public Safety officers, a grizzled former cop named McGowan. After a brief introduction they led the search parties through the entrance under the science center, a small cadre of flash-lights illuminating the corridor as they moved silently into the maze. Groups stopped and consulted maps, then gradually siphoned off into side passages, their flashlights vanishing one by one. Until they saw something definite, everyone was following strict orders for radio silence. Not that the radios would help much anyway—during a test, the tunnel walls had proven impenetrable to their signal, the words rendered virtually unintelligible by static.

McGowan handed her a thermos. She accepted it silently, gratefully unscrewing the top and taking a sip, almost choking on the bitter drink. She preferred her coffee with milk and sugar, but under the circumstances would take whatever was available. She repressed a yawn as she handed it back. It had been a frustrating day. Their hurried search of Josh's house hadn't turned up anything of note. Aside from piles of books and filthy clothes, there were few personal items. The only notebooks were filled with meaningless doodles; apparently Josh hadn't taken notes in any of his classes that semester. Halfway through the search, Josh's parents had showed up, lawyer in tow, threatening a lawsuit. Kelly sighed. If they didn't find Tiffany tonight, she'd have to tear the place apart tomorrow. She just hoped that the search warrant held up to their scrutiny.

The tunnel was eerily quiet. All Kelly could hear was Officer McGowan's steady breathing and the occasional muffled echoes of distant footsteps. She pulled up her shirtsleeve and tilted her watch toward the flashlight: 8:45 p.m. It was going to be a long night.

Jake sat low behind the wheel of the car, rolling his head from side to side to loosen his neck muscles and wake himself up. The numbskull he'd been partnered with, a rookie on the Middletown police squad, had finally stopped talking after repeated entreaties. He squinted at the numbers on the mailboxes as he blew past them, finally slowing as they approached number five hundred.

"Here we are, 500 Post Street," Jake said.

"I used to live down the block." The kid gestured toward a brick house three doors down.

"Yeah? You remember who lives here?"

The kid shrugged. "Used to be some old lady. It's your turn to get out."

Jake fumed as he headed up the walk; this was a bullshit assignment, his time would be better spent searching the tunnels with everyone else. But Jones was convinced that Josh had been sending them a message with that symbol, which left Jake knocking on doors at 9:00 p.m., the equivalent of midnight in this neck of the woods.

Standing off to one side he knocked on the door and pressed the loaner badge Jones had provided against the glass pane. After a long pause a meek woman in her seventies answered the door. She shook her head, eyeing him distrustfully while answering his questions through the window without opening the door. After confirming that she lived alone and had no knowledge of a Joshua Schwartz, Jake thanked her and trotted back down the walk to the car. He slammed the door as he slid behind the wheel.

"All right, twelve down, fifteen to go. Where to?" he barked at the rookie.

The rookie shuffled some papers. "Take the next right and go three blocks, then turn left."

Jake nodded curtly and blew through the next stop sign. They were in the residential area abutting the university, where many students rented houses off-campus. At the next stop sign he hit the brakes hard to avoid running over two of them, a blond girl and a tall male wearing a vest emblazoned with the word ESCORT in reflective orange. The rookie braced himself against the dashboard and cursed. The students jumped back, startled, then fixed Jake with a glare as he waved for them to cross.

"Jesus, dude," the rookie said through gritted teeth. "You want me to drive?"

Jake didn't respond, just ratcheted the heater up another notch. Damn, it was bitter outside. In the wintertime Dmitri worked out of his office in Athens; aside from ski trips to Italy, Jake hadn't spent this much time in the cold in years. And he sure as hell didn't miss it, he thought to himself. It was a clear night, and a few stars blinked in the sky above him. He shifted uncomfortably in the car seat. The pungent smell of working fireplaces, the cold, and the leaves crunching under the tires were all combining to give him a bad case of déjà vu. Especially since here he was again, knocking on doors, looking for a victim.

It was his last case with the Bureau, the one that got him fired. He and his partner, Sarah, had been tracking a serial rapist in the Pacific Northwest, a bold one who grabbed girls from mall parking lots. After months of work all they had was a vague description of the man and his white van from the one girl who had escaped and survived. According to her, the killer had a shack somewhere upstate. The victim had only been able to provide a vague description of the interior; between rape and torture sessions she spent most of her time there locked in a closet. While he was transporting her, presumably to his kill site, she had escaped from the van. She ran into the woods, crouched terrified in the bushes for several hours, then flagged down a passing car. She was just fifteen years old; the scars on her face and body left her permanently disfigured.

Then Valerie Roberts disappeared from a bus stop near her job at a women's discount-clothing store in Seattle. A Good Samaritan called in a tip: he had seen a slight Asian girl in her teens being dragged into a white van; why the hell he didn't raise an alarm immediately Jake never understood. Based on what they knew, they had three days to find the girl alive. The Samaritan provided a partial license plate number that matched three white vans registered in far-flung reaches of the state. Jake and Sarah were assigned to check out one on the outskirts of Olympic National Forest. It was a straight recon mission. They were only to act under the certainty that they had found their guy, and then only after backup arrived. Posing as married tourists who had lost their way, they pulled into the driveway around 9:00 p.m. The house sat back from the road. It was larger than he'd expected, a sprawling three-story building with a barn in the background. They stamped their feet against rotting porch boards as they waited for someone to answer the doorbell. Most of the house was cloaked in darkness, with only a single light visible upstairs.

"What do you think?" Sarah had whispered under her

breath. Jake's nerves were on edge, his gut telling him something was amiss. He spent years afterward berating himself for not trusting his instincts, for not dragging Sarah back to the car.

Before he could answer, the door was thrown open by a burly man. Towering over them in jeans, a flannel shirt and a Carhart jacket, he held a shotgun in one hand.

"What?" he snarled, baring teeth yellowed by tobacco.

"Sorry to bother you, sir, but we're looking for the 101. We were just leaving the park, and I think we took a wrong turn somewhere…." Sarah said smoothly, looking completely at ease. Jake kept checking the guy's hands on the shotgun, weighing how much time it would take to get to his own piece in its ankle holster.

"Can't help you. There's a gas station down the road." The door was closing when they heard it—a muted cry from the basement. All three froze. In slow motion, Jake reached for his gun, saw Sarah reaching for hers, when she was lifted off her feet by the force of the blast, knocked off the porch and onto the grass below. His own shot hit the door. He heard footsteps running into the house, heading toward the back, and without thinking he ran after them. The guy was halfway down the cellar stairs when Jake caught up. "Freeze, federal agent!" he yelled. The guy froze on the bottom step. As he turned, Jake saw the shotgun coming up again and fired. There was no doubt in his mind that it was a clean shoot. But because he had technically caught the guy in the back, he was subjected to a review by the Office of Professional Responsibility.

Sarah was only in the ground three days when he was called before his ASAC, a nitpicking little bastard who'd had it in for him since day one. Flush with grief and rage, Jake hadn't taken the news well, which resulted in a knock-down, drag-out argument. After a few choice words that his ASAC hadn't taken kindly, Jake was handed his walking papers. He'd thought he was over it. Working for Dmitri Christou had allowed him a freedom he'd never experienced in the Bureau, and a lifestyle that an agent's salary could never provide. But watching the camaraderie of Jones and Morrow, he was occasionally struck by pangs of regret.

"All right, we're coming up on it," the rookie said, pointing to a house at the end of the block on the right.

Jake shook off his reverie and followed the kid's finger, starting when he saw where they were. "Interesting," he mused.

"I'll go." The rookie started to step from the car.

Jake grabbed his arm, stopping him. "Let's call this one in first."

"Yeah?" The kid slid back into his seat as Jake picked up the radio and tuned it to channel 20. The rookie listened as Jake conveyed their location to Morrow back at base. His eyebrows raised at the request for backup.

"You think this might be our guy?" he asked when Jake signed off.

"Might be." Jake tapped his finger on the steering wheel, impatient. Morrow had promised to send reinforcements, but couldn't say how long it would take due to technical problems with contacting the teams in the tunnels.

Twenty minutes passed. Jake's eyes had just drifted

shut when the kid nudged his arm. "Hey, is this our guy?" he hissed.

A screen door slammed, and Jake snapped to attention. Jerome Brown had left the house and was walking directly toward them. When he reached the car he bent over and peered inside, shading his eyes with his hand. Jake unsnapped the clip holding his gun in place and eased it onto his lap before rolling down a window.

"What's up, Jerome?" he said cautiously.

Jerome's face was expressionless as always, voice flat as he said, "I forgot one."

"What?" Jake asked, puzzled.

"There's another way in. I forgot to put it on the map."

Jake and the rookie looked at each other. Jake deliberated for a second; if they refused to follow, Jerome would become suspicious. On the other hand, if they went he could lead them straight into a trap. And he didn't trust this kid's ability to take care of himself if things went south.

Jake tucked his gun in the pocket of his windbreaker and handed the kid the radio. "You stay here. If you see or hear anything strange, call it in."

The kid held the radio as if it were a bomb. "You sure, dude?" he called after him.

"Yeah. I'll be back in five." Jake followed Jerome up the path to his house. He assumed Jerome was stopping off for something, maybe a flashlight, but he gestured for Jake to follow him inside. On edge, Jake kept a hand in his pocket, finger next to the trigger, feeling the weight of the gun against his hip. It would take him three seconds to get to it if this guy tried anything funny.

Once inside, Jerome led the way through the living room and into the kitchen. A small door next to the refrigerator opened into a cellar. Jake followed Jerome down the rickety stairs: at the bottom, a small concrete room was lit by a single bare bulb dangling from the ceiling. Jerome jerked his head to indicate the space under the stairs. "There," he said.

There was a small door set against the back wall, one Jake would have to bend double to get through. Keeping an eye on Jerome, he pulled open the door and stuck his head inside. The musty dampness of the tunnels wafted up toward him. A flight of stone stairs led down.

He pulled his head back and turned to Jerome. "Is this what I think it is?"

Jerome stared at the floor and answered, "Yes, sir."

Jake scanned the room for any other hidden doors, but it looked clear, just a few shelves on one wall lined with boxes. "You mind if I look around a little?"

Jerome considered the request while kicking at an invisible speck of dirt on the floor. "I suppose it won't do no harm."

Jake followed him back upstairs. He half opened the bedroom door, then jumped back, yanking it shut as the dog on the other side erupted in a frenzy of barking, clawing at the wood. "You want to take care of that?" Jake said angrily.

"He don't know any better," Jerome replied. He vanished behind the door with a choke collar on a metal chain, and reemerged a moment later with a wiry pit bull. It emitted a low growl when it saw Jake.

"Yeah, well, he almost got shot," Jake grumbled. It only took a few minutes to sweep the rest of the house and determine that it was clear. They stood in the living room, facing each other. "So are there any other entrances you didn't tell us about?"

"No, sir. At least, none that I've seen, and I've been through almost every inch of 'em."

Jake examined his face; if the guy was lying, he saw no sign of it. "I need to call this in. I gotta tell you, Jerome, it doesn't look good, you keeping this to yourself."

Jerome said, "Didn't want no one to know how I got in and out. But with that girl being gone…I heard they were searching down there, thought they might find it this time."

"How'd they miss it before?"

"You gotta climb some rubble once you get in."

Jake eyed him. He stood stolid as a cigar-store Indian. The dog settled back on his haunches and opened his mouth to pant, exposing jagged teeth. "I don't suppose you had anything to do with that girl going missing, did you, Jerome?"

"No, sir." Jerome shook his head.

Jake considered; it all sounded suspect, and the house was numbered five hundred. But he'd looked everywhere and seen no sign of the girl, or anything that indicated Jerome was involved. They'd had to pull the detail on Jerome to accommodate the search, but tomorrow they'd have more manpower. He'd make sure Jones assigned someone to watch him again. "Okay," he finally concluded. "Someone'll come by, either late tonight or early tomorrow, to lock this up." He pointed a finger at him.

"And if I were you I'd seriously consider staying out of there until all this blows over."

Jerome nodded, and Jake straightened his jacket with a tug. "All right, then."

The kid was waiting wide-eyed in the car when Jake slid behind the wheel. "What was that all about?" he asked, peering back at the front door.

The porch light clicked off. Jake shifted his shoulders, trying to release some of the tension. His body still coursed with adrenaline. "Nothing, the place is clear. Let's roll." He checked his watch: 10:30 p.m.

Nineteen

They were outside now. It was dark, and Tiffany weaved uncertainly on her feet. Those seeds had made her woozy. She hadn't had any water in what felt like forever, and the few spoonfuls of oatmeal he'd shoved down her throat only made her thirstier. She had no idea how long she'd been gone now, it could have been days or weeks. She drifted in and out of consciousness, the thin slit of light outlining the corners of the box telling her when she was awake. It felt like she was trapped in a nightmare.

Even now, with the cold biting through the thin sleeves of her sweatshirt, she wasn't completely certain she wasn't dreaming. She considered running but felt way too tired, and the belt wrapped around her knees only permitted small stutter steps. Her hands were bound behind her back and a piece of duct tape glued her lips together. She was barely aware of the tears streaming down her face.

He was behind her, nudging her in the back from time to time, forcing her forward when she faltered. They were on campus: she recognized the Center for the Arts with the small round secret-society buildings on its perimeter. She had lived just up the hill last year, in Fauss 8. She hated that dorm, it was so far from the center of things and looked just like a Howard Johnson motel. Totally tacky.

She prayed fervently for someone to come by and see them. He kept forcing her just off the path into the shadows. It was a poorly lit part of the campus, funny how she'd never noticed that before. When she got out of here, she would get her father to install floodlights all along it. *Forget that,* she thought. When she got out of here she was going straight to the University of Miami. She'd never been there but pictured buildings set right on the beach, waves rolling up to the window, students riding surf-boards straight into desks, slipping from one to the other as if it were nothing.

She stumbled and he caught her by the hands, twisting them painfully. Her cry was muffled by the tape. Three more steps and he jerked on her hands again to stop her. Tiffany stared up at the marble columns. She had always liked this building, it reminded her of *Gone with the Wind.* She remembered lying on her stomach in the family room, munching on popcorn as those dresses flowed by on-screen. Her father had given her a DVD copy that past Christmas. She had tossed it aside, told him she was too old for that. Now her eyes smarted as she remembered the joy on his face when he handed her the package, so thrilled at choosing the gift himself….

He hadn't spoken a word yet, had simply yanked and pulled her in the direction he wanted her to go, but now he was murmuring in some strange language she'd never heard before. Tiffany pulled her knees apart, testing the length of the belt: maybe she could run for it, she should at least try. She started counting in her head: one, two…

A cord slipped around her neck and her eyes bulged out. She lifted her hands behind her as far as she could, struggling, fighting, kicking her feet off the ground and thrusting her head from side to side, but the rope was merciless. It clamped tighter and tighter until stars danced in front of her eyes. After a minute she went limp.

He gathered her in his arms, gently cradling her head. *Quickly, carefully,* he thought as he moved her into position. He tossed the end of the rope over one of the heavy wood beams above the door. He jerked the knot taut at the nape of her neck, then ran a gloved finger through her tangle of hair. Hand over hand he pulled until the slackness left the rope, drawing her upright and off his shoulder, then higher still, until her toes dangled an inch above the doorstep. He tied the rope off on a pillar, then carefully stripped off her clothes, folding them neatly and stacking them in a pile a few feet away. He stepped back for a moment, surveying the scene to make sure everything was in place. Satisfied, he reached into his knapsack for a foot-long spike and a hammer. He tested the end of the spike, making sure it was razor sharp, then positioned it over her left leg. As he worked, his head bobbed in time to the chant. This one was a fitting sacrifice, he thought. Vidar would be pleased.

President Williams shifted in his sleep. The alarm clock beside the bed read 3 a.m. He had taken two of the pills his doctor had prescribed. It was double the recommended dosage, but a single pill had only made him woozy, and he desperately needed a good night's sleep. He had begun seeing things. Over his secretary's shoulder in his office, the face of one of the girls peering in the window; another reflected on the television screen during the nightly news. His wife had left that morning to visit her sister, who was about to give birth to her second child. She had stood uncertainly by the car door, a hand on his cheek, concern furrowing her brow. "I can stay," she had said. "Jean doesn't really need me there…." But he had insisted, and she had left. The house felt enormous without her. He was sleeping in the rear guest room, hoping that a change of venue might keep the ghosts haunting his feverish dreams at bay.

Something was tapping—a woodpecker? He watched it flit through his dreams. He was at his father's cabin in the woods, sitting on the back porch as the sun went down. The woodpecker clung to the old sugar maple by the house, knocking small holes in the bark. *Tap, tap, tap.* His lips curved up at the corners in delight. He was eight years old and his father was chopping wood, the sound of the ax merging with the woodpecker's knocks in a natural drumbeat.

The alarm went off at 7:00 a.m. He rolled over to shut it off, then stretched languidly, curling his toes with delight. He couldn't remember the last time he had slept so well. He pulled on his robe and stepped into his slippers, then padded downstairs to start the coffee. While it was brewing he went to the front porch to see if the newspaper had arrived yet. He unbolted the door and pulled on the knob, but the door refused to open. *How odd,* he thought, checking the lock again. He would have to call maintenance. President Williams returned to the kitchen and poured himself a cup, stirring in a spoonful of sugar and a touch of milk. The thermostat outside read sixty degrees. The cold snap was over, he thought with pleasure. He felt like a new man. That was all it took, a good night's sleep; his wife had been right to call the doctor. Wonderful pills. He wondered idly if he'd need a refill.

He peered out the back door to make sure no one would catch him gallivanting about in his robe, then trotted quickly to the front of the house. He smelled something odd as he turned the corner, his nose wrinkled up reflexively. When he saw her he dropped the mug, steam rising off the brown liquid as it seeped into the grass.

His hand leaped to his mouth and he stumbled back a few feet before falling to his knees. Head shaking back and forth, he collapsed forward on all fours, the remains of last night's dinner pouring out of him onto the ground. The retching wouldn't stop, his breath came in gasps between heaves, his entire body shuddered with the violence of it. Without looking up again he wiped his mouth and staggered to his feet, reeling back into the house.

Pinned to the front door, the naked, brutalized body of Tiffany Agostanelli hovered over a pool of blood.

Twenty

"Goddammit!" Jake almost threw the radio out the car window. The bastard had taken advantage of the fact that every cop in a ten-mile radius was underground combing the tunnels. The rookie in the passenger seat, still bleary-eyed, clutched at the door handle to brace himself as Jake tore around a corner. When they left Jerome's house the night before it was too late to keep knocking on doors. Morrow sent them to the waterfront to search a section of the tunnel that dead-ended at the campus boathouse. Jake had spent the rest of the night grubbing through the dark, finding a whole lot of nothing, while the killer was carving up a girl right above their heads. A string of curses poured from his mouth. Fifty fucking cops working this case and the guy had slipped right through their net.

The police tape started at the sidewalk ten yards from the president's house. Located on the eastern border of campus, the home was a stately Georgian manor. Tall white pillars stood guard over a redbrick facade. A row of trees surrounded the house on all sides, fencing in a substantial front yard. Through the throng in front of the house Jake caught a glimpse of the girl, staked to the door. *She's like a fucking sacrificial lamb,* he thought to himself. The kid stayed close on his heels as he made his way through the crowd. He spotted Kelly's red hair in a sea of blue jackets. He caught her eye as she turned. She looked drawn and exhausted, but then he probably looked like shit as well, he thought, running a hand over the stubble on his chin.

"Where's Morrow?" he called when he got close enough for her to hear him.

"Doing damage control with the media."

Jake heard the sound of retching and turned to see the kid throwing up all the snacks he'd consumed the night before. He resisted the temptation to roll his eyes. "Why don't you see about rustling up some coffee."

At the word *coffee* the kid turned a shade greener, but nodded and lurched back in the direction of the car.

"So what have we got?"

Kelly sighed. "Not much, I'm afraid. President Williams was home, but he'd taken some sleeping pills and doesn't remember anything."

Jake ran a hand through his hair. "Huh. You buy it? He is new on campus, right?"

"He had an ironclad alibi for Anna's disappearance, I already checked. And the house is clear, no sign Tiffany was ever in there. So he might have just slept through it. He's agreed to submit a blood sample…we'll check it, see if he really took those pills."

"How is he?"

"Let's just say, not good. I had the paramedics sedate him. He was babbling on about woodpeckers trying to come up through the basement of his house."

Jake followed her pointing finger. President Williams slumped on the edge of an ambulance gurney looking spacey. Father John, the school priest, stood next to him. He was speaking urgently into his ear, probably trying to calm the poor guy down. Jake shifted his gaze back to the dead girl. "When did it happen?"

"Three or four hours ago. Same as before—no hair, no fibers, no signs of rape. She's been ripped apart pretty badly, but it doesn't look like he had time to gather much blood. Most of it drained onto the doorstep."

"Or maybe his M.O. is changing. This is a hell of a lot more public than the tunnels. You think he's done with them?"

"Maybe. Hard to say for sure."

They stepped onto the porch, careful to avoid the accumulated pools that were coagulating. Tiffany's dark hair hung long around her face—gorgeous hair, Jake thought. She'd been a pretty girl. Behind her the edges of the painting were visible, dark brown streaks marring the white door. He pulled on a pair of gloves. "They've already documented this?"

"Yes, just be careful where you step," Kelly answered. As he pulled back a few strands of hair to see the girl's face, she added, "Her jaw's torn, almost in half. Ribs are broken, lungs are gone, and he hung her with a rope. Same as the others."

"The legs are different, though," Jake said, letting go of the hair so it shielded her face again. One of Tiffany's legs hung straight, the other was bent at almost a ninety-degree angle, staked through both the lower thigh and ankle. Jake exhaled heavily. "Fuck. This guy's got a set on him, doesn't he, doing this with the president right inside?"

Kelly nodded. She looked drained, and he had to resist the urge to hug her. "He couldn't have known the president would be knocked out. I'm thinking maybe he wants to get caught."

"Not badly enough, apparently. Shit—here comes trouble."

There was movement on the periphery of the crowd. Kelly turned to see a group of agents and officers struggling with Vinny Agostanelli and his men. "I'll handle this." She marched down the steps and pushed through the crowd.

Vinny Agostanelli was wild-eyed, his hair sticking out in all directions. He appeared on the verge of blows with the two cops trying to hold him at bay. "Mr. Agostanelli!" she said firmly. He ceased struggling when he saw her.

"Where's my little girl? Where's my baby? I want to see her, my little girl…" His voice sputtered off in tears. One of his men clasped him around the shoulders, daring her with his eyes to say something.

"Mr. Agostanelli, I'm so sorry. I can't let you see her. You don't want to see her, not like this."

"She's my little girl."

"I know." She gently took his elbow and guided him toward the street, his men parting reluctantly to let them through. "Why don't you let this officer get you some water. Hang on a second." She motioned for the nearest cop to join her, and asked him in a low voice to find Mr. Agostanelli some water. She watched as he was led off. Her heart pounded hard against her rib cage. She recognized the same mix of rage and impotence as when her brother disappeared. Turning back to face the girl, a wave of recognition washed over her and she caught her breath. Jake saw her reaction and followed her eyes. Whatever it was, he wasn't seeing it. Kelly muscled her way back through the crowd and grabbed his elbow. "C'mon," she said, her voice laden with urgency. "We'll take your car.

"Where are we going?" Jake asked, confused. "What is it?"

"Her legs, don't you see?"

Jake looked back over his shoulder as she dragged him toward the car. "What about her legs?"

"We need to get back to Josh's house. He knew what was going to happen to the next girl."

"What? How?"

"It's the symbol. We need to find out what he knew."

Kelly sifted through the piles of clothes on the floor while Jake watched. "Remind me again what exactly we're looking for?"

"Something with that symbol on it—we must have missed it before. Check the stack of books over there." She tilted her head toward a tower of books balanced precariously against a small prefab desk.

Jake let out a low whistle as he finally realized what

she was referring to. "Tiffany's leg position formed the same symbol Josh left for us."

"That's my guess. They're too similar for there not to be a connection."

"So you think he was involved after all?" Jake lifted the top book off the pile and flipped through it: images of the Madonna were featured on page after page. He discarded it and started on the next one.

"Maybe, and he couldn't handle the guilt anymore. I don't know." Kelly's brow furrowed as she straightened and arched her back to stretch out the muscles. Scouring the tunnels last night had left her entire body feeling sore and bruised. "But I'm pretty sure he saw a pattern in the photos, one we didn't recognize."

"So what am I looking for? Something Roman, maybe?"

"Roman or Norse. Anything that mentions pagan religions." Kelly peered around the room in consternation. Josh had thumbtacked thick black drapes over both windows, blocking all sunlight from entering the room. The bare bulb on the ceiling glared across the optical-illusion prints decorating the walls, the kind where if you stared at them with unfocused eyes, images crept out of the background. Mounds of stale clothing dotted the floor, and a sleeping bag was tangled over a bare mattress. And in the center of the room, pools of blood. Her nose wrinkled as she sifted through a pile of clothes.

"Well, what have we here?"

Kelly glanced up. Jake had lifted a corner of the bare mattress, exposing a book underneath. "I'm almost afraid to look." He picked it up between two fingers and turned it over, then raised an eyebrow. "Not exactly what I expected. Check it out."

Kelly eagerly crossed the room. The cover displayed a Viking in full regalia, black patch covering one eye. A mountain lion sat at his feet like a tame housecat. The title read, *The Mysteries of Norse Shamanism*. Jake dropped the mattress back into place as she flipped through the pages.

Jake peered over her shoulder. On her second pass through the book, he stopped her. "Go back a few pages, I think I just saw something."

She turned back to the previous chapter and caught her breath. A copy of the symbol Josh had created out of bent wire dominated the page, over the word *Thurs*.

"A rune?"

"I guess so. It's written in Icelandic, with the English translation underneath." Jake began to read aloud. " 'Thurs,' or 'giant,' causes the woe of women—few are cheerful from misfortune. Thurs is a dweller in the rocks, and the husband of the etin-wife Vardh-runa.'" He stopped reading, flipped forward a few pages, then slammed the book shut. " 'The woe of women' is a hell of an understatement if you ask me. So what the hell does it mean?"

"I don't know," Kelly answered. "But I think I know someone who might."

Jake followed her finger: on the back cover a photo of Professor Howard Birnbaum, author, smiled back at them.

The door opened to her second knock. Professor Birnbaum blinked at them from behind horn-rimmed glasses, his free hand balancing a mug of steaming tea on a saucer. "Agent Jones, so you finally got my messages. I see you've brought a colleague."

"What messages?" Kelly said, puzzled.

The professor looked perlexed. "I left several messages with the campus switchboard. Didn't they reach you?"

"No, I've been a little busy," Kelly said, examining him carefully. The nervous agitation had vanished. Many serial killers claimed that in the aftermath of a successful kill they were most at peace. Was that the case here?

"Well, thankfully you're here now. Come in, come in." He retreated down a narrow wood-paneled hallway toward the back of the house. Kelly and Jake glanced at each other, then followed. Jake noticed that Kelly had one hand tucked under her windbreaker, ready to draw her firearm. He reached under his jacket and unclipped his shoulder holster. *Boy Scout motto, always be prepared,* he thought.

The hallway opened into a large living room, where sunlight spilled through slightly warped panes of glass set in iron. Antique Oriental rugs and overstuffed armchairs were framed by floor-to-ceiling bookshelves. A fireplace with an enormous stone mantel dominated one wall. *Jesus,* Jake thought. It was just like the set for *Masterpiece Theater.*

"Please, have a seat." Professor Birnbaum gestured toward the two armchairs facing the fireplace. When they stood silently, he shrugged and sank into one himself. "Very well."

"It appears you've been less than honest with us, Professor Birnbaum." Kelly tossed the book onto the coffee table facing him.

He leaned forward and retrieved it, riffling through the pages contemplatively before setting it back down. "Not my best work, I'm afraid."

"Can you explain why the positioning of Tiffany Agostanelli's body exactly matched the rune listed on page eighty-six of your book?" Kelly said evenly.

"So she's dead, then? Such a shame. Yes, I'm afraid I can explain it."

This is it, Jake thought, his entire body tensing. Would he go quietly, or would he spring for the fire poker a few feet away? The silence lengthened as they watched him draw a spoonful of tea out of the cup, blow on it, then delicately sip it off the spoon.

"Well?" Jake finally asked impatiently.

Professor Birnbaum set the saucer on the table next to the book and sighed heavily. "I apologize for the delay, it's just that there's so much to explain I hardly know where to begin."

"You could start with how you killed them," Jake said, fists clenched by his sides as he pictured this mild-looking man draining Anna's blood into a bucket.

"Me? My goodness, no, I would never…" Professor Birnbaum barked out a short laugh. "As I told Agent Jones at the outset of her inquiry, I could never commit such a crime. But unfortunately, I think I know who might have."

"Another girl has lost her life," Kelly said quietly. "I'm going to need some convincing."

"It's not what you think. Based on the limited information you provided the last time we spoke, I had nothing but vague suspicions to present to you. Suspicions that I realized could only serve to make me more of a suspect in your eyes."

"Mind if we ask if you have an alibi for the past two nights?" Jake asked.

"Of course not. In fact, that's what I was just about to reveal. I attended a symposium in New York. A copy of my train ticket." He carefully laid the stub on the table. Kelly retrieved it and checked the dates and times.

"This doesn't prove anything. New York is only a few hours away by train. You could easily have bought another ticket and paid in cash," Kelly stated bluntly.

"My friend will have no problem corroborating my story. And I believe that once you've heard what he has to say, you'll view these events in a far different light."

"Really. And when will we have the pleasure of making his acquaintance?" Jake asked snidely.

Professor Birnbaum stood and gestured with one hand toward the door. An enormous man cloaked in black stepped into the room and pulled off his hood to reveal flowing white hair and a long beard. "May I present to you Stefan Gundarsson, the Warder of the Lore."

Twenty-One

Stefan stepped forward and extended his right hand. Jake shook it reflexively, then recovered from his surprise and quickly withdrew it. Kelly eyed the man steadily, her hand still stuffed inside her jacket. Stefan appeared to debate whether or not to try for a handshake, thought better of it and issued a curt nod in her direction. Walking lithely past them, he folded his tall frame into the chair opposite the professor. *Jesus,* Jake thought, *the guy had to be at least six foot six. There's a basketball coach out there somewhere kicking himself for letting this one get away.*

"Warder of the Lore?" Kelly asked. Jake was impressed by her calm demeanor. It must take a hell of a lot to shake her up.

"Yes, for the Ring of Ásatrú. We are the largest organization of our kind in the United States." He carefully emphasized each syllable in labored English, Kelly noted, though she couldn't place the accent.

"And what kind of organization is that, exactly?" Jake asked.

Stefan shifted slightly in his chair after glancing at the professor. "A religious one. We practice Ásatrú, the pre-Christian religion of the Germanic peoples."

"So you're what, some kind of cult?" Jake pressed.

Stefan's lips twisted into a wan smile. "A common misconception. We assist local groups by publishing a quarterly journal detailing various rituals, we train prospective clergy, we help to spread the word of the Heathen North."

"I don't suppose any of these rituals involve murdering young girls?" Kelly asked.

Stefan slowly shook his head. "There is evidence that in the past, sacrifices to Odin were conducted every four years in Iceland, as noted in works such as Adam of Bremen's history, but that is not the sort of behavior we would ever endorse. Ours is a peaceful, earth-loving religion."

"And how were these sacrifices conducted?"

Stefan appeared visibly uncomfortable as he responded, "The victims were hung, then stabbed."

Silence hung heavy on the room. Professor Birnbaum cleared his throat. "Perhaps I can help explain. When I heard of the, shall we say unique nature of the killings, I was immediately reminded of the Odinist rituals. When Agent Jones showed me the drawing of Fenrir, I was alarmed by the apparent link to Norse shamanism."

"Fenrir?" Kelly interrupted.

"Yes. One moment, I'll show you." He leaped to his feet and crossed the room to the opposite bookcase. The sudden movement caused both Kelly and Jake to tense.

"Oh, do relax," the professor mumbled as he drew a book from the third shelf and flipped it open to a marked page. He presented it to Kelly, who reluctantly withdrew her hand from her coat and took it. Staring back at her was a near-exact replica of the drawing found in the tunnels. A black-and-white etching of a wolf face leered luridly from the page, over the words *Fenrir, or Fenris.*

"What is this?" she asked, puzzled.

"Fenrir, son of Loki, enemy of the gods. An enormous wolf-creature bred of both god and giant. Prophecy foretold that Fenrir would end the gods' reign, so in hopes of preventing that he was bound with a magic tether. At the end of the world, or Ragnarök, legend has it that Fenrir will break his bonds and devour Odin."

"So you knew what the drawing represented all along?" Kelly said, voice tight.

Professor Birnbaum appeared embarrassed. "I had some idea, yes. But it wasn't until I spoke to Stefan that I knew for certain."

"You should have said something," Kelly said.

"Agent Jones, you were obviously already considering me as a suspect. I didn't think it wise to draw any more attention to myself until I knew whether my suspicions were correct."

Jake interjected, "I don't see how all this stuff about a wolf and Thor is going to help us."

Professor Birnbaum shook his head emphatically. "Thor is one of Odin's sons. Odin is the Norse equivalent of Zeus, the lord of all gods."

"The head honcho," Jake offered.

Professor Birnbaum inclined his head. "In a manner of speaking, yes. Odin was the raven king. His death was to be avenged by one of his sons, Vidar, the god of silence and revenge."

"And how does Vidar do that?" Jake asked.

Professor Birnbaum grabbed the book from Kelly's hands and flipped forward a few pages, then handed it back, watching her in silence. Her eyes widened and she gasped slightly at the image on the page.

"What is it?" Jake asked, fighting the urge to cross the room. One of them needed to cover the door in case these guys tried to bolt, he reminded himself.

She looked up and met his eyes. "He split his jaw."

"Indeed," Professor Birnbaum said mildly. He traced a finger across the page as he read from the book. " 'Immediately thereafter Vidar will come forth and put one foot on the lower jaw of the wolf. With one hand, he will take hold of the upper jaw of the wolf and tear apart his gullet, and that will be the death of Fenrir.' " He snapped the book shut and glanced up at them.

"So someone is sacrificing the girls in the same way that Vidar killed this wolf Fenrir?" Kelly said slowly.

"It would appear so, yes." The professor nodded emphatically.

"But the way they're being killed also resembles a sacrifice to Odin," she continued.

"I'm afraid so."

"All due respect, gentlemen, but this evidence appears to place you both at the top of the suspect list," Jake said pointedly.

"I realize that, but you must believe us." The professor regarded them, wide-eyed.

"Really? And why's that?" Jake asked.

Stefan's voice resounded from the depths of the chair. "Because I know who is responsible."

Kelly regarded him closely. He appeared almost preternaturally calm and composed, hardly the attitude of a man being questioned by the FBI. He could be a sociopath, she theorized, a killer who liked to toy with the cops by offering to assist them. Bundy had done that, helping to create a profile of the Green River Killer while he was sitting on death row. There was no doubt in her mind that Stefan could be their perp: he had the size and strength to pull it off, and there was something about him that Kelly didn't trust. With any luck he'd slip up and reveal one of their holdbacks, something about the murder that only the killer and investigators would know, something that had been kept from the media. But if she was going to draw him out, she'd have to tread carefully.

"If you knew who was committing the murders, why didn't you come forward sooner?" she asked.

He took a moment to weigh his response, before saying, "Until Professor Birnbaum contacted me, I was unaware of what was transpiring here. I try to maintain a state of purity and belief in the goodness of life. I find that following current events renders that state difficult." Stefan seemed to draw farther into his robes. "However, when he informed me of the killings, I felt it necessary to come speak with you myself."

"So who did it?" Jake asked suspiciously.

The professor and Stefan exchanged glances. "Perhaps I should start with a brief explanation of my position. As Warder of the Lore, one of my primary responsibilities involves overseeing the training of our Godmen and Godwomen."

"Priests?" Kelly asked.

Stefan waved one hand in the air. "They are clergy of a sort, educated in the history, religion and traditions of our ancestors. They spend at least a year in study, researching texts such as the *Eddas, Heimskringla,* and sagas, as well as some of the more recent secondary sources."

Kelly interrupted, "I'm sorry, I'm not sure what this all has to do with the murders, and we're pressed for time here. If you could just give us a name—"

"Patience, please." The words thundered out of his mouth, though his features remained impenetrable. Kelly instinctively tightened her grip on her Beretta.

Stefan issued a deep sigh and sank farther into the armchair. "Americans, always in such a rush. You will get your name, but to find him I believe a more complete understanding of who he is and why he's behaving in this manner could prove invaluable. Please, it won't take long."

After a moment, Kelly silently nodded her assent.

He tented his fingers, closed his eyes and continued, "A few years ago, I was approached by a new student who was already well versed in our lore. His enthusiasm was such that I waived one of our traditional requirements for Godmen, that they be self-supporting. In the interest of furthering his studies I took him under my wing, and into my home. He progressed rapidly, reading all the required materials, even contributing some fascinating articles to our newsletter. Soon after appearing on my doorstep, he began presiding at some of our Hearth's most sacred rites."

"Hearth?"

"Local groups perform their own rituals, the same as other churches, to celebrate the holy feasts and blessings of the year, such as Midsummer Night and Yule," Professor Birnbaum explained.

Stefan nodded in agreement. "I had high hopes for this young man. Having no children of my own, I envisioned him one day taking over my position." He fell silent, as though drawn away by distant memories.

"Well? What happened?" Jake asked after a minute.

Stefan shook his head slightly as though clearing it of cobwebs and continued, "He was understandably eager to visit the Homeland, birthplace of much of our lore, and last spring I agreed to finance his pilgrimage."

"The Homeland being?" Jake asked impatiently. A sharp look from Kelly rebuked him. *Christ,* he thought, *it was like pulling teeth getting information from this guy. Warder of the Lore? It was more like purveyor of the bullshit.*

"Iceland, Norway and Sweden. He wished to visit various holy sites, such as the Helgafell and Gotland, among others." He paused before continuing in a voice so low all three leaned forward to hear him. "I fear that the trip proved his undoing."

"Yeah? How?" Jake finally asked, ignoring Kelly's look of reprobation.

"At the turn of the fifteenth century, Bishop Gottskálk

presided over Hólar, Iceland, a religious settlement that served as the true capital of the North for seven centuries. In addition to being a Catholic bishop, Gottskálk was one of the most infamous magicians in the history of Iceland."

"A Catholic bishop?" Kelly said incredulously.

"Regrettably so. You must understand, the form of worship that we practice has no basis in magic. However there have always been practitioners within our fold— shamans, seiors, hexenmeisters." Stefan lowered his gaze.

Professor Birnbaum piped up excitedly, "An interesting example is the Pennsylvania Dutch, who are actually the descendants of German immigrants. Isolated in rural communities, they brought many of the old practices of braucherie, or witchcraft, with them. Many of those objets d'art they sell at craft fairs are in actuality hex signs." He noted the silent disapproval on the faces surrounding him and awkwardly cleared his throat. "My apologies. Please do continue."

Stefan drew his hands under his robe, and Kelly tensed. "Hands where I can see them, please," she said sharply.

He lifted an eyebrow and withdrew them, laying them in his lap palms up. "As I was saying, there were at one time many books of magic—the only one that survived the Christian purges of the Middle Ages was the *Galdra-bók*. Two other famous manuscripts once existed—the *Gráyskinni*, or gray leather, and the *Raudhskinni*, red leather, named for the manner in which they were bound. The *Raudhskinni* was said to be the more powerful of the two books, written in gold runes on red parchment. It contained the darkest kind of sorcery, ways to foresee the future, shape-shift, even to raise the dead. When Bishop Gottskálk died the book was buried with him, so that the world would be safe from its secrets. Over the centuries, many who sought his knowledge have attempted to rob his grave. All those who tried have gone mad or vanished completely."

Despite the sun streaming through the windows, Kelly felt a shudder down her spine. She brushed it away. These were silly tales, the equivalent of ghost stories around a campfire. She glanced at her watch: it was almost 9:30 a.m. The sooner she had an opportunity to check out this guy's alibi, the better; and if it didn't hold, she might be able to get an arrest warrant. Until then she'd put a detail on him and the professor. She turned her focus back to what he was saying.

A shadow passed over Stefan's features. "My young protégé returned from his trip a changed man. Initially, I thought it was simply the draining effects of such a long journey. But his journal entries became increasingly erratic."

"You read his journal?" Jake asked. He imagined the old man skulking around a dark bedroom, sneaking a peek at a pink diary.

"As part of their training, Godmen are required to maintain a journal of their rites, which is then evaluated by the Warder of the Lore. I had requested that he maintain meticulous records of his journey. When I saw the entry for Holar, I was shocked."

"What, did he get down with a local girl?" asked Jake. Stefan tented his fingers and brought them slowly to his chin. "Far worse," he said heavily. "He claimed to have recovered the *Raudhskinni*."

Using both hands, he raised himself from the tub. The water ran red as it coursed down his naked body in rivulets. He wiped himself down with his hands, forgoing the stained towel hanging on the back of the bathroom door. It had been a long night; the sacrifice had taken longer than expected, and yet he hadn't been discovered. Odin must have shielded him from prying eyes.

It was hard to repress the surge of excitement he felt whenever he contemplated how close he was to completion. It would be a relief to be finished, he thought; the task was more daunting than he had anticipated, becoming increasingly difficult with each victim. This last girl had fought unusually hard, there were already bruises forming on his legs where she had kicked him. He hoped the next one would be easier.

He walked down the hall toward the back room, drops of reddish water trailing in his wake. The black robe was on the bed where he had left it, the other equipment laid out beside it. He picked up the knife and carefully wiped the blade on the folds of the robe, then held it up to the light seeping through the windows, examining it. The blade would need to be sharpened again, he would see to that after he rested. He laid it back down on the pile, then carefully wrapped everything in the robe before storing the bundle in the crawl space above the closet. As he stood at the top of the ladder his fingers reached in farther, groping until he felt the mottled texture of oilskin. He closed his eyes as he ran one hand over it, feeling the hard edges of the book inside. A smile danced across his lips. He was so close to completing the ritual. And when he had, everything would change.

Kelly was aware of pangs of hunger in her stomach, and the throbbing of blood in her ears. She hadn't eaten in over twelve hours, or slept in almost thirty-six, and the Warder's story had her riveted in spite of herself. The strong regular cadence of his voice was hypnotizing. She could easily understand how he rose to a position of power within his organization.

"So you believe that your former student might be the one responsible for these murders?" Kelly asked.

Stefan nodded his head sagely. "I'm afraid I had a rather strong reaction to his journal entry. Last June I expelled him from our program for not behaving in accordance with the values of the Ring of Ásatrú."

"How'd he handle it?" Jake asked.

"Not well, I'm afraid. That same month my housekeeper, Katerina, a young Ukranian woman, disappeared. She had been with me almost five years, and was always most reliable. At the time I feared merely that she had been detained and deported. But when Professor Birnbaum informed me that a young woman had been fished from the waters off Bridgeport, I suspected the worst." He lowered his eyes. "She was four months pregnant when she vanished."

"How did you know the body we found was Eastern European?" asked Kelly suspiciously.

"Friends in low places, I'm afraid," Professor Birnbaum said with a look of embarrassment.

Stefan continued, "Knowing his prior history, I feared he might have reverted to his old ways."

"Those old ways being?" Jake asked.

"Prior to entering my tutelage, he had spent the past two decades in a facility for the disturbed."

"Let me get this straight—you knew he was crazy, yet you invited him to live with you?" Jake was incredulous.

Stefan shrugged, embarrassment flushing his cheeks slightly. "You must understand, we pride ourselves on accepting individuals regardless of their past. It is one of our strictest tenets, the belief that any life can be salvaged."

"What was he institutionalized for?" Kelly asked.

"It's my understanding that when he was an adolescent, he was responsible for the deaths of both grandparents."

"So you took in a murderer, and trained him as a priest?" Jake said slowly in disbelief.

"He had been released, and seemed appropriately repentant," Stefan said pointedly. "I believed it was not for me to judge a man so determined to change the course of his life. Unfortunately, it appears that I made a tremendous mistake. Rest assured it's not one I will ever forgive myself for."

Kelly examined him closely; if he was their killer, he was putting on a hell of a show. She decided it was time to press him and see how far he was willing to go with this. "Mr. Gundarsson, I really need a name," she said. "It's time that we end all this."

"That's precisely the problem," he said. "I recently

discovered that the name he provided me with, Victor Moore, was false."

"I see," Kelly said soothingly. As expected, he was dodging the question. Given a name, within five minutes they would have been able to determine if he was lying. He was cagey, she'd give him that. "I don't suppose you can account for your whereabouts the past few days?"

"Actually, I can," he replied smoothly. "The professor approached me at a symposium in Manhattan. There are several hundred people there that can attest to my presence, I was the keynote speaker. I'd be happy to supply some names."

"I'd appreciate that." Kelly deliberated for a moment, then reached into her front pocket for her notebook. She flipped it open to the page where she had copied down the symbol. "Does this mean anything to you?" she asked, crossing the room and holding it out to him. She scrutinized his face to gauge his reaction.

He examined the drawing carefully. "It's the rune you mentioned before, Thurs. A Thurs is a force of nature, the force of opposition in the world. As a rune, it's used as a powerful form of aggressive defense, or a catalyst for change. How does this relate to the murders?"

Kelly ignored the question and quickly sketched two other drawings next to the first. Seeing them, Stefan drew his breath in sharply. Professor Birnbaum vaulted from his chair to peer over their shoulders.

"What?" Jake asked, maintaining his post by the door despite his curiosity. "It's just a couple of letters."

"These aren't letters, they're runes," the professor said

animatedly. "Each has a very specific meaning in and of itself, but they can also be combined to form words."

"So what do these three spell?" Kelly asked, her brow furrowing as she regarded them closely.

"Is this the order they were found in?" Stefan asked quietly.

Kelly realized that she'd listed them inaccurately. Lin was the first victim, then Anna. "No, it should be this one—" she pointed to the last drawing "—then the middle one, then Thurs. What does it mean?"

Stefan sighed heavily. "I'm afraid what you have here is Úr, or Drizzle, which drives out the elements that cause one to be weak. Followed by Íss, or Ice, a powerful force for concentrating the will. Then the Thurs." He and the professor exchanged glances again.

"What?" Kelly demanded, looking from one to the other.

"It would appear," Stefan said carefully, "that you have the first three letters of a word that ties in with the Fenrir drawing."

"What word is that?" Kelly asked.

"Vidar."

"So we're missing the final two letters?" Jake asked.

"Yes. The word would be completed by Ár and Reidh, the runes for rewarding action in the past and for creating a pathway to power."

"Meaning what?" Jake said, stupefied.

Kelly sank into the chair vacated moments earlier by Professor Birnbaum. "Meaning he's not done yet."

Twenty-Two

Morrow covered his mouth with one hand to suppress a yawn and blinked to refocus as the computer screen swam before him. His eyes felt as though they were stuffed with sand, his clothes stank, and he longed to brush his teeth. Now that they had a full unit working this case, he had moved their base of operations to a classroom in the science center. With Jones gone, the responsibility for chaperoning twenty cranky, sleep-deprived FBI agents fell to him. They were all working the phones and manning computers, digging up ancient court records, looking for a teenager who had been sentenced to a term in a mental hospital for killing his grandparents. They were focusing on a six-year window of cases in New York, New Jersey and Connecticut; if nothing turned up there they'd expand the search outward. The problem was that not every county had archived older cases in their databases. Persuading clerks in distant counties to stop what they were doing to sift through dusty file boxes was daunting. On top of that, they didn't have a definite age for their suspect. If he was a juvenile when he committed the crime the records might be sealed, in which case they'd never find him. It was worse than searching for a needle in a haystack; they were digging through an entire field.

Kelly and Jake were en route to Brooklyn to check out the last-known residence of their killer. Morrow doubted they'd find much, but he was hoping they'd get lucky. This had been a rough case so far, and they could really use a break. The guy that claimed he could ID the suspect was sitting in the next room sipping coffee, waiting for the sketch artist from the New York field office to arrive. Morrow made a point of checking in on him periodically. With the robe and beard, he looked like an extra from *Lord of the Rings*. It didn't take much to imagine him committing a crime like this; he certainly had a crazy air about him. Too bad his alibi had checked out.

Morrow tapped furiously, leaning in to gaze closely at the screen. In the five boroughs alone, more than ten cases from that time period were potential matches. Even with the extra manpower it would take days to investigate them all, and that wasn't counting the results from some of the other sixty-odd counties in New York. And then there was Connecticut, and Pennsylvania…he sighed heavily and hit a button that read *Print All*. A printer across the room sputtered to life, plaintively grinding out sentencing reports.

"God, I hate that noise," Morrow said aloud while rubbing his throbbing temples. It was going to take weeks to catch up on his sleep when all this was finished.

Despite the brief catnap he had managed to sneak in the command trailer the night before, his head felt as though it was packed with cotton. Hopefully the pace would slow a little now that the girl had been found. Their killer was definitely due for a day off.

A beeping sound announced that the printer had finished. He tapped the papers against a table to straighten them, then started dividing them into five piles. When he had finished he clapped his hands together to get everyone's attention. They glanced up from their computers and phones.

"Ladies and gentlemen, I have the results from the Big Apple. I need five volunteers to stop what they're doing and start on these."

One hand was tentatively raised. He arched an eyebrow. "Did I mention that those five volunteers would be the first allowed to break for lunch?" He smiled as every hand in the room shot in the air. "I thought as much."

After distributing the stacks of records, he decided to make a run to the vending machine for a sugar jolt. On the way there he rapped on the door to the next room to see if he could get something for their mystery guest.

Huh, he thought, ducking his head in to scan the interior. *Must have gone to the bathroom.*

Kelly gripped the door handle as Jake swerved across three lanes of traffic, barely making the exit onto 95 South. A few drops of coffee sloshed out of the cup clenched in her other hand, and the phone tucked between her shoulder and cheek almost went flying. She threw him a cautionary look. "Sorry," he mumbled. "My driving skills aren't their best at the moment."

"Just get us there in one piece, please," she muttered. They were both exhausted, their frayed nerves contributing to the tension. She hung up the phone with a snap and crossed another name off the list.

Jake glanced at her. "Alibi still holding?"

"This is the third person to confirm it. Stefan was definitely at a symposium in New York when Tiffany was taken. The hotel bartender even remembers him and the professor staking out a table from midnight until closing."

"He's sure it was them?" Jake asked. Kelly raised an eyebrow at him. "Hey, it could've been a black robe convention."

"He picked their driver's license pictures out of a photo array. So they're both in the clear."

She leaned back against the seat and closed her eyes, even though she was too on edge to nap. It was disappointing; she'd really thought Stefan was feeding them a line of bull, that this "student" was a figment of his imagination. With his alibi checking out, she was now forced to take him at his word. At the moment this was their most promising lead, so she was throwing everything into following it up.

Stefan claimed his student had left in such a hurry that most of his belongings were still at the house. They were on their way to search it now. Morrow was digging for names based on the background information that Stefan had provided. Hopefully that wouldn't prove to be a pack of lies, too; Stefan was right, there had been no record of a Victor

Moore anywhere in the system. How he'd managed to procure a passport was a mystery in and of itself. *If he had actually gone to Iceland,* she mused. *God only knew what he had really done with the Warder's money.* There was a chance Stefan was lying to them, and that he actually knew the killer's name. But why come forward at all then? And he'd offered to sit down with a sketch artist. Once the sketch was finished they'd disseminate it, get the general public involved. She couldn't let herself consider the possibility that this was just a wild-goose chase, that their killer might have nothing to do with Stefan, that all this Norse stuff was just a coincidence. *Sooner or later they'd back him into a corner,* she told herself. She just hoped it happened before he struck again.

On their way out of town they had stopped by the student union for triple espressos. The campus was eerily empty for that time of day. In front of almost every house cars gaped open, with students shoving duffel bags and laundry baskets into the exposed hatches and trunks. "They're clearing out," Jake had observed.

"I don't blame them," Kelly muttered, watching a girl strap a guitar to the roof of a VW bug. She massaged her temples. Her head throbbed from all the bits and pieces of information floating around inside, bumping against each other but never linking up. With this case it seemed like the more she knew, the less she understood. And what Stefan had said at the end of their interview chilled her to the marrow.

"The manner in which the girls were killed was, I'm afraid, the final key. It appears that my student has now fully embraced the dark arts, and is using a combination of ancient rituals to achieve his end," he had said solemnly.

"That end being?" Jake asked.

Stefan shifted in his chair, clearly uncomfortable. "That, I'm not entirely certain of. The ceremonial gruel with henbane seeds, the blood eagle, the raven feather in the stomach, the runes, all these things are drawn from ancient Norse rituals. A major holy day on our calendar is fast approaching: Winternights. This year, it's scheduled to begin at midnight on October 13th."

"That's tonight," Kelly interjected.

Stefan nodded. "It's one of our three major holidays, a time to honour ancestral spirits and the powers of fruitfulness, wisdom and death."

"That doesn't sound so bad," Jake remarked.

"I'm afraid you don't understand," Stefan said, raising his eyebrows. "Winternights marks the time when animals are hallowed and sacrificed to Odin and his host of the dead. The ancients believed that the Wild Hunt begins to ride after Winternights. Then the roads and fields no longer belong to humans, but to ghosts and trolls."

"How cheerful. St Patrick's Day is looking better all the time," Jake muttered.

"Whatever Victor is planning, I believe he will attempt to see it through to fruition this evening," Stefan concluded.

Kelly was jolted from her reverie by another of Jake's NASCAR-style lane changes. Clearly sleep was not a possibility on this ride. She tucked her coffee mug into a cup holder, reached into the back seat to retrieve her laptop and flipped it open with a sigh.

"What the hell was that about the Wild Hunt?" Jake asked after a moment. "I mean, man, I feel like I fell into a fairy tale with all that stuff he was talking about back there."

"I know." Kelly rolled her head from side to side a few times, then started a Web search. After a moment a string of links appeared on the screen. "Here it is—the Wild Hunt." She read to herself for a moment, eyebrows narrowing.

"Well?" Jake asked impatiently, glancing at the screen.

"Keep your eyes on the road. It says, 'Belief in the Wild Hunt is found throughout Northern Europe. In Norse myth, it was thought that the souls of the dead were wafted away on the winds of a storm. Odin was worshipped as the leader of all disembodied spirits, and eventually the storm became associated with his passing. The Wild Hunt was said to presage misfortune such as pestilence, death or war. Some believe it refers to Ragnarök, the end of the world, which seems to come ever closer as the sun grows weaker and the darkness stronger.'"

"Man, and I thought the Catholic church was fucked up," Jake said with a low whistle. "Can you believe people really buy into this stuff today?"

Kelly shrugged. "I guess it's not all that different from worshipping a carpenter that lived two thousand years ago."

"Don't let Father John hear you say that. So what do you think our guy is after?"

"No idea," she said with a sigh. Her cell phone buzzed. "Jones." She listened for a long moment, then said, "All right, we'll follow up on it. Let me know if you get anything else."

"What?" Jake asked.

"Possible lead. Morrow says so far they've found three cases that are a close match, men released from Bellevue in the past few years who were incarcerated as juveniles. Let's head there first, see if we can get anything."

Jake shook his head in frustration. "I can't believe we have someone who might know what our killer looks like, spent almost a year with him, for Christ's sake, and we still don't have so much as a name."

"Don't worry, we'll get one," Kelly said determinedly. "We're close now. He's running out of time, and thankfully there aren't many students left on campus for him to take."

Jake's jaw set in a grim line. "Unless he already took them."

Morrow sighed as he approached the trailer. After fighting off a virtual battalion of microphones and cameras at his latest press conference, all he wanted to do was climb in, take off his shoes, and sneak in a few minutes of shut-eye. But there was Claire, the local Lois Lane, sitting cross-legged on the ground in front of the door. As he approached she stood and brushed off the seat of her jeans. "I heard Tiffany Agostanelli was killed. Is it true?" Her brow was furrowed, and he noticed that she didn't have her notebook.

"I'm afraid I can't confirm anything for you. We'll release an official statement sometime in the next few hours." Morrow tried to brush past her, but Claire refused to budge.

"The paper's not coming out this week. Everyone's leaving. Classes aren't officially canceled yet, but no one's going," Claire said.

"So consider yourself on a well-deserved vacation." Morrow downed the last of his coffee, the fourth cup of the day and counting, he thought.

"It wasn't Josh, was it?" Claire asked. "Does that mean you still don't have any suspects?"

Morrow suppressed a twinge of annoyance; he didn't have time for this. "I meant what I said at the press conference—we're still following up a number of promising leads. Now, if you'll excuse me, I really need to get to work—"

"Do you think it's safe to stay? My folks want me to come home, but I don't know…I can't really afford to lose my tuition payment."

He examined her. The bravado of a moment before had vanished, she looked like a scared little girl. An image of his own daughter flashed through his mind, and he took a second to control the aggravation in his voice. "What do your parents think?"

"They want me home." She paused, considering, then continued, "Would you stay, in my position?"

"I can't honestly say," Morrow answered, thinking that he'd never had the opportunity to be in her position. While attending night school at City College he'd been mugged at gunpoint on the way to class, and yet there he was again the following evening. These kids, with every advantage and no idea how to get through life. "But if I were you, I'd listen to your parents."

She shifted uneasily from one foot to the other. "I guess. But the administration hasn't said what they'll do yet, if they'll refund tuition or give credit for classes or what. And I heard that President Williams has totally lost it, no one's even sure if he'll be staying. So that means Dean Scott will be in charge for a while, and he's such a bastard."

Morrow rubbed the bridge of his nose. "Claire, I really don't have time for this."

"I just thought—"

"Well, you thought wrong."

"But—"

"Excuse me." Morrow unlocked the door of the trailer and pulled it open. Claire stepped aside to avoid being hit by the door.

"Sorry," he called over his shoulder as he slipped past. The last thing he saw before closing the door was Claire, completely crestfallen. He felt as if he had just clubbed a baby seal.

Twenty-Three

She and Jake had already waited almost an hour to receive an audience with the head of Bellevue's Criminal Detention facility. They sat on cracked plastic chairs in the hallway, sipping cups of lukewarm coffee from a vending machine. Jake was busily flipping through back issues of *Better Homes and Gardens*. Kelly felt something vibrate against her belt, recognized the first three numbers as the Chicago area code, and clicked open her cell phone.

"Kelly?"

Kelly shut her eyes—she had completely forgotten about calling her friend Brian to help identify the strange drawing. So much had happened that it felt like weeks had passed since they had spoken. And now it was unlikely he could tell them something they didn't already know.

His excitement hummed through the receiver. "This was a humdinger, let me tell you. I spent most of the night on it, but I think I got what you were looking for. You want it all, or should I hit the highlights?"

"Just the highlights."

"Sure. All right, let's see—the drawing is of the wolf Fenrir, from Norse mythology." Kelly could almost picture Brian at his kitchen table, brow furrowed as he squinted through his glasses at the page. "At the end of the world, Odin, the big cheese, is supposed to be killed by Fenrir. Odin's kid Vidar, the god of silence and revenge, then kills Fenrir with his bare hands to avenge his father's death."

Kelly found herself tuning him out, focusing on the dust motes dancing through a shaft of light down the hall. The dull murmur of the insane served as a background hum, one voice occasionally piercing the soundproofed walls in a shriek of discontent.

"I almost forgot the best part. Guess how Vidar does it?"

"Does what?"

"Kills Fenrir—Jesus, Kelly, are you paying attention? I spent all night on this, you told me it was important."

"It is, Brian. I'm sorry, it's just…I was up all night too," she responded guiltily. No point in letting him know his all-nighter had been in vain.

"All right then, I won't make you guess. Vidar grabs hold of Fenrir's jaw and rips it apart. Tears his face in two. You should see the picture I found, it's pretty gruesome. I'll fax it over with the other stuff."

I've already seen it, thought Kelly, but simply said, "Thanks, I owe you one."

"No problem. You can make it up to me with dinner the next time you're in town."

As she was hanging up she heard his voice call out from the receiver and raised it back to her ear. "Yes?"

"Almost forgot one thing. It's probably not that important, but Vidar was a twin."

"A twin?"

"Yup. He and his twin brother, Vali, were the kids of Odin and some giantess named Grid. Must have made for a hell of a family portrait." He chuckled.

"Thanks again, Brian."

Jake glanced up from an article on transplanting hydrangeas. "What's up?"

Kelly tucked her phone back into place. "A friend of mine, teaches religious iconography. He ID'd the photo of Fenrir."

"Yeah? Tell me something I don't know," Jake grumbled.

"He did mention one thing that Stefan left out. Apparently Vidar was a twin."

"So what, our guy is a twin now?"

"I don't know. Might be worth looking into." She slid forward slightly in the seat and winced as her back protested. Despite their sensible design, the flats she was wearing were starting to pinch her feet, and her lower back felt unbelievably tight. She longed for a shower. A shower, a fluffy robe, a down bed with four-hundred-thread-count sheets. And a steak. A juicy red steak with a side of garlic mashed potatoes, creamed spinach and Yorkshire pudding.

"What are you smiling at?" Jake asked grumpily. He tossed the magazine back onto the small white table separating them. "You'd think they'd get *Sports Illustrated* or *Newsweek,* for Christ's sake."

"People steal them."

"Yeah, you're probably right."

The door to the office suddenly cracked open to reveal a small, mousy-looking man dressed in an ill-fitting suit. He squinted at them. "I can see you now."

He stepped aside to let them pass into his office. Sterile as any hospital room, it contained a shoddy brown desk backed by a bookshelf. An enormous, outdated computer covered one corner of it, while the rest held neatly stacked piles of papers. A fake plant reached mournfully toward the window, which was small and set high in the wall. This space had probably once been used for patients, Kelly thought. The room still seemed to exude a current of mental anguish and tension. A tall, thin man sat in one of the two green chairs facing the desk. She extended her hand as he half rose.

"Special Agent Jones with the FBI. Thanks for taking the time to meet with us on such short notice."

His gray eyes matched his suit perfectly, and they gazed at her as if she had just said something extraordinarily unpleasant. "Henry Dunham, in-house counsel for Bellevue. I'm afraid you're wasting your time."

Kelly eased into the chair facing the desk, while Jake stood behind her.

"I hope not," she said genially. "I believe what we're asking is fairly straightforward."

The smaller man closed the door and shuffled behind the desk. He nervously straightened a paper pile before introducing himself. "I'm Dr. Theodore Parsons. I'm afraid Mr. Dunham is right. As far as revealing the names of released patients, we're bound by doctor/patient confidentiality laws."

"I understand. We're not asking for your entire patient list, just those that were released over the past two years."

Dr. Parsons cleared his throat. "While we of course want to help you find the perpetrator of these terrible crimes, I've already spoken with the board and I'm afraid we can't provide you with those names. Besides, the likelihood of one of our patients killing again is absurd. We don't release anyone until it's clear they no longer pose a threat to society."

That's what they were afraid of, Kelly thought. The repercussions would be devastating if it turned out they had released a serial killer into the general public. Bellevue had already been under fire lately, and this could be the straw that broke the camel's back. "My understanding was that such names are a matter of public record if the patients were serving time for violent crimes."

"I'm afraid that's not technically the case."

"We can get a subpoena."

"And we'll fight it," Dunham said calmly.

Kelly looked from one bureaucrat to the other. They'd hit a dead end here and she knew it. The hospital could block a subpoena for weeks, possibly months, the kind of time that she didn't have. She stood abruptly.

"Thank you for your time."

Jake followed her out. "What the hell was that?" he said as soon as they were out of earshot.

"They're not going to budge."

"Well, you could have fought a little harder. I never figured you for a quitter."

"I'm not a quitter. I'm just hoping for a shortcut."

Just outside the emergency room doors a nurse leaned against the brick wall of the building, inhaling deeply off an unfiltered cigarette. Dressed in scrubs with pink sneakers, hair pulled back in cornrows, she was a heavyset woman in her mid-forties. Her name tag read CELIA. Kelly approached her and held up her badge.

"Hi, I'm from the FBI. Could I ask you some questions?"

The woman eyed her through a cloud of smoke. "I'm on my break."

"It should only take a minute."

The woman stamped out her cigarette with the ball of her foot. "Ain't supposed to be talking to you."

"Please. It's important," Kelly said pleadingly.

The woman took in their rumpled clothes and hair, and peered toward the sliding glass doors indecisively. Seeing no one, she gestured with her head for them to follow. Next to a blue Dumpster out of view of the door, she planted herself with feet slightly apart, crossed her arms, and asked, "What d'ya wanna know?" The honeyed tones of the Deep South rubbed the rough edges off each syllable.

"We need to find out about patients released over the past couple of years."

Celia snorted. "Got a few hours? We got a revolvin' door here, faster than the Hilton. They never should have released those men, none of 'em, you hear? Know-it-all in there, saying they're better, when we know there's just no mo' money for 'em. Cutbacks. I gotta pay for health care now, you believe that? A nurse, payin' for health care?"

Kelly struggled to contain her impatience. Any minute now, a staff member could come out and see them talking, and that would be the end of it. "Did any of them strike you as being particularly dangerous?"

Celia laughed. "Honey, they struck me all the time. Hell, I lost three teeth working here and got my nose broke twice. I tell you though, the most dangerous are the quiet ones. They sit there all day nice as you please, doing they artwork, playing chess, and then one day they jump from behind and try to strangle you with a bedsheet."

"What about a guy who read a lot of books?" asked Jake. "He might have talked about different gods like Odin, Vidar…"

Celia looked him up and down as if she hadn't noticed him until now. "My, aren't you a handsome one. You together?" She wagged her finger from one to the other of them. Kelly vigorously shook her head no. "Shame. Beautiful babies the two of you would make. Oh, you talkin' 'bout the Viking."

"The Viking?" Kelly and Jake exchanged glances.

"Yep. Smart as a whip, that one. Smart enough to talk his way out of here. Always going on about this and that, the end of the world, giants and serpents. Bunch of nonsense, you ask me. I tol' him that he should just accept the Lord Jesus Christ as his savior—"

"What was he in for?" Kelly interrupted. Clearly, once Celia warmed to a story there was no stopping her.

Celia frowned slightly. "Oh Lord, he was here a long time. I been here fifteen years and he came in before that. I heard he killed his grandparents. They was nice enough to take him and his brother in after they folks died, and one day the Viking ups and kills 'em both in bed. Sliced 'em up pretty bad, from what I hear. I told 'em, just 'cause he's quiet don't mean he's safe, but they don't listen."

"He had a brother?" Kelly asked.

"Sure, looked just like him, too. Same funny glasses— couldn't hardly tell 'em apart. He'd come visit every month, always brought flowers and some books, stayed for an hour or so, which is more than most of 'em get. Things affect folks different ways." She leaned forward conspiratorially. "I heard that back when they was kids, their daddy lost his job, killed himself and set the house on fire. Thems the only two got out. But one turns out normal, and the other ends up here." She jerked a chubby thumb toward the brick wall behind her. "You never know, do ya?"

"What were their names?"

"Let's see." Celia rocked back on her heels and crossed her arms, peering up at the sky. "We always just called him the Viking. His real name was Paul, I think. Yes, Paul, because his brother was Peter. I always thought it funny, robbing Peter to pay Paul. But with them it was the other way round."

"What was his last name?" Jake asked impatiently.

"Well, I don' rightly remember. He been gone a few years now. You know how many patients they give me? I hardly get to sit all day, runnin' around watchin' after these crazy folk."

"Are you absolutely certain you can't remember?" Kelly pressed.

Celia shook her head slowly. "No, ma'am. And I don' know where he went. Haven't given him a thought for some time now. Figured I would've, he left here mutterin' 'bout making 'em pay for killing his daddy. That's the thing about people, always shiftin' the blame somewhere else." Celia shook her head and sighed heavily. "My cousin Esther was the same way. Always goin' on 'bout the man. I tol' her, I said, 'Girl, you gonna give yourself an ulcer!' And you know what—"

Jake interrupted, "What about when he was released? Do you remember what month it was?"

"It was right about Christmastime. I remember, 'cause he gave me one of his books as a sort of holiday present. Couldn't make no sense of it. It was all poems, got three pages in and set it down. Myself, I prefer mysteries."

Kelly pulled two photos out of her folder. "Do you recognize either of these men?"

Celia squinted at the blowups of Professor Birnbaum and Stefan. "Those license photos? They look like license photos, better'n mine, I'll tell you that much, my eyes are almost closed. Nope, never seen either of these gentlemen before."

"So they never visited the Viking?" Kelly asked.

"Not on my time."

"All right." Kelly tucked the photos away.

Celia smoothed her scrubs down with both hands and nodded. "You got what you came for?"

"Yes, thank you, Celia," Kelly said with a smile, squeezing her hand gratefully.

"I better get back. My break was over ten minutes ago."

The doors slid silently shut behind her.

"Fifteen years and she only remembers his first name?" Jake groused.

"It doesn't matter. Morrow should be able to run it down." Kelly was already striding back toward the car, ponytail bouncing against her back as she flipped open her cell phone.

"Nice shortcut, by the way. Didn't think you had it in you."

Kelly tried to shrug nonchalantly; she was uncomfortable with what she had just done, but they were under a time crunch and if she waited for the wheels of bureaucracy to churn forward another girl might die. "Sometimes you don't have a choice."

He hurried to catch up. "Exactly. Glad to see you're coming around to my way of thinking. Are we still going to the Warder of the Loons place?"

"Absolutely." It was hard to contain her elation; they were getting close. She loved it when the pieces started to fall into place and there was an undeniable sense of momentum building. She turned. "You want to drive, or should I?"

He could feel the voices getting closer, but they weren't upon him yet. It was louder now, a buzzing on the periphery, like a mosquito in the darkness. The chatter of the television in the next room was comforting; he'd taken to leaving it on day and night, enjoying the lilt of the voices and songs that streamed through. It had been years since he'd been able to choose the channel, and now he flipped through with abandon whenever he entered the room: 104, 105, 106… It was hard to believe there were so many, he'd had no idea. He loved the jingles in particular, humming them to himself as he worked. "Rice-a-roni. The San Francisco Treat!" "Have a good night's sleep on us…mattress discounters!" His voice soared to the high registers on the final notes.

"We should take a trip when all this is finished," he said conversationally to the cellar door. It was slightly ajar, a single shaft of light from the kitchen piercing the gloom. "We never really traveled together, you and I. I would very much like to see the Grand Canyon." His eyes cast about the kitchen: stainless-steel sink, large white refrigerator, gas stove. It was a wonderful house, much larger than he'd expected. After spending most of the past twenty years confined to one room it felt enormous.

"It's almost done," he said contemplatively as he finished cleaning the barrel and sighted down the length of it. The gun had been a true find, hidden in a box in the attic. He generally considered them to be clumsy, inelegant weapons, hardly worthy of his time, but ideally the knife should be saved for sacrifices. "And then all will finally be resolved."

He nodded toward the door, pulled on his jacket, and tucked a bundle of cloth under his arm. The cemetery was only a few blocks away. Situated on a hill overlooking the town, it amply fulfilled the útiseta requirement for a grave mound. It had been some time since he had connected with his fetch animal, and he was eager to see him again. Besides, prudence dictated that he seek its aid for magical defense. With the forces descending upon him and time running short, he needed all the help he could get.

He weaved between the crumbling marble headstones.

This was the older section of the cemetery, dating back to the early 1800s. He had spent hours here over the past months, examining the names of family members inscribed on obelisks, peering in the doors of barred crypts, marveling at the elaborately carved angels. Personally, when the time came, he planned on being pushed out to sea in a small boat. Perhaps Peter would do that for him.

The útiseta was an ancient ritual, meaning literally in Icelandic "sitting out." Similar to a Native American vision quest, it involved attaining a trance state in order to connect with his fetch, the personal guardian attached to him for the duration of his life. He ducked under some low-hanging branches and found the spot that had proved so fruitful for him. It was a small glen encircled by evergreens, their spiny branches grazing the ground. He spread his blanket over an area that was thickly carpeted in needles; he found that being comfortable made the ritual progress more quickly. Still standing, he performed the hallowing ritual, clearing the stead of any bad spirits by tracing the sign of the hammer at each of the four cardinal points. He settled himself on the blanket facing north and withdrew a coffee mug and thermos from a small backpack. Carefully unscrewing the cap, he poured a small amount of red liquid into the mug. His nose wrinkled slightly at the smell—it was turning, he'd have to replenish his supply soon. He set the mug in position close to his right hand and closed his eyes. He sank into a meditative state.

The minutes stretched into hours. Slowly, a sense of "otherness" grew within him, a feeling of being part of something greater than himself, greater than anything he had ever known. He basked in the sensation, reveling in the feeling of power it conveyed.

When he felt his limbs coursing with vitality, he began to recite the invocatory galdor mantra. His voice rose and fell softly, coaxing the animal to him: "Fare forth, holy fetch. Fly to me, that I may know thy might, that I may wax in thy wisdom."

Keeping his eyes closed he reached for the cup, raising it toward the heavens. He recited a litany of praises to his fetch, honoring everything it had done for him in the past. "Hail, holy fetch, high in might, thou art my shield, thou art my strength, thou art my true friend." Tilting the mug back, he drained half of it in one gulp, wincing slightly at the tang of old blood. He poured the rest on the ground in front of him, at the northern border of the cloth. In a singsong voice he chanted the same phrase over and over again, his voice mounting in urgency with each repetition. "Fetch, fare thee forth!"

There was a fluttering of wings, and he opened his eyes. A raven perched on a branch to his left. It cocked its head to the side and regarded him closely.

"Hello," he said, bowing his head deferentially. "Thank you for coming."

Morrow hung up the phone feeling reenergized; thanks to a friend at the Department of Corrections, he had gotten the suspect's last name and a copy of his file. They were getting close, he could sense it in his gut. "All right, we've got a new lead. Half of you will continue working through the other files, if this doesn't pan out I want to have other suspects to run down. Since I don't know all your names yet—" he made a sweeping motion with one arm "—this half of the room sticks with business as usual." He held up the file in his other hand. "The rest of you are going to run down everything you can find on this man, Paul Nielson."

"Are we looking for anything specific?" asked a young woman from the corner.

Morrow surveyed the scene. He had sent the Hostage Rescue Squad back to New York, and the agents with seniority were at the motel catching some shut-eye. That left him with a dozen junior agents. "I'm looking for any people who might help him. I need addresses, phone numbers, everywhere he lived, places he might go. Start running down people who knew him, relatives. Especially a brother, apparently he has a twin somewhere named Peter, let's find him. Also, check out other inmates released from Bellevue in the same period, especially these two men." He sorted through the piles on the table and withdrew two more folders. "And Adams, I want you to find me a photo of him, A.S.A.P. He might have traveled to Iceland in the past year; see if Homeland Security has passport photos on file under any of his possible aliases, including the name Moore."

Adams nodded. Within a minute the files had been divided up and the team set to work. Morrow detected a familiar rumbling in his belly. He pointed to the young agent sitting closest to him. "You— I'm sorry, what's your name again?"

The kid glanced up at him. "Agent Han, sir."

"Right. Agent Han, I'm assigning you the most important task of all. There's a deli down the street on the right. We're going to need a big ol' stack of sandwiches, coffees, chips, just go ahead and empty the place out." He tossed him his credit card. "We'll charge it to the Bureau. If this pans out I promise you all breakfast in bed tomorrow morning. Or at least a few extra hours of sleep. Any questions?"

No hands were raised. "Okay, get to it." Morrow took his seat and began tapping away at the keyboard in front of him.

A minute later there was a tentative knock on the door. He looked up. A small man with scraggly blond hair and a briefcase peered in at him. "Agent Morrow?"

"Can I help you?"

The man shuffled in. "I'm Agent Barnes, the sketch artist."

"Yeah, right." Morrow pushed back his chair and lumbered to his feet. He'd completely forgotten about the freak in the next room. "Follow me."

The door was closed. He rapped his knuckles against it once then pushed it open, stepping inside to double-check. The room was empty.

He furrowed his brow. "Huh, he must've gotten tired of waiting."

The sketch artist rubbed his ear. "I was really hoping to miss the rush-hour traffic back to the city."

"Yeah, I get you. Let me try to track him down. We've got food coming, why don't you kick back for a few minutes?"

Looking put out, the artist settled into a desk in the far corner of the room. Morrow stepped outside and closed the door while he dialed Jones's number.

Twenty-Four

Claire hung up the phone. Her parents weren't happy with her decision, in fact her father had threatened to drive down from Vermont to personally escort her home, but she refused to give in. This was the biggest thing that had happened on campus, well, pretty much ever, she thought. She had her heart set on a job reporting for the *New York Times,* and there was no way in hell she was going to miss out on the story of a lifetime. She began to unpack the bag on her bed. Both of her housemates had already left. Mary had managed to secure a seat on an afternoon flight to Arizona, and Sean caught a train to Philadelphia that morning. Mary had hugged her before leaving. "Don't you go and do anything crazy, girl." She had whispered in her ear, "And don't eat the rest of my brownies...I put them in the freezer."

The house felt enormous without them. They had lucked into one of the best available, an enormous Victorian built in the 1800s to house the university's first president. Claire's bedroom was three times the size of the one she grew up sharing with her sister. She plopped down on the futon couch occupying a corner of the room. Most of her furniture had been scavenged the year before when departing seniors dumped everything, from lamps to sofas, out on the street. The futon couch was her particular favorite: covered in a soft maroon velour, it only had one stain that refused to come out despite repeated scrubbing.

Claire flipped through her notebook. Her last piece on the killings had been printed in the *Cardinal*'s Friday edition. She had considered putting out a special one-page issue on Tiffany's abduction and murder, but the only other person staying was Brad the photographer, an odd guy she didn't relish the prospect of spending hours alone with. It was funny how quiet it was outside. She dropped her notebook back onto the couch with a sigh and went to the window. There might as well be tumbleweed drifting across campus, she thought. Usually this time of day there would be throngs of students headed to class or to the student union for a midday snack. She saw a boy dressed entirely in black, a duffel bag slung over his shoulder, baseball cap tucked low over his ears. At the corner he stopped and flagged down a passing cab. A CNN news van drove past as she watched, satellite dish tucked into place as it sped down the street. She didn't have enough information on the new murder to compete with them. What she needed was an exclusive—information that no one else had access to. She went to the refrigerator and rummaged through the food, pulling out the milk marked CLAIRE and filling a bowl with cereal.

This was her school, after all; these reporters from out of town didn't know about half the stuff that she did.

She carried her bowl over to the top of the cellar stairs and gazed thoughtfully into the darkness. At the bottom of the stairs, tucked against the back wall and almost completely concealed by a discarded bookcase, was a small door. She had almost mentioned it to the FBI, but Sean was worried about his marijuana seedlings being discovered and had begged her not to. Claire had never been down there herself; something about the tunnels had always struck her as unbelievably creepy, even before they discovered the girls. So far none of the press had even photographed the sites where the first girls' bodies were discovered. And here she was with quite possibly the last open access point on campus. She wondered if they awarded Pulitzers to undergraduates.

"Careful with that stuff—I promised Stefan he wouldn't even know we were here," Kelly cautioned, eyeing the sprawling stack of books on the floor that Jake had nearly kicked over. She was seated at a desk in the Warder of the Lore's library, sifting through his personal papers. Most of it was unintelligible to her, essays on various rituals, notes on ceremonies that had been performed recently. He had reluctantly given them permission to search the house for any evidence relating to the killer. He owned a sprawling brownstone on the Upper East Side of Manhattan, a stately building with eight bedrooms scattered throughout the four levels.

"How do you think he affords this place, anyway?"

Jake asked, leaning back on his haunches and taking in the parquet floors, crystal chandelier and marble fireplace.

"He's apparently tenth in line to the throne of Denmark. Old money. Pillar of the community since he moved to the States in the eighties, a generous donor to a variety of organizations, and a serious playboy until about a decade ago when he suddenly dropped out of the scene. After that, he only appears on pagan sites. He seems to be very respected in their community."

"Yeah, a community of freaks. It figures. The rich ones always get sucked into some weird cult."

They worked in silence for another hour. Kelly couldn't prevent herself from glancing nervously at her watch as the minutes swept past. Four-thirty, four forty-five, five p.m. She was ready to keel over from exhaustion. From time to time her eyes shut involuntarily, her head felt as though it was only loosely tethered to her shoulders and might bob off like a balloon at any second.

"There's nothing here," Jake said in frustration. "Want to check Paul's room again, or should we call it a wash and pull out?"

Kelly deliberated: their search of the suspect's dormer room had revealed nothing but a bare mattress perched on a cot, a few robes on hangers and a small nightstand. And just in case Stefan was right about his itinerary, she wanted to be back on campus before nightfall. Which was now less than an hour and a half away. "One more quick sweep of the house, then we're out of here."

They mounted three flights of stairs to start at the top of the house. Apparently Stefan extended his belief in simplicity to decor. The walls lining the halls were completely bare, and only a few pieces of furniture adorned each room. Most of the bedroom doors were shut; a quick perusal earlier had revealed beds and chairs covered with sheets. Apparently it had been some time since the Warder had any overnight guests aside from his student.

The narrow room at the top of the final flight of stairs was still flooded with late-afternoon light from two skylights that formed eaves at either end of the room. Kelly peered around, certain that she must have missed something. She lifted a corner of the mattress, moved aside the hangers in the closet, peeked under the bed. Jake watched her from the doorway.

"Satisfied?" he asked with raised eyebrows. "Now can we please blow this joint?"

As she crossed the room, a floorboard creaked under her feet. Frowning slightly, she rocked her foot across it, then knelt on the floor, feeling around the edge of it with her fingers.

"It's loose," Kelly said. She glanced around the room for something to pry it up with.

"Here." Jake unclipped a small knife from his belt and handed it to her. He squatted next to her, watching as she carefully eased the edge of the blade along each of the four sides, lifting the board centimeter by centimeter. "I'm not sure how the Warder of crap is going to feel about you ripping apart his floor," he said with amusement.

"How about less talking and more helping?" she answered, struggling with the board. He grabbed the lip of one side while she took the other, and together they heaved. The board released with a groan, revealing a mottled subfloor.

"There's nothing there," Jake said, voice heavy with disappointment.

"Wait a sec." Kelly plunged her right hand into the open space, feeling around the adjoining boards. Her hand brushed against the edge of something.

"Great way to get the hantavirus," Jake commented. "You better wash your hands after this. I knew a guy once who…" His voice drifted off as she triumphantly withdrew something from the floor.

Kelly flipped it over. It was a photo of Stefan with one arm wrapped around another man. The Warder's face had been almost entirely covered by another rune penned in black ink. It was the man with him, though, that almost caused Kelly to drop the photo.

"Holy shit," Jake breathed.

Kelly could only nod. Gazing up at them from the glossy surface was Father John.

Morrow bolted up in his chair, wide awake. The room was pitch-black. Startled, he jerked to his feet, knocking his knee against something hard. Reaching down he felt the familiar rounded edge of a desk. *The trailer, I'm in the trailer,* he realized, rubbing his face with both hands. He groped through the darkness until his fingers found a desk lamp. He clicked it on and checked his watch: six o'clock. He'd been asleep for over an hour. He had only sat down for a minute to flip through a file while waiting for Jones to call back, and he'd conked out.

He settled back into the chair and picked up his cell phone: no messages. Where the hell were they? Jones and Riley had been gone all day, and he hadn't heard anything since they left Bellevue. He dialed her number again, waited as it went to voice mail, and left another message. He kicked himself for not getting Riley's number as a backup. He felt a twinge of concern: he didn't like it, not being able to reach her like this. It wasn't like Jones at all. What if they'd run into their guy at the house? He also hadn't been able to track down their eyewitness, despite repeated calls to the professor's house. There was probably an extremely disgruntled sketch artist in the next building.

Morrow took a sip of water from the glass on the desk and cringed slightly at the tang of chlorine. He debated whether or not to send someone from the New York field office to check on them. But they might have already left the house, following the lead in a completely different direction. He tapped a foot impatiently as he deliberated.

There was a knock on the door and he sighed with relief. They were back. Her cell phone had probably died, or she hadn't been able to get a signal.

"It's open!" he called out.

There was no response. Pushing against the desk with both hands, he lifted himself from the chair. "What, is it locked? Hang on, I'm coming…"

There was a blast of cold air as he opened the door. A single street lamp illuminated the parking lot, casting the figure before him in silhouette. Morrow reached reflexively for his gun, realizing instantly that he'd left it on the desk. His mouth opened, and he said, "You."

The silencer made a small popping sound, hardly louder than a kid cracking gum. Morrow fell backward, clawing at the air. The bullet had pierced his throat, severing his vocal cords. As he choked on blood he pictured his wife and daughter. He watched as they receded, his arms jerking frantically by his sides, fighting against the darkness that was encircling him. *Shit,* he thought, as his eyes glazed over and the roaring in his ears slowly receded. *I can't believe I'm dying in a goddamn trailer.*

Twenty-Five

Claire took a deep breath and collected her thoughts. She made a final check of everything: flashlight, camera (her housemate Sean's, because it was high resolution and had a flash), and a backpack stuffed with water, snacks and extra batteries. She had a compass clipped to her belt (also Sean's, from his wilderness-instructor training course), a canister of pepper spray and a map of the campus tucked in her back pocket. She was as ready as she would ever be.

It had taken most of the afternoon to clear out the space in front of the door. She heaved books into boxes, threw away lamps, and shifted the bookshelf to the side, almost choking on the dust. Now she paused for a moment, hand on the sliding bolt. She didn't have to do this, after all. It was hard to fight the sense that she was making a terrible mistake. Three girls were dead, two of them in the tunnels. Although it wasn't likely that the killer was still down there, not after the FBI and police had been through them repeatedly, there was always a chance. And there might still be police standing guard; she could be arrested for trespassing. Would a few lousy shots of the crime scenes really be worth it?

Seeing her byline in her mind, "Claire Denisof," in all its *New York Times* twelve-point-italicized glory, she decided they were. Gathering her courage, she pulled on the backpack. She unbolted the door and leaned back with all her body weight, forcing it halfway open. The bottom grated against the concrete, carving an arc through the dust on the floor. She clicked on her flashlight and stepped inside.

"I can't believe I forgot to bring the car charger." Kelly frowned at her phone.

"I can't believe it, either. Doesn't sound like you at all." Jake's smirk faded at the expression on her face. "You want to use my phone to call in?"

Kelly shook her head. "It's more important that we get back there."

"Well, I think we can both agree that I couldn't possibly be driving any faster." He flashed a grin at her. It faded as he absorbed her expression. "Listen, you should relax. Command center sent two teams to watch the house. The priest and his brother are covered."

"I know, but I'd feel better if I could reach Morrow. No one seems to know where he is."

"You know Morrow. Probably went out on another emergency donut run."

"Maybe." Kelly tapped a finger against the dashboard. "I really need that warrant."

"So what about your judge friend?" Jake suggested.

Kelly shook her head in frustration. "Let's just say that two warrants in two days would be a bit much for him, especially when one is for a priest's house. And Stefan disappeared without helping with the composite sketch. I should have received written consent to search his home, otherwise we might lose the photo ID." She nervously chewed on her bottom lip.

"What, now you think he might be involved?"

"I don't know what to think. I just wish I'd left instructions to keep a closer eye on him. Just because his alibi cleared doesn't mean he couldn't be an accomplice."

"Yeah, but at the time you weren't even sure it was a good lead. You worked with what you knew." Jake fell silent for a moment, thinking. "What about what Celia said?"

"I couldn't tell the judge about that," Kelly responded. "Technically, what she told us is still covered by doctor/patient confidentiality. If we arrested him based on that, it would never hold up in court. So all we've got is Stefan's word, and we can't track him down."

"So what do we do?" Jake asked. Kelly watched the odometer bounce between eighty and ninety miles per hour as Jake wove through the slower cars in adjoining lanes.

"We sit on him, I guess." She rubbed her eyes. The exhaustion was inflicting itself on her mental processes. Every sentence required effort. "Anyone entering or leaving that house is followed. And meanwhile we dig around, try to gather some evidence that gets us in that house."

"Now I remember why I hated Bureau work—we

know who the killer is, we know where he is, and we can't go get him until a bunch of suits say so. What a crock." Jake snorted.

Kelly privately agreed. She stared out the window as the sprawling shopping centers lining the approach to New Haven whipped past. Another twenty minutes and they'd be there.

"How much do you think the priest knows?" Jake asked.

"I doubt he's involved, if that's what you're asking. He's been at the university for too long. I think his brother probably showed up on his doorstep looking for a place to stay." She paused. "And in all honesty, I think there's a good chance that Father John might be dead."

Jake let out a low whistle. "So we might have already met Paul."

Kelly nodded. If there had been a switch, it was hard to believe that no one had noticed; church attendance must really have been down dramatically. *When had it happened?* she wondered. How long had Paul waited before murdering his last living relative?

"One thing has been bothering me," Jake said suddenly. "Why the hell is his name Father John? I thought we were looking for a Peter."

"Some orders have their priests adopt a new name when they're ordained."

Jake rubbed his stubble with one hand. "Interesting"

"So you're not a Catholic?"

"Nope. Baptist, born and bred."

"Huh, I wouldn't have guessed that." She eyed him appraisingly.

Jake shrugged, his eyes fixed on the road. "I'm originally from Texas."

"Where in Texas?"

"Austin. You ever been?"

"No, I'm afraid not."

"That's a shame, it's a great town. Listen. I haven't had a chance yet to apologize for the other day. I know you're probably a little sensitive about what happened with your brother. I didn't mean to pry."

"That's okay." Kelly leaned forward and readjusted her ponytail. "It was a long time ago."

"They ever catch the guy?"

"No. I dug up the file after I got into the FBI, and there were a few solid leads, no ViCAP back then, so I think he must have been crossing state lines to throw everyone off. Plus, the local police refused help from the FBI, and they had no idea how to handle a case like that themselves." She felt a familiar flash of rage as she said it, once again pictured the insolent local police chief telling her parents they had it all under control.

"Typical," Jake said understandingly. "Territorial bullshit."

She nodded. "There was one suspect who was in town around that time, staying with his mother. He had a record for burglaries, some domestic violence charges, and he was looked at for a few arsons. Sounded like the prototypical child molester, and it turns out other boys had disappeared from towns he was staying in."

"So what happened to him?"

Kelly unconsciously gnawed at a nail. "He was killed in a bar fight a few years later."

"Is that why you joined up?"

"It wasn't for revenge, if that's what you're thinking."

Jake tilted his head to the side and released a chuckle. "Ah, the free-floating aggression, I'd almost started missing it. What I *meant* was that you probably wanted to stop that sort of thing from happening again, to another family. It would make sense, right?"

Kelly brushed a piece of lint off her lap. "I guess so. I graduated from school and worked at a law office in the city as a paralegal, and after a few years I took the Bureau exam. It wasn't as if I had this compelling need to track down people like the man that killed Alex. I just wanted to do something concrete, something that made a difference." She eyed him appraisingly. "What about you?"

"Military brat. For me, it was the armed forces, the police, or the FBI, and I figured in the Bureau there'd be a lot less yelling. Which didn't turn out to be the case."

"You miss it?"

Jake made the turn onto Route 91 North. An image of Sarah lying in the snow, blond hair clotted with blood, flashed across his brain. "I hadn't, not for a long time. But something about this case…security work isn't the same. Not by a long shot."

"I can imagine."

"But Dmitri is a pretty amazing boss. He and Anna were very close. I don't know how he's going to come back from this, honestly."

His cell phone rang. Kelly smirked as "The Yellow Rose of Texas" chimed through the car.

"What, you think your ringtone is better?" Jake said with a grin as he snapped it open and said, "Riley."

Kelly watched as the smile vanished and his face hardened. Her heart sank; they were too late, somehow the killer must have managed to grab another girl. Maybe they were following the wrong lead after all. Despite the coincidences, maybe the priest had nothing to do with it.

"We're almost there." He hung up, keeping his eyes on the road.

"What? Is it another girl?" Kelly asked after a moment.

There was a hoarseness in his voice as he said, "It's Morrow. They found him in the trailer." He shifted his gaze to her. "Kelly, he's dead."

Twenty-Six

Claire stood uncertainly at a fork, aiming the beam of her flashlight down at the map of campus. It was more confusing down here than she had expected. The tunnels twisted and wound disconcertingly, and she'd lost her bearings. Her best guess placed her under the psychology building, or possibly the student center. She had suddenly become aware that even if she found the murder sites, she wasn't entirely certain how to get back home. With all the other exits locked from the outside, this had given rise to a twinge of panic that she was fighting to keep under wraps. She stuffed the map back in her pocket and decided to take the left branch; with any luck, that would lead her to the chapel.

It was quiet down there, and the darkness outside her flashlight beam felt palpable, as though it were alive and pressing in on all sides. She had been down here for almost an hour so far; thank God she brought extra batteries. She should have told someone where she was going. She could have left a message on Mary's answering machine. In fact, part of her was wishing she had never come.

New York Times, she told herself. Forget an internship, with these photos she might be able to finagle an actual staff position. She pictured her name on the masthead, took a deep breath and continued forward, moving slowly, running her lights up and down the walls. She wasn't even sure what she was looking for. Would the area be roped off by yellow tape? Another hundred yards and she'd turn back.

Claire froze. What was that sound? She strained her ears, listening hard for it, but again there was silence. It had sounded like footsteps. Her arms prickled with goose bumps, and she fought to control the urge to run. There was no one down here, it was just so quiet she was hearing things. After another minute she pressed forward, continuing her slow progress. There was something shimmering on the wall up ahead, reflecting fragments of light. She tentatively moved closer until she was standing in front of it. She played the beam across the wall and drew in her breath. An enormous dark painting, more horrible than anything she had ever imagined, was staring down at her. The cold ball of fear in her stomach flew up into her chest. She struggled to remain calm and knelt on the floor, carefully avoiding the congealed pools—blood, oh God, it was blood—and with shaking hands fought with the zipper on her backpack. All she had to do was take a few pictures and this would all be over. She could go back home and drink a cup of cocoa in front of the TV, she could call her parents and tell them she was coming home tomorrow. Maybe even tonight—she would check the bus schedule when she got back.

Startled by another noise, she almost dropped the flashlight. She strained her ears; this time it was unmistakable. There were footsteps behind her, and they were moving fast. She quickly rose and pulled on the backpack, trying to control her breathing as she headed down the corridor. Whoever it was blocked her return; she'd have to find another way out. It was probably just a police officer coming to check on the scene, or another media person who had found a way in. The footsteps quickened, and she began to run. At the next fork she turned right and shuffled her feet fast until she was about a hundred yards in, trying to silence the sound of her movement. She pressed her back against the wall and clicked off the light. Whoever it was slowed, stopping at the fork. She held her breath, terrified that any sound might give her away. Long moments passed. Finally she heard them start up again, heading down the opposite corridor. She let out her breath slowly, eyes closed, an overwhelming sense of relief flooding her veins. When the hand clamped down on her arm, she was too startled to scream.

It was dark when they pulled in to the parking lot. Emergency vehicles were scattered at all angles around the trailer, red lights sliding in succession along the paneled exterior, the sirens silenced. The medical examiner's van was off to one side. As they stepped from the car, Constance approached. She was wearing an oversize navy parka and a fluffy hat. She put a hand on Kelly's arm. "I'm so sorry, dear."

"When did it happen?" Kelly's voice was dull.

"Two hours ago, give or take. I left everything as it

was, I figured you'd want to see the scene before he was removed. Forensics has been—"

"How?" Kelly interrupted.

"Single gunshot wound to the throat, with a silencer. One of these nice young agents started a canvass of the neighborhood, you'll have to talk to them, but so far it seems that no one heard anything. Most of the students have gone home, you see."

Kelly nodded. She took a deep breath, steeling herself as she headed for the trailer. Jake blocked her. "Listen, if you're not up for this…I mean, I know what it's like to lose a partner. Why don't you let one of the other agents handle the scene?"

Kelly forcibly shook her head. "No. It's my job, my crime scene. He was my partner."

"All right." Jake stepped aside. "I'll be right behind you."

The trailer door hung halfway open to reveal Morrow lying on his back in a pool of blood, his throat gashed open by an enormous bullet wound. Kelly's heart leaped into her throat. She felt the shock starting to poke through her consciousness, and willed her mind to remain clear. She pointed to the stairs. "Have these already been checked?"

An agent behind her piped up, "Forensics finished with the outside of the trailer and the stairs. Just be careful on the inside."

She fought to keep her voice level. "What about photos?"

"Already done."

"All right then." She gingerly stepped over Morrow and into the trailer. His eyes were still clear, and reflected the green glow of the fluorescent bulbs overhead. She dropped to one knee, pulled on a glove, and eased the lids shut with one hand. "Goodbye, Morrow," she said quietly.

"Jesus Christ," Jake breathed. Kelly looked up. Scrawled across their whiteboard in large, broad strokes was a bloody symbol. Something about seeing it in the trailer surrounded by modern equipment made it all the more startling.

It was another rune, deepening red against the white background.

"We should get Birnbaum over here, see if he can tell us what it means," Jake said, his voice shaky.

Kelly straightened up. Forcing herself to focus, she scanned the trailer. "It doesn't look like he took anything," she mused. "Why come here? Why kill Morrow?"

"Maybe he knew we were getting close," Jake answered.

"It still doesn't make sense, unless he's taunting us." She ran a hand through her ponytail. "My larger concern is that if this was done by Paul Nielson, it means he's out of the house and we don't have any way of tracking him."

"Yeah." Jake glanced down at Morrow. "Listen, I know you're by the book, but maybe I could disappear for a few hours, do a little poking around on my own."

Kelly thought it over; she had to admit, the possibility of getting someone in the priest's house to look around and confirm they were following the right trail was tempting. But if Jake found anything, it would be inadmissible in court. She'd hate to catch this guy, then have him walk on a technicality because she'd let her emotions get the best of her.

"Can't let you do that," she said with regret. "But I think you're right, we need to talk to the professor. If nothing else, I want to find Stefan and see why he took off earlier."

"What about the family?" Jake asked. "If you want, I can make the call."

"I'll do it." Kelly looked around the trailer one last time, her gaze lingering on Morrow. "Tell Constance to take him. I'll use the phones inside."

Fifteen minutes later she pushed open the door to the science building. It closed with a *whoosh* behind her. Three of the emergency vehicles had left, along with the medical examiner's van. The cold hit her face like a slap, the skin still raw from the water she'd splashed on it. That had been the hardest phone call she'd ever had to make. Morrow's wife's shrieks seemed to pierce the receiver.

Jake was hunched against their car smoking a cigarette. She joined him, crossing her arms over her chest.

"You got any more of those?"

Jake shook his head. "Nope, begged it off a forensics hack." He held his cigarette out to her. "You can take a drag off this one if you want."

He passed it to her and she inhaled deeply, sucking the smoke into her lungs. "I didn't know you smoked," she said as she handed the cigarette back.

"I don't. Haven't for years."

"Me neither." She tucked a loose strand of hair behind her right ear and looked at the ground. "I've never lost a partner before."

He nodded as he exhaled up toward the sky. Small shreds of white clouds were splayed across it, as if someone had dragged a ball of cotton across sandpaper. "I have."

"I know."

"By the way, I took the liberty of digging this out of your bag to look up our rune of the day." Jake held up Professor Birnbaum's book.

"Yeah? What is it?" Kelly asked.

"The yew rune." He flipped to a dog-eared page. "It's kind of hard to sort through the mumbo jumbo, but the gist of it is a death curse."

Kelly's face hardened. It would take a hell of a lot to scare her off at this point. "Anything else?"

"Yeah, it says that it indicates the termination or conclusion of a process." Jake glanced up at her. "Look, maybe you should sit this one out. You haven't slept in almost two straight days, and you just lost your partner. You could organize everything from the command center—"

"No." Kelly shook her head firmly. "I'm seeing this through. I think we should suit up for this run, though, just in case. Tell everyone to wear their vests and bring extra ammo. Why don't you round up a half-dozen agents to come with us, we'll leave for the professor's house in five."

Jake looked bemused. "I'm afraid special agents don't exactly relish taking orders from me anymore, but the rest of the plan sounds good."

"Right." Kelly rubbed her temples. "Good point, I'll tell them."

Jake watched her closely. "You're sure about this?" he asked, voice laden with concern.

Kelly nodded fiercely.

"All right, then." Jake took a final drag off the cigarette and flicked it into the darkness.

Twenty-Seven

He had disappeared again. Claire forced herself to relax.
There were moments when the panic became overpowering, her breath coming in short sucking gulps, her heart
batting so hard against her rib cage that it felt like it
would tear through, and she lost consciousness. Each
time she came around she struggled with the fears
flashing through her brain, every terrible image she had
ever seen and others she could only imagine. Panicking
wasn't going to save her. She wasn't sure what would, but
she needed to try to remain calm. She counted to ten and
then strained furiously against her bindings. Her arms,
waist, and legs were all cinched with ropes that locked
them into place. She struggled for as long as she could
and then stopped, panting through her nose. Tears ran
down her face and slid across the duct tape covering her
mouth. He was going to kill her. She had risked her life,
and for what? For a few stupid photographs. It wasn't as
if she was out in the field recording war crimes or uncov-

ering a government conspiracy. For the first time in her life, she reconsidered her dream of becoming a journalist. *Not that it matters,* she thought. *I'm as good as dead now anyway.* She saw the faces of her parents and sister and the tears accelerated. They would be crushed. She was the family's great hope, the investment her father had poured all the money he earned fixing transmissions into, and she had let them down. *Stupid, stupid, stupid.*

She heard footsteps again and looked down. He was coming back, carrying something this time. She watched him dip a brush in a bucket and draw it out, dribbling long strands of blood on the floor in a half circle. She almost retched but caught herself, realizing she'd drown on her own vomit. *Stay calm, relax,* she reminded herself, taking shuddery breaths through her nostrils. He had set the gun aside, it was on the wooden table just behind him, not that that helped her. He kept referring to an enormous red book that lay open on the altar. Night had fallen: she saw the first star rising above the trees, a tiny sliver of moon just below it. She wanted to live. She didn't know exactly how those other girls had been killed, but the rumors were horrible. Now that she was stranded here, strung up like a chunk of meat, an increasingly graphic reel replayed in her mind. She had seen the knife—he made a point of showing it to her before gingerly setting it next to the book. It was huge and menacing looking, with a slightly curved blade. She shuddered at the thought of it on her skin.

He started chanting, and she tilted her head forward to keep an eye on his movements. He was going over the circle, again and again, the red standing out starkly against the floor. These were the first words he had spoken since taking her. His silence had been terrifying, but the chanting was in its own way so much worse. It was in some strange language she couldn't understand, sharp and coarse with heavy consonants. Russian, maybe, or Swedish.

Great, she thought, listening to his bass singsong. *It's not bad enough I'm dying, I'm going to be a ritual sacrifice, like a goat or something.* She wondered how long it had been since he took her. One minute she was in the tunnels, the next he was marching her through the darkness, gun aimed at her spine, winding through numerous twists and turns until they came to a door. For a moment she had hoped that he was letting her go, that he had realized she wasn't the daughter of a millionaire, wasn't worth killing at all, really. Then he led her here and began the long, slow process of securing her in place. One thing was certain: her name would make it into the *New York Times,* but as a victim, not a byline.

"Now what?" Jake grumbled.

Kelly pressed the buzzer again, then ducked her head and cupped a hand around her eyes to peer in the side window. With the dim lighting, she could only make out a few feet of Oriental carpeting. She stepped back. "Car's still in the driveway," she noted.

Six agents stood nervously behind them, vests visible under their windbreakers, guns drawn at their sides.

"Wait." Jake pressed an ear against the door. "Did you hear that?"

"What?" Kelly listened hard.

"That." Jake pointed at the door. "I distinctly heard a cry for help, which provides exigent circumstances."

"Nice try." Kelly sighed. "But I don't feel like losing my job today." She knocked again, rapping hard as she called out, "Professor Birnbaum!" She waited a long moment for a response, then turned and headed back down the stairs.

"Where are you going?" Jake called out.

"We can't get in here, and there's no sign of anyone at Father John's house either. So we try the next best alternative."

They bounded up the stairs to the chapel. The Public Safety officer turned the key in the lock with shaking hands, then stood aside as they swarmed in. Agents swept past the pews, then checked behind the heavy curtains lining the back of the church. Moonlight sifted through the stained-glass windows, casting a ghostly kaleidoscope on the floor. The building was empty.

Kelly stood by the altar, glancing down at the spot where Chad and Anna had been making out less than a week before. She imagined she could see the imprint of their bodies on the thick red carpeting. Turning, she noticed a shimmer of white on the altar. "There's something here!" she called out.

Jake was by her side in a flash. Switching her gun to her left hand and easing the sleeve of her windbreaker over her fingers, she gingerly picked up a white envelope. Suddenly, light flooded the chapel; one of the agents must have found the central switch. Printed in stark black letters were the words *Agent Jones.*

"That's never good," Jake commented.

Other agents were drifting around the chapel, clearly at a loss. Kelly hesitated a moment; procedure stated that she should wait for a HazMat team, or at the very least forensics. But it was unlikely that Paul Nielson had access to a biological weapon, and her gut told her that whatever was inside needed to be seen as soon as possible. She was sick of having her hands tied in this case; while they followed procedure, people were dying. Kelly pulled a pair of latex gloves out of her pocket and donned them. Carefully sliding a finger across the upper seam of the envelope, she tore it open.

Inside was something stiff and square. Kelly carefully unfolded it to reveal a Polaroid. She sucked in her breath sharply: it was a close-up of Claire, eyes wide with fear, duct tape covering her mouth.

"Oh, crap." Jake ran a hand through his hair. "He's got another one."

Underneath the photo, printed in the same bold black letters was the message Come alone.

Jake shook his head at the look of determination in her eyes. "No. Absolutely not. You heard Stefan—he's planning on killing two more people. Right now he only has one. We've got twenty-five agents here and another whole team on their way up from New York. We wait an hour we can go in whole hog, knock him out before he hurts her."

"I don't think we've got that kind of time," Kelly said

calmly. She pulled off the gloves, tugged the ponytail from her hair and rewrapped it into a bun.

"You're crazy. It's been a long time since I worked in the Bureau, but I seem to remember the protocol in these situations, and it doesn't call for you to go out cowboying on your own."

"Cowgirling."

"Whatever. I'll go with you."

"If you come, he'll kill her."

"She's probably already dead."

"I don't think so. He'll wait for me. Like you said, he needs two victims." She was astonished at how calm her voice sounded, even though her heart was racing in her chest.

"You don't even know which way to go," Jake protested. He watched her check the chamber on the gun strapped to her ankle before reinserting it in the holster. She did the same with the weapon she had set on the altar, then stashed that below her left shoulder. She straightened her jacket back over it, made sure that everything was secure, and stood.

"Sure I do," Kelly said calmly, gesturing at the rug under her feet. Jake followed her gaze and started. Almost invisible against the red carpeting, a dark brown smear of an arrow was painted below their feet. It pointed in a direct line from the altar to the trapdoor leading to the tunnels.

He glanced around the room one last time, satisfied. Everything was in place. He glanced down at the watch on his wrist, the one that had been his father's, then his brother's. The hour was rapidly approaching. He scrutinized the girl. She was struggling against the bindings again, unable to see him in the shadows behind her. He felt a physical quickening in his chest and loins, and inhaled deeply. At the sound she suddenly stilled. He was tempted to draw closer, to witness the panic in her eyes: it was like a drug, that panic. But there wasn't enough time; he needed to position himself to entrap the final sacrifice. The girl was secure, she would be there when he got back. He glanced at the watch again, then carefully drew the hood back on. Soon it would be over. He turned on his heel and opened the door at the rear of the room. The breath of the tunnels licked his face, the darkness reaching out to him like an old friend. He swept inside and drew the door shut behind him.

Twenty-Eight

Kelly sank onto a pew in the front of the chapel and tried to collect her thoughts. She missed Morrow. If he had been here, he would have settled her jangled nerves with a few jokes. She knew that she was going to catch hell from the boss for what she was about to do, but she couldn't sit by and wait for another girl to be gutted by a madman. This is why she'd joined up, after all: to save and protect the innocent. If she didn't at least try to rescue Claire, she'd never be able to forgive herself.

Jake reappeared with his work backpack and rummaged in one of the pockets, extracting a small black box. He opened it carefully. Nestled in the padding was a tiny device—a bug, she realized—and a GPS monitor. He carefully lifted the bug out of the case and pressed it behind her ear, nestling it inside her hairline. He pushed a button on the monitor and the screen illuminated with a map of the street they were on. A small red dot indicated her position.

"What's this for?" she asked, tracing the molded edge of the device.

"Insurance. We already know radios don't work down there, I'm hoping this might. At least it'll help us find you if you come aboveground."

"Where'd you get it?"

"One of those spy-gadgets guys gave it to me at a conference. I thought it might help keep track of Dmitri if he was ever kidnapped, but he claimed to prefer death to wearing that thing around. I held on to it just in case."

"Always prepared."

"I was a Boy Scout, after all."

She laughed nervously. "Really—I can't see that."

Jake feigned astonishment. "You kidding? Eagle Scout. I even got the merit badge for 'Citizenship in the World.'"

"What did you have to do for that one?"

"I had sex with a foreign-exchange student, Gabriela from Venezuela."

"And that made you a citizen of the world?"

"Boy, did it ever."

Kelly rolled her eyes. "Nice to know you can still manage to be crass in the face of danger."

"What can I say—it's a gift."

They smiled at each other. Kelly got to her feet and self-consciously dusted off the back of her windbreaker.

"So we'll be ten minutes behind you, with teams posted at all access points in case you need the cavalry." A look of concern furrowed his brow. Kelly forced a grin. He had to resist the urge to hug her, instead awkwardly patting her shoulder. "Go get'em, champ."

"Right." She heaved a deep breath and stood. A unit of five agents watched as Jake pulled open the trapdoor. Kelly hoped she looked calmer than she felt as she clicked on the flashlight and stepped onto the ladder.

At the bottom she played the flashlight beam along the walls. On the right-hand side there was a long red streak; a few yards past it, another one. Hopefully he was using one of the other girls' blood, not Claire's, she thought. Kelly moved slowly, gun at the ready in her right hand, flashlight in her left. About ten yards in there was a fork, with a mark on the right wall urging her in that direction. She took a deep breath and turned, the thin circle of light from the trapdoor behind her vanishing utterly. She was in the darkness again, and this time she was all alone.

The room was sliding past in waves. Claire watched it, transfixed. With the exception of one unsuccessful attempt at getting stoned with her roommates, she had never tried any drugs. She didn't like it, she decided. She felt the world spinning out of control, strange shapes emerging from the walls and floor, the edges of everything blurring. Unless she was mistaken, an entire flock of ravens was perched in a row on the ceiling rafter opposite, watching her. She must be seeing things; those seeds he had given her tasted foul, it was probably their fault. It was odd how gentle he was with her, cradling her head as he eased back the tape and slipped them in her mouth. His features were distorted by the strange mask he wore; his nostrils flared against the rubber, his eyes were dark pools beneath. She had taken the mask as a good sign; if he was planning on killing her, why would he hide his face? She tried to explain that she couldn't identify him if he let her go, but he fastened the tape back over her mouth mid-sentence and left the room.

He was coming back now, struggling under the weight of something enormous that was wrapped in plastic and sealed in duct tape. He knelt on one knee and carefully set it on the floor in front of the table, on top of the circle he'd drawn in blood. He began undoing the bindings, easing off the plastic layer by layer. Claire and the ravens watched with interest. *It's a present,* she thought. *Oh, no, that's right, it's not Christmas yet....*

The room was suddenly filled with a terrible stench, so strong Claire's head involuntarily twisted away from it. Her eyes burning, mind shocked into clarity, she turned back and watched in horror as he positioned the legs of his victim, then crossed his arms over his chest. Her eyes widened farther as they lit on the man's face. It was Father John, the kindly priest she saw sometimes around campus. *What kind of sicko kills a priest?* she thought, a flash of rage causing her to momentarily forget her own dire situation.

Then he pulled off his mask, and mangled shreds of her scream tore through the duct tape.

Kelly stopped in her tracks. In front of her was a large metal door, with the now-familiar face of Fenrir the wolf emblazoned across it. The last marks pointed here. She shone the light down the length of the tunnel to confirm it. This was the way he wanted her to go. There might as well have been a sign reading *Trap.*

In the tunnels her senses had sharpened to hyper-acute-ness. At every bend she had slowed, staying close to the wall, edging her way along until she could see a clear path ahead. In her mind she envisioned him tracking her with night-vision goggles, a gun aimed at her heart as she fumbled through the darkness. In her heart she had the terrible feeling that this was her last night on earth.

Stepping back slightly, she kicked open the door and slid inside, panning her gun across the room. It was clear. She was in a small utility room. A boiler sat on one side, a large fuse box was mounted across from it. On the floor next to the door was a discarded chain and bolt, probably the ones used to block the access point. *So much for that plan,* Kelly thought. At the opposite end of the room a staircase ascended between two concrete walls, leading to a landing. She tucked the flashlight in the harness on her belt, took a deep breath and slowly mounted the stairs one at a time. At the landing she paused before whipping around the corner: there was no one there, just another flight of stairs leading to a gray door marked B. She was in one of the administration buildings, or possibly a dorm. Either way she didn't recognize it.

She checked her watch: it had been ten minutes. Jake should be heading down the tunnel now, follow-ing her tracks. She guessed she was about halfway across campus. She stood to the side of the door, pulled down the handle and yanked it open, holding it ajar with her foot as she checked for signs of movement. It was dark inside, the only light a red glow from the Exit signs, but she decided against turning on the flashlight. She eased inside and stayed low. She was in a long aisle, lined almost floor to ceiling with bookshelves. All the bindings were the same, and suddenly she knew where she was: the library. In the basement they kept copies of the senior theses, the products of two semesters' worth of blood, sweat and tears. Hers was down here somewhere: an analysis of how and why the Middle East peace process derailed in the 1970s. *Religion,* she thought. *I can't seem to get away from it.*

She worked her way along slowly. She had only been down here once before, but she remembered that on the far side of the room there was a staircase leading to the main level. At the end of the aisle she stopped and ducked low, then peered around the edge of a bookshelf. The musty smell of old parchment and dust made her nose twitch. Stretching in front of her was another long passage. It ran the length of the building, a few hundred feet long. A seemingly endless row of stacks dead-ended on it, each separated by short aisles. Getting past them would consume valuable minutes.

Suddenly, she caught a flash of something black at the end of the aisle. Kelly squinted into the darkness. Any doubt was eliminated when she heard a rush of movement on the other side of the room. She bolted down the aisle after it. At the last row she stopped and darted her head out, gun held high, eyeing down the sight. There was no one there. There were footsteps again, closer this time— and there was no way to tell which aisle they were coming from. She hunched down against the shelves, feeling the press of bindings in her back. There was no other option than to edge along, aisle by aisle, until he turned up.

"Paul!" she called out. The weight of the words hung heavy in the air. She heard the footsteps slow. It sounded like he was one or two aisles away. "We know who you are, Paul. Give yourself up now and no harm will come to you."

The sound of running footsteps. She heard him clattering down the stairs, back the way she had come, and then the slamming of the door to the basement. *What the hell was he up to?* she wondered. *Shit.* She had to stay with him, he was the key to finding Claire. She debated for a few seconds, then made up her mind.

Carefully, she stood and peered down the next aisle: the flight of stairs started at the end of it. She took a deep breath, pushed off the floor and propelled herself down the aisle at a breakneck pace. Taking the stairs two at a time she bolted for the landing, leaped down the stairs and caught the door to the tunnels before it slammed shut. There was a noise to her right, down a pitch-black fork. Without giving herself a chance to think, she ran toward it.

Twenty-Nine

Jake nervously checked the time on his watch: eight minutes. He had been right to worry; the GPS signal vanished when Jones rounded the first bend in the tunnel, and he had to restrain himself from throwing the monitor against the wall in frustration. One of the agents had rushed to the command center and brought back the maps of the tunnels they had used last week: he assigned a dozen agents to cover the six access points within a conceivable distance of the chapel, but he had no way of knowing how far in she'd gone. Frustrated, he absent-mindedly tapped the map on his lap with one finger. He should have said five minutes, not ten. Five minutes was close enough to catch up if she needed them, in ten she could be all the way across campus. He was rusty. One plus about all the Bureau's rules and regulations: they kept you sharp. The past few years of living the high life left him ill-prepared for a situation like this. He felt useless, incompetent, the same as when Sarah bled to death on the ground in front of him. He checked his watch again: nine minutes, fifty seconds. Close enough. He jumped to his feet and waved for the other five agents in the room to follow him. "Let's go."

Quickly and silently the team wound through the tunnels. The trail of blood stopped at the library, which was odd, Jake thought; hardly the place he would have chosen for a moonlit ritual sacrifice. They quickly checked the basement; it was empty. He mounted the carpeted stairs leading to the main floor of the building two at a time. At the top, a long marble promenade extended before him. It was only nominally brighter upstairs. Portraits of past presidents and deans lined the hall, peering through the dusky light. To his right, a corridor led to the rear of the library, where an enormous atrium faced the main quad. The library was a five-story building composed of row after row of stacks, study carrels and rooms housing special collections. It would take at least an hour to search the entire place.

The agents fanned out around him, splitting into pairs and disappearing up flights of stairs and down the dark aisles. Jake decided it made the most sense to start on the main floor. He trotted down the hallway toward the back of the building, past glassed-in displays of rare books and rows of computers, their screens blank and silent. In the center of the building, running through all five floors and connected by metal staircases, were the stacks. Corridors down each side penned them in, and off those corridors were the study rooms and carrels.

Taking a left through the doorway and entering the stacks, he passed down the row, ducking his head in each one. "Jones!" he called out. "Jones, if you can hear me, make some noise!"

He continued down the row, trying to simultaneously see down the aisles while checking every possible approach. At the end of the row he ducked into the opposite corridor. Here a set of French doors opened to the "quiet room," an enormous study hall with long oak desks lit by overhanging lamps with green shades. Cautiously he entered. It was completely still. Empty, just like the rest of the place. He swore under his breath, backed out and made his way down the corridor to the atrium at the rear of the building. The library had been extended at some point in the past. The addition created a glassed-in room that framed the former exterior, leaving the original brick walls and marble columns intact. The librarian's desk sat in the exact center of the new room. Deep, plush armchairs faced the windows overlooking the quad, and a few tables wrapped around the main desk. Towering above it all was a stunning white marble balcony.

Jake turned in a slow circle listening to the clatter of agents from the other floors yelling, "Clear!"

"Shit," he whispered in a voice filled with dread. "She's not here."

Kelly dashed through the tunnels, gun drawn, mind intent only on catching him before he got to Claire. She barely paused at each fork, cocking her head to the side as she listened to the sound of him racing ahead of her.

He was moving fast, but not outpacing her by much. Clearly he wanted her to follow.

She had by now completely lost her sense of direction. He seemed to be leading her in circles, farther and farther from the library and the chapel, possibly off the campus itself. It felt as though she had run for miles, her body freshly charged with adrenaline from the chase.

Kelly turned right down a narrow shaft, her steps slowing as she realized she could no longer hear him. She played her flashlight along the walls. There were no drawings here. The walls were uncommonly dark and slick, with trails of green lichen lining the upper reaches, bright against the condensation. Her feet sank into the floor, and she realized with surprise that the concrete had given way to mud. She tried to silence the squelching of her feet, creeping forward as quietly as possible. Kelly eased herself around a corner, turning right to follow the imprints left by him, and stopped. A door at the end of the passage gaped open. Blue light shone from the other side.

She stuck close to the right-hand wall as she approached, the sound of her heart loud in her ears. A strange creaking sound emanated from the room. *Okay,* she thought. *Eyes and ears open. You're on your own now—one wrong move and you and Claire are both dead.* She drew a deep breath, counted to three in her head, and darted through the door.

Jake pounded on the door of the house insistently. "C'mon, c'mon…" he muttered. Professor Birnbaum's car was still in the driveway—where the hell was he?

He rubbed his chin as he deliberated. The five agents he'd recruited were eyeing him warily, clearly not thrilled to be following a rogue who had been kicked out of the Bureau. The others had split off from the group and were carrying out a thorough search of the tunnels. Jake knew it could take days to find them that way. He had a better idea, which was why they were now standing in front of Professor Birnbaum's house.

"Screw it," Jake said finally. "Break it down."

The agent holding the battering ram regarded him uncertainly. "Um, sir? I don't believe we have a warrant for this premises."

"A warrant? You're kidding, right?" Jake grabbed one end of the battering ram and raised an eyebrow at the agents staring at him. "We've got one agent down, another who's off the grid in pursuit of a serial killer. And in this house is someone who might be able to tell us where they went. A little help would be nice." The agent who had emerged from the darkness bearing the battering ram silently took the back end. Jake planted himself in front of the door, nodded his head, and counted, "One, two…"

On three he swung the metal ram back and slammed it hard against the exterior. The door crashed open with the crackle of splintered wood. They spilled into the house. Jake flicked on the hall light, motioned for three agents to check the upstairs while he headed to the back room. It was hard to believe they'd just been there that morning, he thought—it felt like years ago. He remembered the dappled light from the windows highlighting streaks of red in Jones's hair, and his grip tightened on the gun.

They entered the study. The dying embers of a fire crackled in the fireplace. Jake strode forward purposefully, seeing an arm dangling off the side of an armchair.

"Professor Birnbaum, we need…" His voice trailed off as he faced the chair head-on. The professor sat rigid against the cushions, a book still propped open in his lap. Perched on top of the book was his head, the whites of the eyes flashing at Jake like an accusation.

Kelly gasped. She was in the boathouse, she realized. The low wooden room opened out on the river. She was standing at the far end. Along both walls were the sleek fiberglass sculls used by the school's rowing teams. And dangling by a rope from a hook directly across the room was Claire.

Kelly scanned the room quickly—he had vanished. She ran her light across the walls; there was one door off to her right, other than that the only exit opened on the river at the far end. Feeling sick to her stomach, she played the light up the length of Claire's body. She was naked, legs separated by ropes that stretched the length of the room on either side and were fastened to boat cleats. Her hands were bound together in front of her torso. Her head hung forward, blond curls trailing down her cheeks. A rope was wrapped around her neck, extending up into the rafters. Her body hung in the exact shape of the fourth rune. Kelly felt her legs weaken at the knees. She was too late.

Suddenly, the girl's head wrenched up. She squinted against the light, staring at Kelly with sheer terror. Her eyes widened. Kelly felt a wave of relief wash over her. A slow-releasing rope, she remembered. It wasn't the hanging that had killed the girls, that was just how he mounted them. Cautiously, she took a few steps forward, scanning back and forth between the door on her right and the vast opening behind Claire. She felt her feet scrape against something, and pointed the flashlight down. There was an old fishnet spread across the floor. Easing to the side of it, she edged her way toward the girl, pulse pounding. Claire was trying to say something—her mouth was duct-taped. The girl's eyes widened and she began flailing wildly at her bonds.

"No, Claire! Stay still! I'll have you down in a minute, stop struggling!" Kelly whispered urgently.

Directly in front of Claire she could see a body lying in a heap. The stench of a rotting corpse was overpowering. *Father John,* she thought. It was obviously too late to save him.

Suddenly, the floor disappeared and she felt herself floundering, falling through the air. The shock of cold water on her body, then her head struck something hard and she fell into a black vortex of silence.

Jake flipped through books, his frustration mounting.

"I'm sorry, sir—what are we looking for again?" an agent asked, looking up from his seat on the ottoman across the room.

"Anything relating to ritual sacrifice," Jake barked. "Possible locations, anything—check the index."

He tried to ignore the headless man covered by a sheet

across from him. Clearly their killer had had a busy day. And in his opinion Stefan was looking more and more suspicious, vanishing the way he had. Unless he was another victim of this rampage, and they just hadn't found him yet. Jake mentally kicked himself. Why the hell hadn't it occurred to him that the killer might come here? Now the only person who could conceivably help him find Jones was dead.

He threw the book aside and picked up another. Research had never been his strong suit, especially not under these circumstances. He checked the GPS monitor in his pocket again: nothing. Goddamn thing probably didn't even work.

It took him a minute to realize that the book in his hands didn't possess an index because it was a dog-eared copy of *Selling Water by the River: A Manual of Zen Training*. He started to toss it with a guttural growl, then froze. His mind flashed back on something. When he was at the boathouse the other day watching them scour the river for Tiffany Agostanelli, he'd struck up a conversation with one of the divers on a break.

"Last case I worked was down South," the guy had said. "Religious nut, took his vics to a river to baptize them. Drowned five before they caught him."

Water. It was the ultimate purifier in every other religion, Jake thought. *Why not this one?*

"Let's go." He stood and marched toward the front door.

"Um, where are we going?" an agent called out as the rest scrambled to catch up.

"To the boathouse."

Thirty

Kelly's eyes opened slowly, focusing on the swaying light cast by a ring of candles. She was lying on the floor facing Father John's lifeless body. Groggily she shifted her weight, trying to reach for her weapon. She remembered falling, cold water—then nothing. Her head was throbbing—she must have hit her head. Her clothes were soaking wet, but at least they were still on her, she noted with some relief. Her hands were tightly bound behind her back. She had failed, she realized with a sinking feeling. And now they were both going to die.

Claire still hung facing her. Tears were now streaming down her cheeks. She was staring at something behind Kelly. Kelly jerked her head back and saw a robed figure crouching outside the perimeter of light. His dark eyes watched her with interest, as though she was in some way entertaining him. He nodded at her. She recognized the voice that issued from his lips, but it held none of the faltering uncertainty when they spoke in the chapel. It boomed out of him now, filling the room.

"The aurochs pit."

"What?" Kelly asked apprehensively. Her eyes scanned the room in desperation, seeking a means for escape.

"The aurochs, the great wild and untamable cattle of northern Europe, as large as an elephant and dark as a bull." He stood and strode around the circle of light until he loomed between her and Claire. He continued, as though delivering a sermon. "The only way to capture one without killing it was with a pit trap." He gestured past her. She followed his hand and saw a trapdoor dangling over an abyss; it must have been concealed by the gritty sand on the floor, she thought with despair. "Ferocious beasts of extraordinary strength and speed, the capture of one was a symbol of the hunter's prowess. You should feel honored."

Kelly was dumbstruck. She peered frantically around the room. He had lit candles in a full circle around them. She was lying on some sort of symbol, she realized, drawn in blood on the floor. The stickiness cloyed to her hands and face. On Claire's right stood a wooden table— an altar, she realized—also lit with candles. Sitting on top was an enormous book, pages glinting red in the light. *The Raudhskinni,* she thought, inhaling sharply. He really had found it, or in his madness had adopted a substitute. Next to the book stood a rough wooden goblet. On the other side she caught the glint of a knife.

She had no idea how long she'd been unconscious, but it had to be almost midnight. The reflection of the moon on the water cast patterns of shifting blue light across the walls. She needed to stall him until they were found. *If* they were found, she realized, fighting back a sharp pang of fear. She could no longer feel the pressure of the GPS beeper behind her ear—it must have dislodged when she hit her head. And no one had any idea where they were.

She watched as he strode to the table and reached for the knife. Facing away from them, he drew something in the air with the butt of it. He turned ninety degrees and repeated the gesture. The next turn brought him facing her: his eyes were oddly glazed over, she noticed, and she wondered if he was high. Claire certainly seemed to be out of it. Her head bobbed forward in slow dips. Periodically she jolted awake, snapping her head up, eyes wide and panicked. Then they slowly drifted shut again.

"So you killed your brother," Kelly said in as conversational a tone as she could muster.

He froze midturn. Glaring, he stooped to face her and gestured with the point of the knife inches from her face. Her head reflexively pulled away from the vicious-looking blade, breath catching in her throat as he growled at her.

"I did not kill my brother. It was the others."

"The others? What others?" she asked in confusion. Why would a man already responsible for the deaths of at least four people refuse to claim another?

"The ancestors." His eyes darted up toward the rafters fearfully, and he lowered his voice to a harsh whisper. "Spirits from the past, they took him. I warned him of the need to avenge our father's death, but he paid no heed. They came to claim him, they will come for me if I fail."

"Fail at what?" Kelly asked.

With a sweeping gesture he motioned to his brother on the floor. "The past must be made right."

She stared at the body facing her, trying to analyze it. Already in advanced stages of decomposition, the body was straining against the confines of a simple black suit. His skin was mottled greenish-blue and blistered, almost rendering the features unrecognizable. The milky eyes were beginning to seep, the remaining hair was patchy, and she could see that some of his teeth had fallen out. There was no evidence of insect activity that she could see, so it had clearly been protected by something—but the man had obviously been dead for at least a few weeks.

Something that Stefan said suddenly flashed through her mind as she glanced up. *The Raudhskinni. It was said to contain the darkest kind of sorcery, ways to foresee the future, shift-shape, even to raise the dead.* If he was telling the truth and hadn't been responsible for his brother's death, was it possible…?

"You're trying to bring him back to life," she said quietly.

He didn't glance up from the altar. "Yes."

"You're mad."

He ignored her, clearly absorbed in examining the text. It all fell into place now. Paul had probably come to his brother for help once he was ejected from the Ring of Ásatrú. What if Father John had died unexpectedly while his brother was staying with him? Now truly alone in the world, in the dark recesses of his mind Paul had decided that his only recourse was to sacrifice innocent girls in an attempt to raise his brother from the dead. And he possessed a book that promised to show him how.

"Why those girls?" she blurted, trying to keep him engaged while she came up with a plan.

"The daughters of the elite," he said without looking up. "The fruit bearers of those who would ruin the world with their greed."

"I'm sorry, I still don't understand," Kelly said encouragingly. If she extended her right middle finger all the way down to her wrist, she could almost reach the knots binding the leather. She tried to struggle inconspicuously with it, catching a corner with her fingernail before it slipped off the smooth surface.

He followed his finger across the page, lips pursed, answering her question offhandedly as if she were a disruptive child. "My father was sacrificed on the altar of enterprise. It was necessary to avenge his death in order that he might rest. Now my brother and I can have some peace." He glanced up from the page. "Besides, it was necessary to have their blood. Blood is very potent, you see—few rituals are effective without it."

"Hmm." Kelly nodded her head, then winced at the pain. "And you need five girls."

"Yes, that's correct." He sounded pleased that she understood.

"But Claire and I aren't daughters of enterprise. And neither was Katerina."

A cloud crossed his features. "Katerina was a mistake. She had the great misfortune of witnessing a ritual, one she did not understand. It was never my intention to kill her. Most saddening, but necessary."

Kelly cleared her throat, trying to sound casual as she pressed, "And us?"

"Regrettably, your investigation forced me to alter my plans. Too many prospects left campus. You must understand this is not what I wanted." He looked imploringly up at Claire, then back down at her. "I do extend my sincerest apologies. You will, however, have the opportunity to witness a ritual that has lain silent for over five hundred years." He paused, knit his brows together and continued, "The beginning of it, at least."

"That is comforting," Kelly muttered. She felt the first knot give way under her persistent tugs, but the straps didn't release. With a sinking heart she realized that the rope must have been knotted repeatedly. Taking a deep breath, she set to work on the next one, ignoring the cramps in her fingers. The tingling at the tips indicated an impending loss of feeling; the bindings were slowly cutting off her circulation. If she didn't get out of them in the next few minutes, her last dim hope for survival would vanish.

Jake blew through the front door of the professor's house. "Let's get back in the cars. Two of you come with me, the rest follow," he ordered, gesturing with his flashlight. It was best not to show uncertainty; his hold on this unit was tenuous enough as it was. They were only bothering to listen to him because Morrow and Jones were gone, and nobody else had stepped in to fill the vacuum.

They weren't moving, he noticed with a sinking feeling. He'd felt the shift toward mutiny during their search of the professor's house.

One of them stepped forward. "We're thinking we should return to central command and regroup, sir."

Jake played his flashlight up to the agent's face. "We give up now, you're basically condemning Agent Jones to death."

The agent was in his early thirties, stocky with a buzz cut. He had a brash confidence that reminded Jake all too much of himself at that age. "The thing is, we've already violated about fifteen rules of procedure today. I realize that you're no longer acquainted with the code of conduct," he continued in a withering tone, "but the rest of us don't want to get reassigned to Peoria."

Jake drew himself up to his full height and glared down at him, hoping against hope that he might still come out of this the winner. "Agent Jones gave you direct orders to follow me tonight."

"All due respect, sir, Agent Jones is probably already dead. Even if she survives this, she'll be investigated for her actions tonight. And I don't plan on joining her. I'm going to call this in and wait for the M.E." With that, the kid turned and strutted back to his parked car. The rest of the unit followed, and Jake was left standing alone. The weight of his failure combined with fatigue threatened to overwhelm him, and he felt his knees start to give. Bracing himself, he stiffened his legs and strode toward the car. He refused to give up yet, not until he knew for certain what had happened to them. Even if he was too late to save Jones, he might still have a chance to catch the bastard who killed her. And without the FBI there to chaperone, he could settle the debt privately.

A dark figure was leaning against his rental car. He slowed his pace, positioning his gun directly below the flashlight until it illuminated the letters "F.B.I." emblazoned in yellow against a navy background.

"You miss your posse?" Jake asked dryly as he approached.

"Just thought my time might be better spent, sir." It was the young agent who had helped him earlier with the battering ram, a shy-looking kid, probably not more than twenty-six years old. "You mind if I tag along?"

Jake shrugged, secretly relieved to see him. "Suit yourself."

The kid climbed into the passenger seat. Jake eased the car out of the mud and back onto the pavement, then accelerated. "We should be there in under five."

"Yes, sir."

"Jake. Not sir, Jake."

"Right." The kid looked uncomfortable but lapsed into silence.

Jake glanced at him. He was slightly built—it was a wonder he passed the physical exams the FBI forced them to undergo every year, he didn't look like he could knock out one push-up, never mind thirty-five. "What's your name?"

"Danny Rodriguez."

"Okay, Danny. I lead, you cover my back. First sign of trouble you call for backup."

"Gotcha." The kid paused before asking, "Anything else?"

"If you're a religious man, this would be a good time to start praying." Jake gunned the engine and the car leaped forward.

Kelly felt the last knot start to give. She tried not to cry out with relief as the bonds around her wrists suddenly eased and blood returned to her throbbing fingertips. Somehow she had to get to the gun before he started whatever bizarre ritual he was planning. She eyed him. He was seated to the side of his dead brother, just a few feet away from her, eyes closed. He appeared to be meditating. Claire's head had slumped forward again. Now was the time. Kelly eased her legs in front of her, straining her muscles to hold them just above the floor, trying to be soundless. She braced herself to jump to her feet, then felt a presence and jerked her head to the side. Someone was there, in the shadows off to her left. Her heart leaped—the beacon must still have been working, Jake had found them after all. The figure took a step closer, toward the light. It was too large for Jake. One step farther and Stefan's long white beard came into view. He nodded a solemn acknowledgment as her body flooded with relief.

"Are we almost ready?" His voice echoed through the room. Claire's head jerked up.

Paul blinked, trying to shake off his reverie. "Master." He breathed the word reverently as he scrambled to his feet. "I've prepared the sacrifices. All is ready for the ceremony."

Kelly's shock registered on her face. Stefan smiled down at her. All traces of the submissive pose he had assumed that morning in Professor Birnbaum's house vanished, cruelty now glinting in his eyes. "My dear, you didn't honestly believe I'd sacrifice my best student, did you?" he said in a soothing purr. "I see you've managed to escape your bonds—very clever of you. Unfortunately, too late to do any good."

"Why?" Kelly asked, casting about desperately for some sort of weapon.

He followed her gaze to the altar, where both her guns were perched next to the knife. "I welcome you to try, but I doubt very much that you would make it. Sometimes it's better to be reconciled to your lot in life. I assume Paul has illuminated you as to the nature of our ceremony this evening?"

"It's insanity," Kelly said, slowly easing herself to a sitting position. "You can't honestly believe that this will work."

Stefan's gaze settled on the book. "The *Raudhskinni.*" He breathed the word, caressing each syllable. "It was the reason I joined the Ring of Ásatrú. I first heard the legend of the red leather book as a child in Denmark. As you can imagine, it captured my imagination. I've devoted my life to this moment," he said, voice lowering to a hiss.

"So why did you tell me everything? Why did you let me search your house?" Kelly asked, her mind still reeling.

He strode past her to the altar, stroking the book lightly with one finger, then carefully lifting the knife. "Surely I didn't tell you everything, Ms. Jones. The call from the good professor demanded some sort of response. He was on the verge of approaching the authorities himself, which would have been disastrous. As it was, things have turned out almost exactly as we planned." He laid a hand on Paul's shoulder and smiled at him. Paul basked in the glow of his attention. "My son, we have tread a long road together," Stefan said reflectively. With a swift movement he raised the knife and flashed it across his disciple's throat. Kelly gasped, horrified, as Paul's body collapsed in on itself, blood pulsing out of the neck with each throbbing heartbeat. He sank to the floor soundlessly, the smile supplanted by a look of wounded surprise as he crumpled on top of his brother's corpse.

Claire was writhing above them, plaintive animal noises escaping from the duct tape covering her mouth, her arms and legs thrashing the few inches allowed by the ropes.

"I'll be with you in a moment, dear," Stefan said, glancing up at her. He wiped the blade clean with a fold of his robe. "Such a nice boy—malleable. I couldn't have asked for a more devoted servant."

"You killed him," Kelly said, her voice flat. The shock of the murder had sharpened her senses again, shaking off the fog from the blow to her head. She only had to overcome one man now, not two, she thought. If she could only get him away from the altar for a minute…

He followed her eyes and his lips broke into a terse smile. "Please don't see this as an opportunity to escape, Ms. Jones. It would be such a waste to have to kill you before the time comes. And Paul would be so terribly disappointed. I'm afraid his translation of the text missed a few salient points." Stefan gazed pityingly down at the bodies stacked before him. "The *Raudhskinni* does have its limitations, resuscitation is only effective on recently departed souls. Even if I could bring the other one back, the smell…" He wrinkled his nose and shuddered. "I doubt he'd thank me, don't you agree?" His voice was pleasant, conversational. His smile widened.

"Speaking of which…" He checked his watch, then peered toward the river. The night had brightened considerably. It must be almost midnight, Kelly thought. The moon forced the edges of the boathouse door into long shadows that arced back toward them, just grazing Claire's dangling toes. "Yes, it's almost time."

Stefan lifted the knife again. Kelly caught her breath, and saw Claire do the same. But no; he was merely repeating the ritual that Paul had performed earlier, turning at right angles to himself, decisively carving the air in front of his chest with the knife. His back to her, Kelly tensed her muscles, preparing to spring. She would go for the Glock—it was the closest weapon and should have the most impact. Two steps, jump over the dead brothers, grab it with your right hand, she thought, picturing the action in her mind. *Better to go down fighting,* she said to herself, leaving the sentence unfinished in her own mind.

She pushed off the ground with both hands and feet, the scratch of grit against her shoes painfully loud. Before she could reach the altar he shifted and lunged with terrible speed, catching the side of her head with the knife handle. She reeled from the blow, hands clutching at the edge of the altar as her weight shifted and she went down.

She landed on her hands and knees in a pool of Paul's blood, chest heaving, bolts of light dancing in front of her eyes. She shook her head hard to clear her vision. Stefan's voice sounded as though it was echoing down a vast chamber toward her. "Now that wasn't very nice, was it?"

She watched helplessly as he gathered the Glock in his free hand. "I think I'll hold on to this for a moment, if you don't mind." He smiled at her. "Now, where was I?"

He turned to Claire and began to chant, his voice filling the room, the words wrapping around each other as they reverberated off the walls. Claire's eyes signaled resignation, an awareness that she was past the point of saving. Kelly flashed back on her brother. Had Alex had the same look? Had he known which breath would be his last?

The chanting suddenly increased in volume. Stefan tilted his head back, the candlelight casting garish shadows across his face as he traced a line up Claire's leg with the tip of the knife. Kelly fought to stay conscious as the world shifted in and out of focus. He was going to kill Claire. She was going to die the same way the other girls did, blood pouring down her leg, her life dribbling away onto the floor below. Kelly's head dropped forward and she sank back on her heels. She couldn't bear to watch.

The shadows suddenly rushed in around her. The candles flickered then were extinguished by a gust of wind. She winced as a sharp cry pierced the air. The room was filled with the thrashing of wings. She looked up and saw a stream of dark birds soaring from the rafters toward the water, their sharp screeches piercing the sudden silence. There was someone else in the room—she squinted and tried to focus her eyes. Someone was grappling with Stefan; they swayed together in a bizarre dance, their grunts now the only sound.

Kelly staggered to her feet. Gathering up her last ounce of strength she lunged at the altar, fumbling in the darkness, almost tripping and falling over the dead brothers. She could hear them on her right now, Stefan cursing in Danish at his attacker. The altar wasn't where it should have been—it must have been knocked over during the struggle. She dropped to her knees and cast about on the floor with her hands, burning her thumb on molten candle wax as she groped for the gun.

Frantically, she sifted through the mass of netting and cloth covering the floor. Her hands grazed a parched leathery surface—the book, she realized, then right next to it her palm glanced across steel. Her hand closed around the gun's barrel. Rolling, she grasped the Glock in both hands and pointed it toward the two reeling shadows. A scream pierced the darkness and the two forms separated, one dropping to the floor. The enormous dark form raised something above its head. Moonlight glinted off the edge of the blade. As he drove it downward, she squeezed the trigger. The gunshot was preternaturally loud in the small space, adding to the ringing in her ears. She watched as the shadow stiffened, then reeled backward toward the river's edge. Head forward, hands clutching his chest, he rocked back and forth on his feet, howling in pain. Stefan raised his hands toward the ceiling as if in supplication, then tumbled backward. The sound of the splash dissipated as Kelly caught her breath, still clutching the gun in both hands. The throbbing in her head became more insistent, and she felt herself slipping away into darkness.

The last thing she saw was a single feather, floating down from the rafters and into the gloom, shining oddly bright as it drifted toward her.

Jake's head jerked up at the sound of the shot. He ran from the car, leaving the door open and counting on the kid to follow him. The school name and logo was emblazoned on the side of the white building in red paint. He charged the door, running sideways. The flimsy bolt gave under his momentum and he hurtled into the building.

He rolled once and leaped to his feet, gun ready. Trying to ignore the throbbing of his shoulder, he played the flashlight across the room. "Jones!" he cried.

There was something large strung up in the center of the room, blocking the limited light from the river side.

The kid at his shoulder gasped and choked. "Good God, what's that smell?"

Jake took a few tentative steps forward. Anyone could be hiding in the shadows. He whirled at every imagined movement, his flashlight illuminating the shiny hull of a red scull, a pile of netting, then Claire, strung up like a slab of meat. A pile of human clothing on the floor, and the tang of fresh blood and gunpowder; he struggled to suppress the bile rising in his throat. Where the hell was Jones in all this carnage?

The kid breathed out "Jesus Christ…" as the light revealed two men strewn on top of each other like discarded toys, the smell of decay almost overpowering. A trail of fresh blood led to the edge of the dock. Jake stepped closer and probed through the water, his flashlight beam penetrating a few feet before fading into the silvery depths.

He spun at the sound of a low moan. Rodriguez was already there, bent over her. Jake's heart leaped into his throat as he knelt by Jones. She was soaking wet, covered in blood, her hair stuck together in clumps. Gingerly, they rolled her over to check for a pulse—she was alive, despite all the blood. Jake smoothed the hair back from her face and cradled her head in his lap. As if from a distance he heard Rodriguez calling for backup and medical assistance. Jones's eyes fluttered, then opened, and she peered up at him uncertainly.

"What…" she asked.

"Shh," he said gently. "You done good, kid. It's all going to be okay."

Thirty-One

Kelly awoke in a king-size bed, the smooth feel of cotton sheets against her skin. She was dressed in a man's T-shirt and boxers. Stretching her arms above her head as she sat up, she suddenly flinched at the throbbing in her temples. Carefully, she lowered herself back down and turned on her side. The clock on the nightstand glowed a perplexing 4:35 p.m. The events of the day before flooded her mind, crows and blood and water and cold—she closed her eyes again as the images blurred together. She wasn't entirely certain what had happened, but somehow she had survived.

She shuffled to the bathroom to find some Advil and was surprised to see a toothbrush and a man's shaving kit there. An adjoining door was ajar. She knocked tentatively and heard footsteps approach.

"It lives!" said Jake, throwing open the door and spreading his arms wide.

Kelly laughed. He was barefoot, clad only in a T-shirt and jeans, hair still wet from the shower.

"I didn't wake you, did I? Sorry about the tight quarters. Apparently there's some sort of plumbers' convention in town, so this was the only available room—"

He sounded nervous and apologetic, she noted with amusement.

"So where the hell am I?" she asked with a pained grin.

"The Radisson. Finest establishment this side of Stamford, or so I'm told." His gaiety seemed forced. "You really don't remember? They wanted to check you into the hospital but you protested—vehemently—so the compromise was that I take you here for observation."

"Observation, really," Kelly said wryly, glancing down at herself. "Which I suppose explains the clothes."

"I swear, I hardly peeked." Jake held up his hands to protest. "Your outfit was sopping wet—couldn't let you catch your death of cold."

Nervousness made the twang in his voice more pronounced than usual. Was there something he wasn't telling her? "Are you kidding? I'm considering returning to civilian life for the room service alone."

"Speaking of which…" Jake stepped back into his room and nodded toward a trolley piled high with platters. "I thought this might be more civilized. Besides, I did a little recon this morning and the media swarm has descended. They all want a shot of the female super-agent that cracked the case wide open."

"I should really change," she said, tugging discomfitingly at her top, aware that in direct sunlight her breasts might show through the thin fabric. Not that he hadn't already seen them, she reminded herself, trying not to flush at the thought of it.

Jake seemed equally awkward as he said, "You look great. Besides, you're probably starving. I know I am, and I managed to eat something last night. You can shower and change after breakfast."

As soon as he said it she realized she was famished. She eased herself into a chair and watched Jake prepare a plate for her. The curtains were pulled back to reveal a gorgeous fall day. She tore into the food in front of her, barely coming up for air until her plate had been cleared twice.

"Whoa," Jake said, watching her with a smile. "Not exactly the salad type, are you?"

"Mmm, that was delicious." She leaned back and closed her eyes, enjoying the feel of the sun on her back. She opened them again to find Jake watching her. He looked away as she caught his eye.

"So do you mind if I ask what happened?" she said, hoping the answer wouldn't turn her newly replenished stomach.

He shook his head. "I was hoping to ask you the same thing. Man, that was a hell of a mess in there. Never seen anything like it."

"Claire?" she said, almost afraid to ask, the lip of the coffee mug concealing her mouth.

"Claire's fine. A little shaken up, but she didn't lose much blood. Jerome caught the worst of it, he's still in intensive care."

"Jerome?" she asked in confusion.

"Yeah—why, you didn't see him?" Jake seemed as

puzzled as she was. "Pretty ballsy for a guy with one arm, I gotta say. That Special Forces training is no joke. He got sliced up pretty badly, though. He's in a coma, lost his spleen. The docs are hoping he'll pull out of it sometime in the next few days. Otherwise…" He shrugged as the words trailed off.

The figure struggling with Stefan, she remembered. The tall dark shadow had been Jerome. "And Stefan?" she asked.

Jake shook his head. "No sign of him, but they've got divers out looking. The amount of blood he left on the ground, chances are his body'll turn up somewhere downriver. Just in case I asked them to put his photo over the wire, have the locals check out hospitals, bus stations, that sort of thing. The New York office has a team staking out his house."

"Wow. Are you sure you want to go back to the private sector? Sounds like you're angling for my job." She arched an eyebrow.

"Not with that benefits package. Dmitri gives me vision *and* dental."

She laughed, and he grinned back at her. She topped off her mug with more coffee and stirred. The afternoon light lengthened across the room as it hit the uppermost tree branches outside. Kelly remembered something else. "And the *Raudhskinni?*"

"The what?"

"The *Raudhskinni,* remember? The red leather book? They had it on an altar," she said impatiently. "It must have been there when you came in. They should have cataloged it."

"Jones, you've been through a lot." He reached for her hand.

She felt a sudden flash of anger. "Don't patronize me—it was there, I saw it."

"Jones, I got there right after your gun discharged. I was there when the EMTs came, and when the floodlights lit that place up like the Fourth of July. We searched every inch of the building, no sign of a book. But I'll ask Rodriguez if he found it."

It was all too strange. The book gone, Stefan vanishing into the river…

"We dug this up, though." He handed her a faxed copy of a newspaper article and watched in silence as she perused it.

She met his eyes. "So the twins were the only survivors."

"Yup. Can't imagine having your father try to murder you. Guess he went nuts when he got fired. They lost their mother, a sister, and another brother in the fire. The twins' bedroom was downstairs, that's how they made it out, but they must have heard the others screaming. Great way to breed a serial killer."

"Yeah, I guess." She examined the carpeting and frowned. "So what was Stefan's excuse?"

"You read *Hamlet*. Danes are nuts. Which reminds me…" Jake crossed the room and carried over a crystal vase overflowing with red roses.

"For me?" she said with surprise, reaching for the small card tucked into the ribbon.

Jake grinned. "Sorry, I can't take the credit. These, and

three others just like 'em, are compliments of Mr. Vincent Agostanelli."

The card read simply, *If you ever need a favor… V.A.* Another copy of his business card was tucked behind it.

She rolled her eyes. "That'll be the day."

Jake took the card and read it. "Hey, you never know. I'd hold on to that number if I were you."

"I'm sure you would," she said with a smirk. Now that her hunger was sated, she was itching to get out of her clothes and into the shower. "Did you call Dmitri?" she asked.

"This morning. He was understandably thrilled by the news. I'm hoping this will give him some of that closure bullshit therapists are always talking about. He's arranging a memorial for Anna. It'll be on campus a week from Saturday, if you want to go."

"I'd like that. I have to check in with my ASAC, see what he says." Even after a "clean" shooting, Kelly would be on probation until the Office of Professional Responsibility cleared her. Her mind was suddenly flooded with the tasks awaiting her: she'd have to type up reports, organize files and evidence for storage, head back to New York and wait for her next assignment. She rubbed her temples at the thought of it.

"One last thing." Jake looked at the floor. "I called Morrow's wife last night to tell her we got the guy. I know that the news should probably have come from you, but you were pretty out of it, and I was worried the press would leak it first. I hope that's okay."

"That's fine. I'm glad you did it." Morrow's face

flashed before her eyes: she saw him lying on his back, blank eyes gazing at the ceiling, and a wave of sadness rolled over her. "I think I'll jump in the shower now."

She let the hot water run down her back for a long time, wincing as she probed the lumps on her head, feeling the sharp ends of stitches notched in her scalp. She scrubbed herself with soap, determined to remove every trace of the dirt and blood that had covered her the day before. Every time she closed her eyes images danced across them: Tiffany Agostanelli mounted on the president's door like a hunting trophy, Claire sitting on the curb, Morrow chatting with the press. From the outset this case had affected her more than most, and she still wasn't sure why. The murders had been particularly brutal, but she'd dealt with that sort of thing before and emerged unscathed. Being at her alma mater had rendered it more personal, but deep in her soul she knew there was more to it than that. She was still too close to what happened to want to examine it further. She would shelve it in her mind, the way she had every case before it. In a few weeks she would be in Jersey City or Brooklyn or Baltimore, staring at another carved-up corpse, chasing down another deranged killer. That was her life, her calling—she had done it for so long now she knew that she would never be suited to anything else.

She pulled on a clean hotel bathrobe and strolled back into her room, toweling her hair dry as she went. She checked the messages on her cell phone. The first was from ASAC Bowen, both congratulating her and outlining her temporary suspension. "Shouldn't take long," his nasal voice said after a pause. "I've authorized some extra vacation days, won't expect to see you in the office until Wednesday. Desk duty until the OPR finishes their investigation."

Big of him, she thought. With any luck she'd be back out in the field shortly. Anything was better than being stuck at a desk with him hovering over her shoulder.

Dmitri Christou had left an overly formal message as well, thanking her for finding the man who robbed him of his daughter. His voice cracked at the end, when he said "Anna" out loud. Kelly winced as she listened. It would take him time, but he'd recover, she reminded herself. It was amazing, people's ability to put the past behind them. She remembered reading Proust in college. The one phrase that had resonated with her was, "You don't get over the past, you get around it." It was true. It was how she dealt with losing Alex, and the rest of her family with him. It was how she kept going, case by case, city by city. It was only now that she realized how weary that could make a person. Perhaps sometimes the direct route was better.

There was a tentative rap on her door. Jake came in. "Just wanted to check on you…" he said, his voice trailing off at the sight of her in a robe. Her calves peeked out the bottom, and her still-moist hair hung down her back, the red brilliant against white terry cloth. He swallowed hard. "Well, you look like you're doing fine. I was just thinking maybe we could head over to visit Claire at the hospital. Her folks arrived early this morning, and they really want to meet you."

"Jerome, too," Kelly said.

"Right, Jerome." He was carefully examining the mottled stucco ceiling of her room.

"Apparently I have a little vacation time coming," she said casually, turning toward the mirror to run a brush through her hair.

"Really? Funny coincidence, Dmitri recommended I take a few days, too." Jake paused. "So where are you headed?"

Kelly shrugged nonchalantly. "I hear Vermont is gorgeous this time of year. I've never been."

He cleared his throat. "No, me neither. Must be nice."

"That's what I've heard."

"Well. Maybe I'll see you up there."

She smiled at him in the mirror. "Maybe."

"Okay then." There was an awkward silence. Jake pointed toward the door. "I'll be waiting in the next room. Just knock when you're ready to leave."

"Sure. Give me five minutes."

The door closed behind him. Kelly sat for a long moment, the brush still in her lap, eyes on the mirror but focused beyond it. A breeze parted the curtains, throw-ing a shaft of sunlight across the room, sparking the flames in her hair. Perched on a branch outside the window a dark bird cocked his head to the side, watching through a bot-tomless black eye. The curtain drifted back into place and the raven released a guttural cry. As the sun eased below the horizon he spread his wings and lifted off the branch, making one swooping pass by the window before winging off in the direction of a waning moon.

MEET THE
DEADLY SEVEN

Seven titles from bestselling authors and new voices that will chill and terrorize you with their tales of murder, conspiracy and suspense.

JUNE   AUGUST   JULY

JUNE   JULY   AUGUST   NOVEMBER

REQUEST YOUR
FREE BOOKS!

2 FREE NOVELS
FROM THE ROMANCE/SUSPENSE
COLLECTION PLUS 2 FREE GIFTS!

YES! Please send me 2 FREE novels from the Romance/Suspense Collection and my 2 FREE gifts. After receiving them, if I don't wish to receive any more books, I can return the shipping statement marked "cancel." If I don't cancel, I will receive 4 brand-new novels every month and be billed just $5.49 per book in the U.S., or $5.99 per book in Canada, plus 25¢ shipping and handling per book plus applicable taxes, if any*. That's a savings of at least 20% off the cover price! I understand that accepting the 2 free books and gifts places me under no obligation to buy anything. I can always return a shipment and cancel at any time. Even if I never buy another book from the Reader Service, the two free books and gifts are mine to keep forever.

185 MDN EF5Y   385 MDN EF6C

Name	(PLEASE PRINT)	
Address		Apt. #
City	State/Prov.	Zip/Postal Code

Signature (if under 18, a parent or guardian must sign)

Mail to The Reader Service:
IN U.S.A.: P.O. Box 1867, Buffalo, NY 14240-1867
IN CANADA: P.O. Box 609, Fort Erie, Ontario L2A 5X3

Not valid to current subscribers to the Romance Collection,
the Suspense Collection or the Romance/Suspense Collection.

Want to try two free books from another line?
Call 1-800-873-8635 or visit www.morefreebooks.com.

* Terms and prices subject to change without notice. NY residents add applicable sales tax. Canadian residents will be charged applicable provincial taxes and GST. This offer is limited to one order per household. All orders subject to approval. Credit or debit balances in a customer's account(s) may be offset by any other outstanding balance owed by or to the customer. Please allow 4 to 6 weeks for delivery.

Your Privacy: Harlequin is committed to protecting your privacy. Our Privacy Policy is available online at www.eHarlequin.com or upon request from the Reader Service. From time to time we make our lists of customers available to reputable firms who may have a product or service of interest to you. If you would prefer we not share your name and address, please check here.